A STAR TO REMEMBER

Mal Stevens

A STAR TO REMEMBER

Published by Mal Stevens
First published 2014. Revised edition 2026.

ISBN 978-0-6485979-2-6 (paperback)
ISBN 978-0-6485979-3-3 (ebook)

www.malstevens.com.au

Dedications

In Loving Memory Of
Mario 'Muz' Ergovic
11.06.1971 - 09.10.2012

You always were, and always will be, my best friend, my Muzzy.

…some day I hope to meet you, some day, I know not when,
to clasp your hand in a better land, never to part again…

~*~

For Marinda, Aimee, Steven, and Lily, my daily reminder
of all that is good in this world.
…the LOVES of my life…
I love you x

~*~

DonateLife WA
For donors & recipients - with love xxx

per ardua ad astra

Table of Contents

Prologue

Hospital ICU wards have their own weather. Machines breathe, doors exhale. The walls are the colour of swallowed chalk, and the clock doesn't tick so much as hold its breath for hours at a time. I learned to read this sky one beep at a time.

"Indianna?" the nurse says - soft, correct. "Would you like a chair?"

I nod because yes, and because anything with legs feels like a plan. The chair clacks. I sit. I watch the rise and fall that isn't Lionel and tell myself the truth, this is a body doing what machines tell it to do, and not what love tells it. Love is loud and often useless in rooms like this. It stands at the foot of the bed and begs and remembers jokes no one asked for.

His forehead still has the groove my thumb knows like a path I've walked since I was eighteen. The tape at his mouth makes a strict line. The monitor argues with itself. Someone coughs two curtains down and the sound makes me think of childhood, which is unfair and therefore accurate.

A doctor speaks to me in kind, accurate words I barely hear. Injury. Non-survivable. Time. Decisions, and then the nurse steadies my hand with hers when the weight of the pen starts to become too much.

"Indi," she says. "You can take your time."

Time is not a thing I own tonight. I have a memory instead, Lionel slipping his donor card into my wallet the day he renewed his driver's license. "Might as well be useful," he'd said, grinning as if it were a dare. I'd rolled my eyes at the time, kissed his little forehead groove, and then filed the moment away next to grocery lists and electricity bills.

Now I take the card out and place it on the blue sheet and it looks like an ordinary thing that will break me. I sign where love tells me to sign, where he had told me long before this room. I sign because he would have, and I am the other half of his sentence.

Somewhere in another room a phone rings and stops. Somewhere a vending machine resists coins. Somewhere a patient dreams of the sea and wakes to a ceiling.

I hold onto Lionel's hand for what feels like the longest time until the machines finally agree with the truth. The nurse turns off three sounds and then turns on one more - quiet. The doctor speaks again, but I don't hear anything except the absence of air that belongs to him.

Later, a woman with the gentlest face I've ever seen asks if I'd like to hear, in time, where parts of him might go. Lungs to a thirty-year-old dad. A kidney to a man who jokes too much when he's scared. Another to a boy who has only just got his L-plates. She says it won't fix a thing. It will only change the shape of it. She's right. I say yes. I say his name. She says it back.

Outside, Perth does its midnight hum, and the sky isn't showing off. Still, I crane my neck and find one star that looks a fraction brighter because I have decided it will be. I tell myself a story I will keep telling, the tide is not here to drown you if you give it channels. You can't build a river in a night, but you can pick up a shovel.

Years from this corridor, I will hold three letters written in unfamiliar hands and cry like a door has been unbolted from the inside. I will keep them behind the softest paper in my house and touch them like braille. Years from this corridor, a night called 'A Star to Remember' will hang a constellation where anyone can find it, and I will say Lionel's name into a microphone and the air will hold it steady.

But now I put my palm over the groove in his forehead and whisper the only promise I know how to make.

"I'll keep you moving Lionel," I say. "I'll take you north with me when I go."

The automatic doors part as if the night itself is letting me through. I step into a wind that smells like rain that can't make up its mind and I look up again. I don't know which one is ours yet, but I pick one anyway. I whisper thank you into a sky that isn't listening and walk back to a life that will keep changing its mind until I decide otherwise.

Tomorrow, I'll tuck his driver's license card behind my license and start packing a bag. I'll put sunscreen and stubbornness next to each other and call it a kit. I'll aim the car north, then keep going until the road waves back.

A star to follow. A map I will draw as I walk.

Chapter One

"Good on ya, Indi!" Mollie and Aliviya sang in unison, before Aliviya added, "You need to start getting out there and doing things for you!"

"I know, I know. But that doesn't stop me worrying about the life I already have here now does it?"

I smiled at my housemates and best friends, two out of the three dearest people to me in this world, and I let myself wonder exactly what this brand-new life could possibly mean for me now. I had worked so hard to get to where I was today, and I couldn't help but feel a bubbling excitement for all the opportunities that now lay ahead.

A bachelor's degree had been quite the achievement for a young woman going through a traumatic life event at the very same time. I stared at the framed certificate hanging proudly on the living-room wall, a Bachelor of Science in Nursing, and suddenly I was overwhelmed by memories of how much work it had taken to reach that dream, and ultimately, what it had cost me in the end. I wondered, would my excitement always be tainted with tinges of sadness?

I remembered the criticisms so clearly, as though they were only yesterday. Sharp little pricks, aimed at my pride in an attempt to derail me. In hindsight, pricking my pride hadn't been hard to do, I was a proud young woman. I always had been, and I suspected I always would be. Back then, the criticisms were aimed at the life changes I had chosen to make for myself. Words spoken in the heat of arguments, things that never should have been said.

The silly things you say but don't truly mean when you just want to hurt someone. I felt myself begin to crumble inside, just a little. But almost immediately, I caught myself. I can't let these thoughts detract from me anymore.

Deep down, I knew my guiding star was leading me toward bigger things, toward my destiny. I could feel it, an unshakable force pulling at me, one I couldn't resist even if I'd wanted to. I was being led, and I knew I was in trusted hands, the trusted hands of the universe. I walked over to the back door and stepped outside. Looking up into the pitch-black sky, I let my eyes roam over the stars. I knew one of them was mine. And I would let it lead me to where I was most meant to be in this world.

Not everyone had agreed with my choices back then. In fact, I don't think anyone had agreed with any of my choices at all. But that was okay. It hadn't been okay at the time, but it was now. I was old enough now to dance to the beat of my own drum. I didn't need anyone's approval anymore. Nor did I want it. My loved ones and my career made me feel happier than I had been in years. They gave me purpose and direction. Without them, I reckoned I would have just curled up and died. It was time to stop dwelling on the past. Five long years I had dwelled. Today had to be the day the dwelling stopped, and my new life began.

I walked back into the house, still caught up in my thoughts. After finishing my degree, I'd completed my graduate year, followed by a year on a busy surgical ward in one of Perth's large hospitals. It was just enough time and experience to give me the courage to join a nursing agency. I'd joined at first in the hope that working across different hospitals would boost my confidence. God only knew how low my confidence had been, buried down in my pink nursing sneakers, and it needed all the help it could get.

Over time, I consolidated my learning, and I knew I needed to establish myself within my career. It was time to crawl out from under the rock I had been living beneath and step out into the big wide world that everyone kept telling me actually did exist out there.

The agency helped me in more ways than I had ever imagined it could. I had succeeded in stepping out from under my rock and, more importantly, stepping outside of my comfort zone. I had now worked in almost every hospital across Perth, in both general and mental health.

After Lionel's accident, I had resigned from my full-time nursing position, and the security it had afforded me, and with nothing but trust and a massive amount of faith in my heart, I chose to work exclusively with the agency. These days, I worked full-time hours as a casual registered nurse, and I danced, at least to some degree, to the beat of my own drum. And I loved it. I loved that I could choose where I worked, how much, and when. The new, improved, confident, unstoppable me had even branched further into remote area nursing, working in some of the most rugged, untouched regions of northern Western Australia. Sometimes, I hardly even recognised myself anymore.

"Wow," I whispered, almost in disbelief. "Who even is this?" Occasionally, pangs of guilt still came to me, especially when I thought of carving out a new life for myself beyond Perth. But my family and friends had always stepped in and supported me when I needed it the most, knowing exactly what to say, and when to say it. They were my greatest strength, my supports, and my daily reminder of all that was good in this world.

I had just completed an eight-week contract in Geraldton before taking a little time off to spend some much-needed girl time with my friends back in Perth. Next on my agenda, a twelve-week remote nursing contract in a fairly isolated part of northern Western Australia.

First, the hospital in Port Hedland for two weeks' of mandatory training and refreshers. Then, ten weeks' as the sole nurse in a remote Indigenous community east of Karijini National Park. Seventeen hours' drive north of Perth.

Back toward all the memories and everything I had once shared with Lionel. This wasn't the life I had dreamed of, but it was the life destiny had dreamed up for me. These days, I chose to see everything as either completely perfect, or as an opportunity for growth and learning. I just had to keep putting one foot in front of the other. That's what I kept telling myself anyway.

***

"Anyone up for pasta?" Mollie bounced into the kitchen, her voice bubbling with the same enthusiasm.

The mood in the house had been slipping toward sullen, weighed down by both my thoughts, and by Aliviya's recount of her day. She animatedly described the unprofessionalism of her coworker Hannah, whilst Mollie and I both listened intently. Mollie busied herself with making a start on dinner, while I opened a bottle of wine, before launching into an almost lecture-like conversation of my own about the importance of being true to yourself, and for standing up for what you believe in. I turned the stereo on and blasted AC/DC's *Whole Lotta Rosie'* just as Luna joined us in the kitchen. It wasn't long before dinner was well and truly underway and the atmosphere in the house had lifted considerably.

My eyes shifted toward the larger-than-life canvas of Lionel that hung on the living-room wall, pride of place in the house. I raised my glass toward it and gently whispered, "Cheers, Lionel." A small smile tugged at my lips as hidden tears threatened to escape my eyes. Random, funny little memories began flooding in, alongside the irritating ones, and the frustrating ones too. They were memories that had made some of the days since Lionel's passing easier to bear, and others almost unbearable. I let them linger briefly before gently tucking them back away again.

Sometimes, when the grief pressed hard, I'd reach inside my wallet and touch the edge of his old driver's license card. It had been there so long now that the plastic was worn smooth. It reminded me that love could keep moving, even when a life couldn't.

***

Mollie, Aliviya, Luna, and I had all found ourselves living in Perth at the same time, and we had jumped at the chance to rent a house together. Our only requirement was that it had to be close to public transport and the city. The four of us had first met back in grade seven of primary school, and right from the very beginning we'd known that we would be friends for life. Fifteen years had come and gone, and our bond had only deepened. School, university, family dramas, relationships that started and ended, happy times, hardships, births, deaths, and holidays, we had seen it all, side by side. We had laughed together, cried together, and leaned on each other through it all. Over the years, friends had come and gone, drifting interstate or overseas, but the four of us had remained strong. Even when busy schedules meant we could only catch up with each other every few months, we somehow always managed to find our way back to each other. It was hard sometimes, but it was also what defined to us who was truly a friend for life, and who had only been a friend of convenience.

Mollie was now an architect working in a global studio that specialised in sustainable design and urbanism. Aliviya worked as a dietitian at one of the major city hospitals. And Luna, our daily dose of Zen, was our Environmental Scientist, and the one who kept us grounded. She was the voice that reminded us to "get over ourselves" when we became too highly strung, and her sunrise Pilates on the verandah was standing room only.

***

After dinner, Luna and Aliviya cleared away the dishes, Mollie returned to her laptop to finalise tomorrow's deadlines, and I finished packing the last of my things into my suitcase, mentally rehearsing the long journey north that lay ahead.

I had given myself two days for the drive to Port Hedland. If I left at 06:00, I could stop in Geraldton to see Mum and Dad for a quick coffee and toilet break before pushing on to Carnarvon. With luck, I'd arrive before dark. That stretch of road was notorious at sunrise and sunset, with kangaroos, cattle, and even the occasional donkey littering the highways. I'd already booked a room at the Gascoyne Hotel. A solid night's sleep there, then back on the road by 07:00 the next morning for the final leg to Port Hedland.

As I packed, a heaviness pressed on me. Anxiety? Nerves? Maybe both. The last time I had stayed at the Gassy had been with Lionel. I hadn't set foot in the north since his accident. My heart belonged there, though. It yearned for the red dirt, the rocky ranges, the peaceful silence. The north was very spiritual to me. And I knew that Lionel would always be right beside me. Still, the thought of the journey made me falter.

"What the friggin' hell am I doing?" I muttered out loud without realising.

"Indi, you need to do this," Aliviya said from the doorway, her voice steady and reassuring. "Everything's sweet. Hit us up if you ever need us, legit only just a phone call away."

"Stop worrying, Indi! Geeeeez!" Mollie called from across the room, her tone a mixture of exasperation and affection.

Just then, my phone sprang to life, the familiar strains of Lenny Kravitz's "Again" spilling out and striking me right in the heart. I had left it as my ringtone since Lionel, but now it felt like another thing I needed to let go of. Change was coming, and change meant that song had to go.

"Mole," I said into the phone, smiling at the name flashing on the screen.

"Hey, Mole," Kat replied.

Kat and I had met through the nursing agency, and we had clicked instantly. I didn't do well driving across Perth, so I mostly filled shifts close to home. Kat lived an hour away in the hills, but we often ended up at the same hospital, giving us the chance to catch up.

"You working South tonight?" she asked.

"No, Mole. I'm packing for Hedland in the morning. I need a break from here."

"Good for you, Mole! It's always the same there. I worked last night, Jack's half-hour break turned into an hour and a half. He waltzes back in at 06:00, and I'd been dealing with patients on my own the whole time. Then he disappears into the office to write his notes, leaving me to do the 06:00 checks. Meanwhile, I'm running cups through the dishwasher and trying to get vital signs on room sixteen done. Honestly, I'm sick of working with these lazy cunts."

I laughed because I knew exactly what she meant. I'd experienced the same frustrations myself more times than I could count. Her rant only confirmed that I truly did need this break. The people I worked with had grown too comfortable around me, too lax, and I had started judging them in my frustration. A change of scenery was exactly what I needed.

"Yeah, Mole, I'm hearing you," I replied. "I get dumped with the checks too, fifteens, half-hourlies, and the routines. Hard to get anything else done when you're the only one doing them."

She went on, animated and fiery as always, describing Jack's avoidance, the chaos of the smoking area, useless handovers, and her slow slide from mini breakdown to major breakdown. Her words came fast, peppered with curses, making me laugh even as she vented.

By the time she finished, I felt drained but grateful. Kat was the only person I knew who could use the "C" word and somehow not make it sound completely vile. She helped keep me sane in this crazy job.

We said our goodbyes, and I returned to my suitcase. My mind lingered on the call. The hospital wasn't all bad, I loved my job, and I loved nursing, but sometimes it was overwhelming. Sometimes you just needed space to breathe.

I zipped my suitcase closed without even realising I had finished packing. My thoughts were still spinning. Feeling heavy and tired, I decided on a quick shower to wash away the residue of old hurts. As I lathered soap over my skin, a sobering truth hit me, erasing Lionel from my heart would be far harder than I had ever imagined.

***

Mollie was still awake, her laptop glowing in the dim light as she finalised a design project. Something about an "office building space inspired by Karijini National Park," she muttered. All double-dutch to me, honestly.

"My boss just emailed, told me not to drive in tired, to take a taxi. He knows me too well. Knows I'll be up all-night finishing this."

"Then get some sleep, Mollie," I said firmly. "No point staying up all night and turning up exhausted. What's that going to achieve?"

I knew I sounded like a broken record, and I was sure she was rolling her eyes at me, but that was what best friends did right, nag when needed.

She changed the subject. "You haven't packed your Homer Simpsons, have you, Indi?"

I laughed. "No. Maybe. Yes."

She groaned. "I'll be glad when those finally fall apart."

Those pyjama bottoms were my favourite, bright yellow, Homer's grinning face plastered all over them. My housemates teased me constantly, insisting the street would know me by them, but I didn't care. Comfort mattered more.

I hugged each of my friends tightly. "Goodnight, besties. I love you very much." Tomorrow was going to be a big day.

Chapter Two

Despite the best of intentions for an early night, I ended up having a late one trying to finish all the last-minute things I still had left to do. Mollie had come in to wake me at 05:00, but I must have dozed back off to sleep because the next thing I knew, it was 06:43. I jumped out of bed with such a fright, and what followed could only be described as the mad rush of my morning routine. Somehow, I managed to get away by 08:00. Not too bad, I told myself, it just meant my Geraldton stop would be a little later, and a little shorter, than I'd originally planned. As I locked the front door, a curious little flutter tugged low in my chest, like a compass needle twitching. *'North, it seemed to whisper. North.'*

***

The drive to Geraldton passed quickly, my mind wandering back to a conversation I'd had with Doctor Knight the last time we'd worked together at South's. The regular staff often complained he waffled on too much, but I worked nights and only saw him occasionally, so whenever I did, I welcomed any chance to sit and listen to him.

He often said Australians whinged far too much. I giggled to myself at the memory. I couldn't exactly argue with him on that.

"The patients come in… they blame their parents for their dysfunctional lives… their children blame them for theirs… it's a vicious circle. You are responsible for your life, no one else. If you're born to privilege and good role models, life is easier. If not, you have to work twice as hard. Doesn't mean you won't succeed, everyone can succeed. But you must be responsible for who and what you are… and walk toward it."

His voice came back to me so clearly, as if he were in the car with me. I remembered studying him intently. He was a "coloured" and educated man, and he spoke with such conviction that I believed him.

"My friend is a manual labourer, and he earns double what I earn," I had challenged him. "Where's the incentive for me?"

"The incentive, my friend, is that in the long term, when the industry your friend works for has crashed, who will he sell himself to? 'I am a manual labourer, will you employ me?' 'I am a shopkeeper, will you employ me?' No! You have nothing to offer! But you, Indianna, are educated. You are a Registered Nurse. Your pay will rise with time, your skills will always be needed. Ten years down the track, when the labourers have no job, you'll be head of your department, mentoring students. How lucky are you to have a HECS debt!"

He had been right. I hadn't had to work sixty hours a week while studying, like some did, just to afford the degree. But I had worked forty hours of night shifts every week, just to keep a roof over my head and food on the table. I never told my hospital placements that I had been surviving on three hours of sleep a day at the time, catching up only on weekends. Still, I had been proud of the choices I'd had to make.

And then his words echoed again: "Education is the key out of poverty! Don't be stuck in the small view of now. Look long term. Education is the key."

I smiled faintly. Doctor Knight had always given me food for thought.

The rest of my drive north was filled with both music from my iPod and, inevitably, thoughts of Lionel. Lionel was never far from my thoughts, ever. In my mind's eye, I could still see him in the ICU bed - his furrowed brow, the temples I used to so lovingly kiss, the fleshy earlobes I would rub absentmindedly. I had idolised him. And now, heading north, I wondered what this return would stir within me. But more pressingly in the moment, I wondered what the threat of Cyclone Nicholas had left behind in the way of rain.

Somewhere beyond the next line of heat-haze, the life I hadn't met yet felt like it was already walking toward me, boots dusted red, hands used to heavy work. The thought came and went like a mirage.

When I pulled into my parents' driveway, the side gate already open, Lily dog greeted me, her tail wagging furiously. A Jack Russell cross, she always made me laugh, her legs far too short for her little body, baring her teeth as though she were the fiercest guard dog in town.

"Mum, it's just a quick stop. I'm running behind schedule," I said, hugging and kissing her cheek before greeting Dad.

Mum, a physiotherapist, had her day off, and so did Dad, who worked in aviation. Fresh back from their travels in Europe and a camping trip to Payne's Find, they seemed relaxed and happy.

"Ham and salad sandwiches and a coffee," Mum offered, while she herself nibbled on a tuna salad and an apple.

"You just have to halve every meal, Elle," Dad teased with a grin. I smiled, thinking of their regular happy hours of nibbles and wine.

Refreshed and grateful, I was soon back on the road. With luck, I'd reach Carnarvon by 18:00.

Linkin Park's *Meteora* blasted through the car, and I sang my lungs out for all I was worth. Past Northampton, I felt the change immediately, every driver I passed along the way waved to me. *'Welcome back to the north, Indianna.'* That simple gesture was something I'd missed the most. It always felt like a blessing every time it happened. As though the land itself, and the country that surrounded it, was saying to me 'keep coming.'

Many people disliked the distances needed to travel to get around in WA, but I thrived on them. I was a road-tripper at heart. Fifteen hours to Karratha, eighteen to Paraburdoo, twenty-five to Broome, give me the open road and red dirt, and I was happy. Still, every stretch reminded me of Lionel, and of our trip to Karratha together when I was eighteen and he was nineteen, of him scoffing a 'Bubble-O Bill' ice cream, then pressing the pink chewing-gum 'eye patch' over one eye until it welded itself to his long, dark eyelashes, cue us on the side of the road with the eucalyptus oil I had stashed in the boot of the car, and laughing so hard I could barely tease it free.

And then there had been the kangaroo incident. Forced to choose between two carcasses laying in the middle of the road, I'd made the wrong choice. The stench that filled the car for half an hour was worse than anything I'd ever smelt in all my years of nursing.

***

After miles and miles of endless red dirt, ant mounds, and spinifex, Carnarvon finally came into view. Optus Hill loomed first for me, and memories of the Gardiners Family who had once lived there. Now, banana plantations, emus, goats, and sheep with fleece so thick they struggled to run filled the view. The sense of home hit me hard.

I was tired. The straight eighty-kilometre stretch had been the hardest. But I was proud of myself. Perhaps it was exhaustion, but maybe, just maybe, I was finally starting to move on from Lionel.

Not away from him, I decided, just forward. And in the quiet space between my breaths, my star felt a fraction brighter, as if signalling to me that forward might actually signal a positive move.

Sleep claimed me that night the moment my head hit the pillow.

***

07:00 came too soon. Though I'd slept deeply, restless dreams lingered.

The Pilbara stretched before me, longer, hotter, windier. With Cyclone Nicholas the previous week, rain lay heavy on the roads. Cows grazed dangerously close to the edges. I thought briefly of stopping to see my sister in Karratha but thought better of it and drove right on by instead. Six years of silence yawned between us. She had come to Lionel's funeral, then disappeared again once more.

"One day, I'll look her up," I whispered, making a mental note to add it to my long list of unfinished things I needed to do.

I passed Karratha without stopping, the last place Lionel and I were together, just the two of us, I wasn't ready to go back there just yet.

The drive to Port Hedland was mercifully uneventful, apart from a downpour near Whim Creek and the near loss of my windscreen wiper. At South Hedland, I ducked in for some supplies to tide me over before heading over to the hospital.

Elizabeth, my contact, greeted me warmly. Tall, smiling, she handed me an orientation pack and directions to the nurse's quarters.

But when I arrived at the circled group of houses, none of the keys fit the locks. My heart thumped as I realised I'd nearly walked into the wrong home. I jumped back into the car, laughed at the absurdity, and let my nerves settle while switchboard connected me with Daniel."

When I finally pulled into the right driveway, his white ute tucked under the tree, just as he'd said, Daniel had the door open before I could knock. His eyes, so startlingly blue, caught me completely off guard. I instantly liked him.

Nice to look at, I admitted, but the flutter from this morning didn't echo for him. Whatever tugged my compass wasn't here, at least, not yet.

***

Tomorrow would be my first shift. A quiet Sunday start, perfect for finding my feet.

I unpacked, showered, then sat on my bed debating my next move. A coin toss settled it, tails. Explore. And though I laughed at myself, I knew I'd wanted that all along.

Dressed simply in a flowing summer dress, hair and makeup neat but understated, I cracked open a cold beer, called Mollie,

Aliviya, and Luna for courage, and then headed out to the local pub Daniel had mentioned to me earlier. The Finny.

***

I felt small as I stood in the car park of The Finny, nerves coiling in my stomach. I stamped out my cigarette on the ground. "I really need to give these away," I muttered, and pushed through the door. As the music thumped through the walls, that strange little pull returned, familiar now, like standing beneath a sky you've seen in a dream.

***

Big Russ noticed her instantly. Indianna.

Of course he did, she stood out in every way. He watched as she kept her gaze low, heading for the bar. The chatter dulled for a moment, only the jukebox filling the silence, Christina Aguilera's *'Candyman'* blaring.

Big Russ's chest tightened. He hadn't seen her since Lionel's funeral, years ago. He'd worked with Lionel, diesel mechanics together on a site out past Newman, and he'd shared dinners and drinks with Lionel and Indi between rosters. He'd regretted not speaking to her that day at the service, words locked behind the wrong kind of grief.

He didn't believe in signs anymore. He'd told himself that, anyway. Still, something about the way the room seemed to tilt toward her made the old belief he'd sworn off wake up in his chest."

Now, here she was.

Tiny's wolf whistle broke the spell. "Would you get a load of that!"

Big Russ forced a shrug. "Knock yourself out."

The boys roared with laughter, already calling bets on who'd charm her first.

But Big Russ barely heard them. He couldn't tear his eyes away. He'd learned the hard way that vows keep a man safe. He'd also learned that the Pilbara had a way of cracking things open, the earth, the sky, and sometimes a bloke's best defences.

And then, just as suddenly as she'd arrived, Indianna downed her beer, slid off her bar stool, and briefly caught his gaze before walking out the door. Her look piercing straight through his heart.

Lust burned low in his gut, unwelcome and undeniable. It wasn't just heat, it was recognition, like seeing a star you've been steering by without knowing.

"Fuck."

Chapter Three

Sometimes the only way out is through.

People still call me Indianna at work because that's what my original name tag said for years, but I answer to almost anything if you say it like you mean it. Sister. Miss. Love. Hey you. The good one on nights. The bossy one with the braids. I've been all of them. But when I stand in front of the mirror at 06:02 with toothpaste on my chin and a headache already forming, I look myself in the eye and say the name that steadies me the most.

"Indi," I tell the version of me who wonders if she's got it in her. "Let's go."

Two weeks' hospital, ten weeks' remote, that was the deal. Hospital first, remote after.

***

The corridor hum says day shift is waking, hand foam and angry coffee, that peculiar hospital off, white that manages to look sterile and stained at once. I bribe myself upright with burnt toast and a contraband sachet of decent coffee I guard like a secret.

At 06:59 I badge in.

"Trainee queen," Kerry the NUM says, sliding a handover sheet my way. "Stick with Tomo today. Pilbara pace, city paperwork."

Tom "Tomo" Morrison, Charge RN, leans against the desk, steady and unshowy, the kind of presence you can lean on. Broad-shouldered, easy-quiet, a face that has seen the 15:00 stuff and still shows up soft. He taps the sheet. "Let's do the round."

"Rule one, if it smells like it needs a priest, it needs two nurses and a plan," I recite.

"Rule two?"

"Breathe through your mouth," I deadpan. He doesn't smile but his eyes do.

Handover in headlines: Mr D (COPD) prickly but improving, Mrs K, post-op day two bowel resection, anxious and immobile, Room 10, double room of doom, 10A, young mum with a well-placed abscess and even better-placed aunty, 10B, a 56-year-old with two-hourly neuro obs after a whisper of a bleed, 10C, a 23-year-old who says she's "fine" in seven languages, 10D, an Elder with chronic diarrhoea and a kimmy (Pilbara hospital lingo for a nappy pad) determined to colonise the corridor.

"And security know we're playing nice because the footy's on," Tomo adds. "People behave when they want the ward TV."

Mr D greets me with a glare and a death grip on his call bell. "You're late."

"I'm Indi," I say. "I'll be your favourite disappointment till 15:30."

He snorts despite himself. We bargain, inhalers, obs, two laps with the IV pole in return for a whispered match update later. Plans are dignity, people can do almost anything if you tell them what's next and mean it. He does his puffs like a champion and pretends not to like me. Tomo has been watching the whole while, not crowding, just there.

You make it look easy," he says on our way out.

"It isn't," I say.

"I know," he says, and moves on.

Room 10 has its own weather. You feel it before the door, warm, wary, air heavy with worry. In 10A, the young mum eyes the wall like it has wronged her. Her aunty sits at the foot of the bed, arms folded, chin licensed as a weapon.

"Morning, Aunty," I say, with the small bow the word deserves.

Aunty narrows her eyes, weighing me. "Not your aunty. I'm her aunty. You talk proper," she corrects me, not unkindly, and then tipping her chin at the young mum, she adds, "but you can say 'Aunty' proper way."

"Yes, Aunty," I say, taking the correction like a gift. "We'll trade, I'll do the stingy bits, you do the brave bits."

Her mouth twitches. "You talk too much," she says, but her shoulders soften.

We set up for the abscess dressing. No fancy words. Explain. Ask permission. Move slow. Aunty sings a low, steady song under her breath and the girl matches her breathing to it. The stench climbs into the corridor and makes the curtains flinch. We irrigate, pack, and tape the dressing, clean and snug so it can heal. The girl crushes my fingers, I let her. Aunty does not blink.

"You got kids?" she asks, out of nowhere.

"No. Not my own," I say. "But I've been someone's kid my whole life. Married at twenty-one. Grew up together, in a way."

"Mmm," she says, verdict delivered. "Then you know."

When we finish, she thrusts a plastic container at me. "For later." Then, with mock severity: "Tea. Strong. Black. Two sugars."

"Like a good story," I say. She rolls her eyes as if to say don't get cocky.

Across in 10B, the neuro patient is all polite and brittle. I do the questions in my calm voice, name, place, the month, the score of last night's game. He chuckles, gets three out of four, then frowns and asks me the date again. I make a note. Patterns are everything. We agree I'll be the boss of the questions; he'll be the boss of saying if I'm annoying. Deal.

At 10:10, the emergency bell above Bed 6 shrieks. Mrs K - grey paper skin, hands clawing the gown, eyes wild.

"On it," I say, voice lower than my pulse. Airway. Breathing. Circulation. Call for help without sounding like you're calling for help.

"Tomo," I call.

He comes in like weather - calm, fast, present. We build a bridge from here to the next minute, nebs, positioning, a stern chat with her lungs to get their act together. I narrate; he does. Her oxygen climbs back up from the land of don't-you-dare. Machines stop sulking.

"You kept your head," Tomo says, a hand warm on my shoulder, the highest praise in this building.

"I nearly took it off to stop it shaking."

"Shaking's fine," he says. "Means you care. If you ever stop shaking after the big ones, go do something else for money."

We don't move away from each other straight away. We don't need to.

The registrar appears, hair and stethoscope both untidy, and asks for the numbers like he's trying to tiptoe on tiles. I give him short sentences in the order he can use. He thanks me properly, which means eye contact, not just pen contact.

"Can you loop me in when you rewrite the analgesia?" I add, before he vanishes. "She's guarding. Might get more distance with a PCA or a tweak."

He nods without defensiveness. "Bring me the chart after obs."

The small wins stack, a registrar who can hear a nurse, a patient who stops chasing air like it owes her money, a room whose shoulders drop.

By 11:00 the ward invents a new chaos, a family conference that wasn't on the board but is very much happening. In 10D, cousins and uncles and aunties gather like weather systems, all intent and love and unhelpful volume. The TV argues with them, the footy commentators argue with both.

"Hey mob," I say, palms out like I'm landing a helicopter. "We're going to shut the telly up for five. Aunty's belly is the boss and she says she wants quiet."

They grin at me for the cheek, then obey for Aunty. That's the trick. You don't tell people to be quiet. You give them a better reason to be. I bring chairs. I bring water. I bring the antibiotic on time because the most respectful thing you can do in a room like this is be good at your job.

Lunch, bananas over the sink, a silent thanks for small mercies.

The smokers' door is the Pilbara confessional, push bar, hip, air on your face. Count the ships. Remember what's steady. Four iron ore carriers queued on the horizon and one tug doing all the work.

A Hemo tech leans on the rail beside me and we exchange the religious weather report.

"Hot."

"Hot."

"Storm maybe Thursday."

"Maybe."

Back inside, the good bits keep shining through the noise. Mr D thanks me not to my face, tells the HCA I'm "not the worst." A junior doctor is brave enough to admit he doesn't know the dressing and wise enough to watch twice. A little boy waves like I'm the Queen of Band-Aids.

In the medication room I do the triple check on warfarin like a person who reads the backs of cereal boxes for fun. Tomo steps in, knocks the door with his heel, and watches the way I line up syringes left-to-right in dose order.

"You are orderly in a way that makes my bones relax," he says.

"I've been accused of worse," I say, signing my life away on the chart.

At 13:20, pharmacy rings with the calm of people who live behind a door. "Your 10C script is illegible," the voice says.

"Copy," I say, and fetch the registrar with the tidy handwriting. We walk the corridor like a married couple who have agreed to disagree and fix it anyway. He rewrites. I thank him. We both win.

By 14:05 Room 10 changes temperature. 10B's neuro obs shift from "mmm" to "not my favourite." Pupil a shade slower, speech with a new wobble. I call Tomo with the sentence that recruits help without setting fire to the room: "Hey, can you come see this with me?"

He's there on the second breath. We look. We agree. He pages. The CT happens because we noticed before the universe wrote us a lesson in capital letters. After, 10B is sleepy but safer. The family call me "love" in a way that says, we saw you see him.

In the staffroom, a laminated sign I used to roll my eyes at because I thought it was cheesy, BE THE NURSE YOU WOULD

WANT AT YOUR CHILD'S BEDSIDE. I don't roll them today.
I drink water like it's a negotiation. I steal a square of someone's
mystery slice and leave a Post-it apology in return, "Indi owes you
one (slice amnesty invoked for near-misses)."

At 15:10 the fire alarm hiccups, howls, then blames the staff
toaster upstairs. Mr D grins like he planned it. I threaten the toaster
with a formal written complaint, and it behaves for five whole
minutes. Sign-out comes and doesn't. You don't leave a ward so
much as get shaken loose from it. Tomo tosses me a muesli bar
like a coach. "Eat before you hit the rail crossing," he says. "Easier
not to cry when a two-kilometre ore train decides to nap across the
road."

"I don't cry," I lie.

"Everyone cries," he says, and walks the opposite way, which
is kind.

Kerry mouths, Rooftop five minutes? I nod.

***

Pilbara sky doing its bruise-in-reverse thing. We drink tea out
of paper cups and let the wind do the rest.

"Two weeks'," Kerry says. "Then you're out bush."

"Ten weeks' remote," I say. "Doctor once a month. Food
truck fortnightly. I'm ready."

"You are," she says. "Just remember, never alone. Back each
other up. #GaylesLaw."

"I know," I say, and feel the law settle into the slot where all
my laws live.

She looks at me sideways. "And you, how are you, not the
handover?"

"Fine," I say, then correct myself. "Tired. Good tired. The not-crying at trains kind."

"Good," she says. "And Indi? You won the aunty, not the dressing."

"I know," I say, surprised at how proud that makes me.

On my way down I detour through 10. Aunty watches the footy, volume low; young mum sleeps from being brave. Aunty doesn't look away. "You going home," she observes. "Not late."

"Not late," I agree.

"Good," she says. "Strong. Black. Two sugars."

"Night, Aunty."

The lift mirror returns a face with pen marks, a tape smudge, and a tired mouth that feels more like fact than judgement. In the foyer a security guard teaches a toddler an improvised handshake because kindness is a shift skill too. Outside, the hot wind holds steady like a line you can walk along if you keep your eyes soft.

I hit the rail crossing green by grace alone. On the coastal loop I pull over where the mangroves give up pretending they're trees and admit they're lungs. I send a photo of four ships and a tug to no one in particular and everyone who needs it. The horizon says, round earth, old rules, keep breathing.

Back at staff quarters, the donga aircon labours like a faithful old dog. I peel off the day. In the shower I find three pieces of tape I didn't know I owned. I eat the surprise leftovers Aunty slipped me, curried sausages that taste like love with an opinion, and send up a small thanks to whoever invented microwaves that don't scream.

Before sleep can argue, I open the red-dirt notebook and write the day's three lines so tomorrow won't swallow them:

- Mrs K breathed.

- Aunty let me in (for ten minutes).

- Four ships and a tug.

I add a fourth, because rules are guidelines and today earned it:

- Kept my head. Kept my heart.

I turn off the light and let the dark be a place to rest, not to fall.

"Indi," I whisper. "Let's go again tomorrow."

***

Tomorrow arrives with a vengeance and a smell like the ward toaster has decided to moonlight as a volcano. I badge in at 06:59. Tomo hands me a fresh sheet with a raised eyebrow.

"Ready for an education?" he asks, and points at the whiteboard where someone has written, in a hand far too cheerful for the content: INFECTION CONTROL SURPRISE AUDIT 10:00.

"Pilbara pace," I say. "City paperwork."

He grins. "You'll be fine. You alphabetised the dressing trolley yesterday. I saw you."

Rounds go long because life does. Mr D graduates from two circuits to three and heckles me into promising a second whispered score. 10A tolerates a wash like a queen receiving a minor duke, Aunty directs traffic like a woman who has found the one correct use for a kimmy. 10B's speech has regained its swagger by degrees. 10C finally uses the English word "nausea" like a tiny victory instead of a dare. 10D sends me to the kitchen with strict instructions to bring tea back hot enough to tell a story.

At 09:42, a relative arrives like a weather change, jangling keys, jangling voice, a storm front in a hat. He wants answers the way some people want blood. I take him to the family room because rooms change outcomes. "We'll go slow," I say. "And if I don't know, I'll fetch the person who does."

He deflates on the third sentence because anger is a currency that spends fast. The thing he needed was a chair and a hand on a timetable, not righteous fury. He gets both. He thanks me by giving me the worst biscuit in the tin, which is how some men say sorry for being loud.

At 10:00 on the dot, Infection Control appears in scrubs the colour of authority. We pass because we were always going to. Tomo lets out a breath he didn't need to hold and flicks me a look that says, told you.

By 12:20 the ward has settled into the afternoon pre-storm torpor. Everyone seems to nap at once except me and the HCA with a vendetta against dust. I use the quiet to practise teach the new grad how to set up for a sterile field without making offerings to the gods of contamination. She watches my hands like they're subtitles.

"Talk out loud," she says.

"Clean to dirty," I say. "Gravity is a snitch. Tape is not sterile because it looks tidy. And you never move faster than your breath."

She grins. "You sound like Tomo."

"Occupational hazard," I say, and properly smile when she doesn't flinch at the word hazard, just nods like she'll remember.

The near-miss of the day saves itself for 14:50, because of course it does. A child visiting 10D goes faint and silent in the corridor, eyes rolling like a tiny pinball machine. We're there before the thud because we live in hallways. Tomo scoops. I fetch juice. Aunty materialises with a biscuit she swears is medicinal. The kid rallies, annoyed at the attention. We all pretend we weren't terrified for a minute. The corridor exhales.

Sign-out, again, arrives with the kind of generosity that looks like "you go, I've got this." Tomo does a final walk. I collect the floating jobs like I'm tidying a beach, bits and bobs, a phone call returned, a chart countersigned, and a pillow fluffed, not because pillows heal, but because people do when pillows behave.

Kerry catches me at the desk. "Remote roster landed," she says. "You'll be with Janelle first swing. She makes tea properly and does boundaries like a champion. You'll like her."

"I like her already," I say.

"Never alone," she says, not as a slogan this time but as a prayer. I tuck the day into the book again that night, three lines plus one:

- Infection Control passed (alphabetised trolley for the win).
- Angry became thirsty became calm (chairs help).
- Kid fainted; corridor caught him.
- Remote roster. Janelle + tea.

When the dark arrives, I meet it like we have a deal. "Indi," I whisper. "Through."

Chapter Four

There's a trick the old-timers teach the newbies in Hedland, when the day tips, step out at the smokers' door and check the ships. You don't have to actually be a smoker; you just need the horizon to tell you the earth is still round.

SCU paged at 09:40. "Cardioversion at 10:00 with Luscombe," Kerry called. "Indi, you're float lead. Tomo's with you. Daniel, you're second."

Copy.

SCU is a two-room in-between, more hum than drama, more precision than slack. Smells like wipes, worry, and a coffee someone abandoned mid-sip.

"Morning, Mr Gibson," I say, laying out rhythm. "I'm Indi. I'll be bossy till you're back in sinus rhythm."

He grips the rail like the bed might actually leave without him. Late fifties, outdoor work written into his hands. Eyes the exact colour of Pilbara glare at 09:00, not quite blue, not quite white, just hot.

"Lot of wires," he says.

"More stickers than a kid's lunchbox," I say. "They hurt less." Consent checked. Anticoagulation charted. Echo reviewed. Fasting confirmed. Anterior-posterior pads on, airway kit at the head of bed, suction checked, oxygen ready, BVM sitting there like a good dog. Propofol/fentanyl drawn with flushes. I run PEDPP in my head: People, Equipment, Drugs, Patient, Plan.

Luscombe breezes in wearing charm like a spare stethoscope.

Indi," he says, washing properly because I give him the look.

Tomo takes the meds side, calm, and precise. Daniel preps the room like he's rehearsed with a ghost preceptor. We time-out at 09:55: patient ID, procedure, indication, consent, allergies, airway risk. Everyone looks at everyone.

"Okay, Mr Gibson," I say quietly. "Sleepy medicine, then your heart will hiccup and remember the song it likes better. I'm here the whole time."

"You talk like my daughter," he says, smiling with both sides now.

"Propofol in," Tomo calls, watching the monitor. Mr Gibson drifts in that peaceful way people do when you get sedation right.

"Synchronised," Luscombe says. "Charging to 120."

"Clear," I say, left, right, bed. The whine, then shock. The monitor scribbles then sulks.

"Still flutter," Luscombe. "Again."

"Go 150," I say, already dialling. Two mils more propofol, a gentle nudge for blood pressure to behave. "Synchronised."

Shock.

The line draws like a steady thought. Sinus rhythm sixty-eight. Warm hands. Calm chest. Pressure decent. Breathing like a person who's just remembered how.

"There we go," I breathe.

"Textbook," Luscombe declares, already half out the door to dramatise elsewhere.

We detangle wires, tidy chaos. Mr Gibson begins his gentle post-shock snore. Daniel looks like someone has shown him a magic trick and then handed him the deck.

"That was…" he starts.

"Work," I say, kind. "Now chart it so future-you trusts present-you."

"And toast," Mr Gibson slurs into wakefulness. "I was promised toast."

"Two slices, butter to the edges," I say. "We'll negotiate tea."

"Strong," he murmurs. "Black. Two sugars."

"Aunty has infiltrated the building," Tomo says gravely.

Only then do I step back and pay the adrenaline tax. The tiny shake. The metallic taste. The body doing its inventory. I honour it with the only ritual I trust.

"I'm going to check the ships," I tell Tomo.

"Five minutes," he says. "We're good."

The door groans, the air kisses my face, and the port spreads itself out like punctuation. Four iron ore carriers and a tug in attendance. I count them because numbers give me something to stand on.

Grief arrives the way it likes to, sure-footed, uninvited, and familiar. Lionel's forehead groove, the gum in his eyelashes at nineteen, eucalyptus oil and laughter, the hospital breathing machines that didn't care about any of that. The tide swells, and I let it. People say "tide" like it's gentle. It is not. But DonateLife gave it channels. Papers I never wanted to sign took a sliver of that water and sent it somewhere useful. A lung to a thirty-year-old dad. A kidney to a forty-year-old man. A kidney to a boy still on L-plates. I keep their letters with my softest paper. Some days I touch them like braille. Some days I pretend I've lost the key to that drawer. Both are true.

And then, traitor mind, Big Russ's eyes surface, the exact brown of iron in water. The Finny. The way the room tilted toward him. I get properly cross with myself, cells reconfiguring without permission, a new compass twitching in a chest that already has a star. Anger is easier than fear. I let a little sit on my tongue like a warning.

I don't light a cigarette. I count ships instead. Four and a tug. "Honest," I tell them, and go back in.

Mr Gibson wakes fully, negotiates a flannel pack from his wife over speaker, and survives a scolding that sounds like love. Tomo charts like scripture. Daniel discovers the printer's moods.

The afternoon stacks its usual way, a chest drain bubbling like a lava lamp in a stoic seventy-year-old, a medication that takes a detour because someone's 7 looks like a 1, a family who bring in a roast chicken and act surprised when the entire corridor turns feral from the smell, a junior doctor brave enough to own a duplicated test and fix it. "Own it, fix it, learn it, move on," I tell him. He looks at me like I've handed him permission to breathe, which I suppose I have.

At 12:15, a pacemaker interrogation wand arrives with an EP nurse who knows more than God and smiles less. We do the little ritual around Mr Salt's chest, interrogate, log, nod. His ventricle behaves like a worker who's been given the right spanner. He calls me "girlie" and then apologises and calls me "Sister." I forgive him both, equally.

At 12:40, Daniel and I stand at the med room sink and inhale toast like it's oxygen. He's still glowing from the cardioversion.

"Felt like cheating," he admits quietly. "Big shock, big fix."

"Sometimes it is cheating," I say. "We steal back rhythm from dumb luck and call it medicine. The clever part is everything before and after."

He nods, serious. "I keep thinking I'll… mess it."

"You will," I say. He blinks. "And you'll own it, fix it, learn it, move on. That's the job."

He nods again, this time relieved, like I've named gravity and now he can stop fighting it.

At 13:05, a man in hi-vis stalks onto the ward with a storm for a voice. "Where's the nurse in charge?" he demands, as if the idea of shared leadership is an insult. His dad is in 4B with new-onset AF (Atrial Fibrillation, Cardiac), and he's furious the bedrails aren't up to his personal standards.

"Hi," I say, palms open. "Indi. Float lead. Come with me, we'll sit and go over exactly what's next."

He wants blood, I give him a chair and facts. He wants certainty, I give him a plan and my direct line. He wants to protect his old man; I give him a job, "You are the medication historian. Make a list. Include the vitamins and the 'just a little for sleep.' I'll check it against his chart." He softens at that, the way men do when you make them useful instead of loud.

At 13:45, the SCU (Special Care Unit) phone pings: "ED sending one up, 48yo, SVT, adenosine x2, converted, shaky." We accept, which is the hospital word for "we'll make the room wider." She arrives tight smiled; the particular tremor of a person who's felt time stop and restart. I drop my voice. "Your heart did park-and-reverse," I say. "It's allowed to feel weird after. We'll watch it watch itself for a bit."

She laughs, surprised to be understood without the manual. We sit with that for three minutes and nothing happens, which is the best kind of medicine.

At 14:20 we catch a small almost-mistake before it can hatch, two patients with near-mirror names, one on beta-blockers, one definitely not. Daniel stops, frowns, asks me to look, we dodge the error together. He goes pale at the thought of what nearly happened, I put two glasses of water in his hands and make him drink both. "This is what checking the ships looks like when you can't leave the ward," I say. "You pause. You point at a horizon, names, dates of birth, and you breathe till the earth rounds out again."

At 14:50, the afternoon tries to go feral. Mr Gibson's BP dips. 10B's CT report returns with just enough language to tighten a jaw. The roast chicken family set off the bed exit alarm twice. The medication room printer decides to eat paper and confess nothing. SCU feels like a small boat in a choppy harbour. Tomo stands in the doorway and says one word that returns us to the map: "Order."

We move, Mr Gibson's pressure likes its fluids, the CT means obs, not panic, the chicken is demoted to the family room with a stern warning about smell being a hospital-wide hazard, the printer gets a disciplinary talk and a new ream. In the middle of that, a DonateLife WA coordinator rings my mobile with a soft-voiced ask about a future education night. I tell her yes, later, after the storm. She understands, because she lives in weather too.

By 15:10, I catch the horizon through the window. Five ships now, the tug has earned a rest. The sky has that Pilbara warning colour that isn't a promise, just a hint. I tuck the view into my chest like a talisman and go back to bed-jenga with Kerry.

We hand over to the afternoon shift the way you hand over a baby, with detail and dignity. "Gibson's pressure stable, sinus holding. Toast at 16:00 if numbers behave. 4B's son is anxious, give him a job. SVT lady is brave but spiky, reassure with data, not platitudes. In 10, Aunty will quiz your tea technique. Answer correctly."

On my way out I duck by 10. Aunty doesn't look away from the footy. "You not late," she says. Not a question.

"Not late," I agree.

"Good," she says. "Strong. Black. Two sugars."

In the lift, my face looks like a person who's done a thing worth doing. Outside, evening is peach-coloured and already bruised. I sit in the car and text two people.

To Tomo: Good crew. Thanks for the backup.

He replies with a single word: Always.

To Mollie: Cardioversion ☑ Nobody died x

She: You're a legend x

Back at the nurse quarters, my laundry accuses me of neglect and Daniel commentates the footy like a one-man radio. I reheat Aunty's stew and make tea strong/black/two sugars because right isn't always about being right.

When the place finally goes soft and the cicadas take over, I open the red-dirt notebook and leave three lines where I can find them again:

- Mr Gibson's heart remembered the song.

- Four ships and a tug (then five).

- Thought about Big Russ's eyes. Got mad at myself. Lived.

Lights out. The tide does what tides do - comes in, goes out, ignores me. On the wall, Lionel's face in shadow, that familiar groove. I press my palm into the air where his forehead would be. Somewhere in the same chest that keeps his love, a new compass twitches, and I don't punish it for trying to point.

"Indi," I whisper. "We'll check the ships again tomorrow."

***

Tomorrow arrives loud. SCU starts with a call from ED: "Chest pain rule-out x 3. One's ninety-two and charming. One's forty-eight and pretending not to be scared. One's sixty and furious about the parking."

"Copy," I say, because copy is a verb and a mindset.

Mr Ninety-Two turns out to be as advertised. He calls me "chief" and insists his real problem is that toast has "shrunk since the war." I promise contraband butter and obtain a tiny miracle from the kitchen. Mr Forty-Eight tries a joke and then tries honesty and decides he prefers honesty. Mr Sixty finds a chair that can withstand his parking monologue and, after being listened to, admits he's really worried about his dog. I help him call a neighbour. He becomes human again.

At 10:30, Daniel runs a full medication reconciliation on a new admit without me prompting. He comes to find me after, eyes bright.

I did a ships check," he says. "Names, DOB, old scripts, the lot."

"How many ships?"

"Two and a tug," he says, not missing a beat. "Plus, a bottle of magnesium tablets that are doing absolutely nothing for anyone."

"Take the win," I say. He does, shy and proud.

At 11:50, I get pulled into a corridor consult, an inpatient with heart failure, eyes like rain. "I'm drowning," she whispers, and it's not dramatic. We add a diuretic, pivot lunch to less salt, sit her up properly, get physio to bless the plan, and I ask her to breathe with me for two minutes while the drug gets started. The tiniest smile arrives uninvited, like a stray cat. "That helped," she says, surprised. "Probably the drug," I say. "Probably the breathing," she counters. We agree to share the credit.

At 12:30, Kerry appears with the clipboard that rules the world. "We've got a junior doctor with a mouth that runs faster than his brain," she says wryly. "He needs a nurse to translate."

The doc is smart and fast and terrified of looking slow. I slow him, gently. "Say the plan in ten words," I ask. He tries twenty. We find ten. He's grateful. Later he brings the right form without being asked. That's a ships check too, notice, nudge, name the wind.

At 13:10, the smokers' door calls. It's not a tide moment, just a battery swap. Three ships and a tug today, the wind's swung southerly. On the bench, a theatre nurse with glitter shoelaces sits with her eyes shut. We don't speak. We don't need to. We're watching the same line straighten.

Phone buzz. Mollie: "Ship report?"

Me: Three and a tug. Cardioversion yesterday. Nobody cried at the rail crossing.

Mollie: "Copy. You're a menace and an angel. Hydrate."

I tuck the phone away like a small heat source and go back to work because work is what saved me before and might again.

Mid-afternoon, Aunty passes through SCU like royalty on a tour. She doesn't say hello. She scans the place for sins. She finds none she's willing to comment on. At the door she pauses, angles her chin at me. "You got good hands," she says, as if it's a completely new thought and not the oldest benediction we have.

"Learnt from people who didn't waste theirs," I say. She nods like I've answered a question she wasn't sure I knew she'd asked.

The shift's last hour tries to teach humility again. A telemetry lead un-sticks itself just long enough to make a monitor scream,

Mr Ninety-Two's toast turns political, a pathology label prints with a typo that could start a new religion, and the printer (that emotionally unstable roommate of ours) decides to jam exclusively when a consultant is waiting. We fix, we apologise, we laugh, we keep moving.

At sign-out, I give the afternoon shift the weather report and the map. "Check the ships if the ward goes sideways," I tell the newest of them, a baby nurse with eyeliner like wings and hands like a prayer. She nods like I've given her a spell.

On the way out, I think I'll skip the smokers' door because I want my car and my shower. I don't. I walk there anyway, because some deals you keep even when you don't feel like it. Two ships now, the tug's off shift. The sky is flat, tired. It looks like how I feel.

I think of Lionel. I think of the letters in the drawer. I think of a man who sent me ranges as if they were a weather forecast we could both obey. I let all of them sit in me without needing to choose one truth to live by this minute.

"Indi," I say out loud, like a friend calling you back inside. "Go home."

I do. Aunty's stew tastes like someone is on my side. In the shower, three new pieces of tape appear from nowhere like shy cousins. I sit on the bed, open the red-dirt notebook, and put the day in its three small boxes:

- SVT parked and reversed; fear did, too.
- Daniel did a ships check without me.
- Two ships at dusk; round earth confirmed.

I add one more, because some days earn an extra:

- Texted ranges. Received horizon.

I turn out the light and let the dark behave. Tomorrow there will be more wires and names and plans and mugs of tea made properly. Tomorrow the tug will push, and the carriers will pretend they moved themselves. Tomorrow I'll step outside when the day tips and count until the numbers remind me that I am not falling, I am standing on a round thing that keeps me, even when the tide is busy.

We'll check the ships again tomorrow.

Chapter Five

The text from Facilities landed before the kettle clicked.

FACILITIES: "Hi Indianna. Quick shuffle. You're moving from Quarters 3B to Staff Dongas East. New housemates Robyn (RN) + Peter (OT). Keys from switchboard. Map attached."

The map looked like a child had drawn a treasure hunt with a blunt highlighter. Two circles, three arrows, one X, and a scribble that might have said turn at the bin chicken. I laughed out loud. Hedland always finds a way to remind you she's a town first and a system later.

"Of course I'm moving," I told the kettle. "Why would anyone grow moss."

Daniel was stirring oats in a saucepan that had known war. "I told you not to get attached," he deadpanned, then softened. "They're good ones, Robyn and Pete. You'll like 'em."

Tell me the donga has air con."

"Air con and a resident gecko called Kevin." He handed me my mug. "And a laundry roster. Don't cross Robyn on laundry day."

I packed fast, scrubs, two pairs, off-duty dress, joggers, slides, the red-dirt notebook, my mug, a ridiculous bow collection I keep pretending I'll grow out of. Aunty's stew went into a snap-lock and the freezer ambled behind us like an afterthought.

At switchboard the evening clerk slid me a lanyard with a shrug that said you're not the first. "Map's old," she said. "If you get lost, head for the big blue skip and swear loudly. Someone will collect you."

Outside, the heat did that Pilbara thing, and pressed all its hands to your face at once. I loaded the boot, cranked the air con, and followed the map like a pilgrim.

Circle one took me down a road that turned into a track that turned into red dust that turned into a chorus of crows. Circle two pointed at a fence with a sign that read STAFF DONGAS EAST and an arrow that pointed west. I did a three-point turn that involved seven points and the opinion of a galah. By the time I found the clinic of sea containers with door numbers stencilled in white, I had forgiven the map and promised to buy it a drink.

Block E, Unit 12. A palm-sized verandah, a steel mesh door, a wind chime made from old teaspoons. I knocked, even though I had keys, because manners are a kind of talisman.

The door flew open and a woman with a riot of greying curls and the grin of a person who buys plants on impulse lifted both arms like I'd been missing for years.

"You must be Indi. I'm Robyn. Come in before you cook."

Then another voice: "Watch the frog."

I looked down. A small green frog occupied the threshold with the put-upon face of a landlord checking references.

"Don't mind him," Robyn said. "He's our security. Hops out at night and does rounds."

"Copy," I said gravely, stepping over the frog like it was a sacred object. "I come in peace."

The donga was exactly as you'd expect if you've never lived in one, and exactly better if you have. Two bedrooms at opposite ends, a galley kitchen, a table with the patina of a thousand coffees and two relationships, and a bathroom with a shower that will be either a blessing or a threat. The kind of place people pass through and also remember forever.

A man in a faded Freo Dockers tee ducked out from the kitchenette, drying his hands on a dish towel. Compact, steady, mid-forties, eyes that have seen people at their worst and still offer them a chair.

"Peter," he said, offering his hand. "OT. I'm the one who labels shelves and returns Tupperware to its rightful owner. You put something in the fridge without a name? It disappears into the void."

"Happy to be named," I said. "I hate voids."

Robyn clapped once. "Right. House meeting, short and sweet, before I feed you. Donga rules."

She meant it as a joke, but she also meant it.

Donga Rules turned out to be a tea towel someone had written on with a laundry marker.

Night shifters sleep.

Air con at 23. No arguments unless dying.

Fish on Fridays only, windows open, incense burning.

Label your shelf or forfeit rights to rage.

Laundry roster on the fridge, write your name in pencil and your sins in your heart.

Shoes off inside (tray on verandah for red dirt).

Gecko Kevin lives here rent-free. He eats the mozzies. He is not to be judged.

If you break it, say it. If you fix it, show us how.

#GaylesLaw, Never Alone. Eyes/hands/back each other up.

Check the ships.

"Did you… add ten for me?" I asked, weirdly moved.

"Peter did, after I told him about you counting." Robyn poured tea like a ceremony. "He said it's as good a rule as any."

Peter shrugged. "Hedland thing. Keeps you level."

Robyn slid a plate of something that smelled like garlic and intention across the table. "Eat. Then we'll do the map-to-nowhere tour."

"The what-now?"

She grinned. "You'll see."

We set off at dusk with head torches and house keys and optimism. The map-to-nowhere was Robyn's name for the warren of near-identical transportables and their near-identical lanes. She took me to the laundry block (two washers, one dryer, a whiteboard with ROBYN written in large letters under Tuesday), the bin corral (home to the aforementioned bin chickens), the cyclone muster point ("If the siren sounds like the town is being abducted by aliens, we meet here"), and the back gate shortcut to the hospital ("Five minutes if you walk like you're late, ten if you're carrying sympathy").

On the way back we passed a donga with the door open and a smell so good it was practically an invitation.

"Don't stop," Peter stage-whispered. "That's Neville's chilli. He weaponises it and then holds you hostage with recipes."

Of course Neville saw us. "Robbo! Pete! Come say hello."

He had a ladle in one hand and the confidence of a man who's fed a small army. "New one?"

"Indi," Robyn said. "Be kind, Nev. She's ours."

Neville peered at me like he was appraising a cut of beef. "Can you dice onions without crying?"

"Depends who's telling the story," I said.

He barked a laugh and handed me a Tupperware container. "Welcome. Not too hot. Bring it back or Peter will hyperventilate."

Back in our donga Robyn pegged a tea towel to the curtain rail to keep the afternoon sun from turning the place into a kiln.

"You'll find your feet," she said. "First week's the map, second week is the legend."

Peter nodded. "And if you get lost, just walk toward the sound of the ocean. Or the wet mess. Same decibel level some nights."

We ate at the table and told the short versions of our lives, the ones you tell when work and heat and the exactness of shared space make intimacy both easy and necessary. Robyn, ED for twenty years, a laugh that could unclench a room, a sister in Busselton, a dog called Dennis back home with an ex who still waters her plants (metaphorical and literal). Peter, OT by day, drummer by weekend, a daughter in Broome, a habit of rescuing bent cutlery and giving it purpose. Me, agency nurse turned remote-bound, love for the red dirt that feels like belonging pressed into the soles of my feet, a family made of friends and a single promise I keep renewing to a man who isn't here.

When plates were stacked and the gecko had announced himself by trotting across the ceiling like a tiny lizard landlord, I ducked outside with my mug and my phone. The smokers' door had been replaced, for tonight, by the verandah step.

Four ships and a tug.

Grief didn't arrive tonight the way it had yesterday, it sent an emissary. A nudge behind the ribs. Remember the promise, Indi. Not the promise to stop hurting, grief laughs at ultimatums, but the other one. The one that gives the tide somewhere to go.

A starred event sat in my calendar for later in the year, 'A Star to Remember.' I'd been asked three times to speak and ducked each one with the speed of a woman who knows her limits better than her courage. Tonight, the courage felt… possible. A text to

Sue at DonateLife took five tries to phrase and three seconds to send.

Me: "Hi Sue, Indi here. I'd like to confirm for A Star to Remember. Happy to speak. For Lionel."

Her reply arrived before my tea cooled.

Sue: "Oh, Indi. Yes. We'd be honoured. Call me when you can, we'll support you through."

The relief wasn't relief. It was alignment. A click in the chest where a compass lives.

Inside, Robyn had put on the tiny TV. The reception was the kind that turns weather into modern art, but we could hear the footy and that was enough. Peter performed couch surgery, redistributing cushions like a man trained in ergonomics.

"Sit," Robyn commanded. "You did a big thing just now. You look taller."

"Only because I'm on your mat," I said. "It's very optimistic."

We watched until the ads got smug and then did the washing up in an easy choreography that felt older than us. When I finally crawled into my new bed, a rectangle of mattress and air con hum, I felt something I hadn't felt since I was small and fearless and sure the world would take my weight.

Safe.

***

The mine bus rocked Big Russ into a near nap on the way back to camp. He let his head thunk against the window anyway. Night shift had a way of turning your skull into a tin can with a stone in it.

Tiny flopped into the seat across the aisle and stuck a boot into Big Russ's shin like a toddler. "Wake up, Romeo."

Big Russ grunted. "You keep calling me that and I'm telling everyone what happened with the emu."

"That emu started it." Tiny leaned over. "You going to the wet mess?"

"No."

"You never go to the wet mess."

"Because it's full of blokes like you."

"Blokes like me keep this place interesting."

"I'm too old for interesting."

Tiny studied him. "You're thirty-one."

"I'm thirty-one and tired."

And then, because the bus was too quiet and his own head too loud, Big Russ let himself think the thing he was absolutely not thinking.

Her.

He tried to picture the Finny without her in it and failed. The way she'd stood at the bar like a person who knows how to be small without being anything but herself. The way the room had bent toward her. Along with the dangerous little look she'd thrown him on the way out, sharp as a hook, quick as a flash.

He flicked the thought away like a fly. Spent no more than a second on the fact that his own heart had a tiny twitch in it he hadn't felt since before. Before Jodie had looked at New Zealand like it was a lifeboat and stepped neatly onto it, before Vanessa had made him question his taste in both women and friends. One divorce, one serious relationship that had gone seriously sideways. That was enough lessons for any man.

Ironclad walls, he reminded himself. They'd taken years to build and the Pilbara to test. The walls were why he was good at his job. The walls were why he slept sometimes. The walls were why the wet mess could howl, and he could sit in his donga and let the air con hum turn his bones into something neutral.

Back at camp he swiped his card at the mess like a prisoner clocking in for a conjugal with a chicken schnitty. Tonight's options, schnitzel, something labelled beef surprise, salad bar with beetroot that tasted like it had travelled steerage. He ate fast, mechanical, the way you do when food is fuel and silence tastes better.

The donga was a mirror-image of a thousand dongas, door that sticks in the heat, bed with a dip exactly where your back wishes it wouldn't, a desk with a gouge from some joker's belt buckle, a bathroom where the hot tap is more of a concept than a promise. He put his boots under the chair, his phone on the charger, and his heart somewhere he didn't have to see it.

And yet.

He lay back, closed his eyes, the dark behind them wasn't black at all but brown, rich, dangerous, the deep-chocolate of two bottomless pools. His brain supplied, unhelpfully, Indianna.

"Fuck," he said to the ceiling, quietly, like a prayer he didn't believe in. Then he rolled onto his side and forced his thoughts to the roster chalked on the whiteboard and the torque specs he knew by muscle, and the way a Perkins will tell you it's going to throw a tantrum if you listen with the part of your spine that remembers. In the morning there would be heat and bolts and men and engines and something to fix, and that would be enough. It had to be.

He turned the air con down to 23 because even alone the rule held. He closed his eyes and didn't check his phone.

***

In the morning I found the washing roster, wrote 'INDI Thursday 06:00' with Peter's steadfast pencil, and stuck a label on the second shelf from the top.

I told myself I was finding my feet. But it felt more like they were finding me.

Work was the kind of quiet that isn't, beds shifting like puzzle pieces, an IV that went backwards before it went forwards, a new grad brave enough to say, "Can you watch me?" and then brave enough to ask, "Did I do that wrong?" The kind of day that builds calluses you don't mind having.

At lunch, Robyn intercepted me with a plastic container. "Tuna pasta. Don't argue. If you fall over, I have to do your obs."

"Bossy," I said, grateful.

"Experienced," she corrected.

At 15:15, I checked the ships. Four again. The tug was on smoko. The tide was doing what tides do, coming in, going out, ignoring us unless we were very foolish, or very lucky.

On the walk back I rehearsed a promise to a dead man. Not the first time and not the last.

"Lionel", I said, out loud because sometimes you have to. "I'll tell it right. Not just the end. The twenty-one when we said yes. The ten thousand named things you loved and the ten thousand you didn't know how to say. The way you laughed with your whole face and shoulders. The way the nurses held us up. I'll tell what DonateLife gave us when we had nothing left to give. I'll tell it soft, and I'll tell it true. I'll stand under the star, and I'll say your name like it is still happening."

A gull looked at me like I'd interrupted its thesis. I nodded back. "You're right," I told it. "Dramatic."

Back at the donga, Peter was restringing a battered snare with the concentration of a man performing microscopic surgery. Robyn was on the phone to a niece, telling a story with her whole body.

"Big night?" she asked when she hung up.

"Only if Neville starts handing out chilli again."

She wagged a finger. "Do not encourage him. Last time he nearly took out half of E Block."

We ate and traded shifts like playing cards. Night, early, late, on-call. It's a choreography, the way you lay your week down next to someone else's and make gaps into nets.

Before bed I stood under the shower and let the red run off my ankles. The air con clicked, the gecko clicked back, and somewhere in camp the wet mess whooped at a try that would be argued about tomorrow. I dried my hair and picked out a bow without irony.

On the fridge, the tea towel fluttered in the draft. Ten rules, one life.

I wrote a small eleventh in biro across the bottom, because some things you have to say out loud even if you're writing them in a place no one else will look.

Keep your promises.

I switched off the light, texted Sue: Call you tomorrow, counted four ships and a tug in my head like sheep, and slept in a way that felt earned.

In the morning the frog did the door check, and I stepped over him like I was stepping into a story I recognised. Out in the harbour, the ships shifted their weight.

"Indi," I told my reflection in the donga mirror, the one that turns you into a short film under fluoro, "let's go."

53

Chapter Six

Mondays in the Pilbara don't tiptoe. They arrive with a sky so clean it looks ironed and a wind that tastes like salt and sunblock. I'm on earlys, marshmallow bunny coloured lipstick already in my pocket, because colour helps on big days.

Kerry slaps a handover sheet onto the station bench. "Heads up. ENT pop-in for a quinsy, and a community review for Hansen's. Dressings list is biblical. Tomo's lead. Indi, you and Daniel run with him."

"Copy," I say, clipping my pen to the top like a talisman.

"Also," Kerry adds, "Elders' morning tea at 10:00. If Aunty Lila says 'sit,' you sit."

"Always," I promise.

***

Handover is headlines with sharp edges, Bed 2: Peritonsillar abscess - fasting, hot potato voice, trismus, drooling, pain 10/10. Bed 5: Open foot wounds, peripheral neuropathy - long-term Hansen's regimen, community check-in with the health worker and extended family. Room 10 remains its own small planet, our young mum with the difficult abscess, and her aunty guarding like a lighthouse. Plus, five title-fights wrestling with tape, two IVs that have trust issues, and a surprise bed-bath for a gentleman who swears he showered last solstice.

"Rule one?" Tomo prompts as we start moving. "If it smells like it needs a priest, it needs two nurses and a plan."

"Rule two? Breathe through your mouth," I deadpan.

His mouth doesn't smile, his eyes do. "Let's roll."

***

Bed 2 is a lesson in airflow and patience. The man looks thirty-five going on ancient. He's tripod-sitting, jaw clenched against pain, voice trapped behind a wall of swollen tonsil.

"Morning, mate. I'm Indi," I say softly, kneeling so my face isn't a threat. "I'm going to be the bossy one who makes the pain go down and the swelling go away."

His eyes flick to mine, frantic. He can't swallow saliva, it strings and drips, and dignity tries to leave the room.

"Not going anywhere," I tell him, sliding a disposable absorbent bluey under his chin and another across his chest. "We'll keep you dry. That's our job. You keep breathing. That's yours."

We move like we've rehearsed it. Nebulised adrenaline, IV line with the least amount of bother, a quiet dose of dexamethasone, fentanyl in whispers, suction ready. I chart "NBM," highlight allergies, run through airway steps with Daniel in the voice you use when you don't want your hands to hear you're worried.

ENT breezes in with a scoop of charm and a tray. "Afternoon - oh, morning. Right. Classic," she says, peering into a mouth that says no. "We'll have you better in a tick."

"Time-out," I interject gently, and she grins and plays along, ID, procedure, kit, consent. The little things that keep the big things from breaking.

"Okay, mate," she says. "Little needle, little nick, big relief."

He winces for a second and then, like unplugging a sink, fluid, pressure, pain… gone. His shoulders drop. Tears he didn't mean to cry arrive and keep their dignity because I meet them with a steady gaze.

"Better?" I ask, swapping soaked for clean with the magic trick that is fast hands and quiet hands.

He nods, and the hot potato leaves his voice. "Bless you," he croaks. "And your lipstick."

"Flattery will get you ice chips," I say. "Small sips. Slow."

"Marshmallow," he adds, surprising us both.

"Bunny," I confirm, and even ENT laughs.

***

Bed 5 is why I became a nurse and why I sometimes think I won't be able to get out of bed again. The elder on the mattress is all sharp cheekbones and gentle authority, the kind of presence that steadies a room. Beside him is Damo, the Aboriginal health worker from community, and three family members who introduce themselves in a ripple, names, skin, where they fit. Shoes tangle at the door like a small party took them off all at once.

We warm the room with hello. We ask to see feet with respect. We set out what we need, sterile pack, saline, iodine, those foam dressings that feel like a cloud when you get it right. We fold the sheet back as if it were an offering and not a barrier. We talk about everything except what hurts for the first five minutes because first you build a bridge.

"Shame job," the elder says, half a joke at his own expense when the blanket lifts.

"Not today," I say. "Not in here." I look at the family. "Everybody good if we go slow and keep everything covered that doesn't need to be uncovered?"

Nods all round.

Neuropathy is a thief. It steals sensation and then pretends it's a favour. We check with a monofilament and a tuning fork and words. We explain as we go because truth is kindness. I teach while I dress, Daniel watches and then does, hands a little bigger than they need to be in the beginning, becoming smaller, neater, kinder as his confidence grows.

Damo translates the important bits into the language of this family, this place. He also translates me, which is a different skill.

I show the elder how to check water temperature with elbow not foot. I show his niece how to pad a boot with a trick my paediatric placement taught me, foam donut, pressure redistribution, and dignity preserved. I show his nephew how to tape without strangling skin.

"Leprosy," the nephew says, half in challenge, half in question. "People scared."

"Hansen's," I say, because names matter. "Curable. Treatable. Not your fault. Not a curse. Meds work. We treat nerves, skin, dignity. You lot are the best part of the plan."

A smile moves through them like sunlight.

We finish, and the elder takes my hand in both of his. His hands are dry and warm and rough like the country that made them.

"Nooba," he says, patting the chair next to him.

I look to Damo.

"Means 'friend'," Damo tells me. "He's calling you friend, asking you to sit, stay a bit. Different mobs, different words, here that's how we use it."

I sit. I let the clock fight me and lose. The Elder talks. He shows me a scar that's older than my degree and tells me how he got it. He tells me jokes that shouldn't be funny and are. The family laughs, the sound with the beat of long afternoons and crowded kitchens.

"Munya," the Elder says at last, tapping the fresh dressings with approval, palm hovering over his hip.

I look to Damo again.

"Munya means 'bottom,' he's saying the backside's sorted. Dressing's good," Damo translates, grinning. "Means 'buttocks, bottom that's right'… here," he says, and nods like he's stamping my passport. "You can use it. Careful, though. Words are like country."

I touch the notebook in my pocket and write them down, *nooba* (friend), *munya* (bottom), with a note: 'used here in this mob.'

On the way out, Aunty Lila appears at my elbow with a plastic ice-cream container that holds something stew-adjacent.

"For later," she decrees. "Sit. Eat. Nooba."

"Yes, Aunty," I say, already feeling the starch of my plans soften in her orbit.

***

The ward turns into a river after that and pulls me along. An obs round, temp, pulse, respirations, BP, sats, and a dressing that refuses to stop bleeding because the wound keeps oozing. Mr D in Bed 4 demands to know who moved the TV and then apologises with a cough that sounds suspiciously like a laugh when he realises that the tv hasn't actually been moved.

At 10:10, the Elders' morning tea hits critical mass in the day room. It smells like damper, corned beef, tea that has been boiled into submission, and a cake that looks like someone's nan loves them more than the rest of us. Someone tells a story about a crocodile and a dog and a ute and I can't tell if it's a parable or a documentary, but it ends in applause. I am taught to slice damper properly (it's an angle, not a square), and I am forbidden from making tea for Aunty Lila ever again because mine is weak and therefore "rude to the day." I correct that with three extra minutes of brew and an extra spoon. I am forgiven.

"Your pink lipstick," one of the granddads announces, pointing at my mouth like it is both suspicious and fascinating. "Nooba, come show Aunty."

"Best accreditation I've ever had," I tell him.

"Don't get cocky," he says, and winks.

***

After shift, I hit the little gym near the staff village because my legs want to run without actually going anywhere. The squat rack is occupied by three blokes in hi-vis who look like the standard issue of every worksite, one with a mullet tied back like a pet, one with a Southern Cross tattoo that looks like it was done on a moving vehicle, and one who keeps checking himself out in the mirrors like he might propose.

They're talking at a volume that suggests they've never met a woman who wasn't their sister, their boss, or their parole officer.

"…that girl from the hospital," Mullet says between sets. "The one with the pink lippy. Looked me dead in the eye and told me to *breathe through my mouth.*"

"Legend," Southern Cross says. "My missus tried that once. Didn't take."

"Bet she's high maintenance," Mirror murmurs, flexing in an ironically unmaintained singlet.

I rack my bar, step back, and absolutely fail to mind my own business.

"Hi," I say pleasantly, wiping sweat. "I'm the high-maintenance one with the pink lipstick. Your squat depth is a workplace injury, your spotter's about to drop you, and if you want to learn how to breathe through your mouth properly, come spend ten minutes in our Room 10."

Mullet blinks. Southern Cross grins. Mirror, bless him, laughs out loud.

"Noted, nurse," he says. "We'll do our paperwork."

That's the way," I reply, and they look confused and a bit smitten, which is the correct response to everything about today.

On the way out I pass the skid-steer bay and find art, four tyres have laid perfect black commas across the concrete where someone braked too late and lied about it on their pre-start. I take a photo of the track marks with the sunset behind them and post it to my private story with the caption: "Spotted: rare Pilbara skid boys in their natural habitat. Breathe through your mouth."

Mollie replies with twelve crying-laughing faces and a gif of a forklift.

***

Back at the donga, Robyn's on the verandah in scrub pants and a vintage band tee, hair up in a bun that says she has forgotten what combs are for.

"How'd you go?" she asks, passing me a bottle of water like a relay baton.

"Quinsy drained, elder's feet dressed, learned two words and got promoted by Aunty to full-time tea drinker."

Robyn grins. "Indoctrinated by morning tea. You're one of us now."

Peter's inside building a tower of Tupperware like it's Jenga. "Leftovers sculpture," he says solemnly. "Title: No One Cooks for One."

I laugh harder than the joke deserves, and it breaks something stiff in my chest.

Over dinner we swap the kind of stories that are actually about everything except the details. Robyn pulls out markers and writes NOOBA and MUNYA on the whiteboard above the sink and then draws a tiny cup of tea next to them.

"Definitions," she declares. "Nooba: friend, mate, our usage here." She underlines *here* twice. "Munya: bottom, buttocks. Here. We never assume."

Peter nods. "Words have country."

"Exactly," I say, and the red-dirt notebook sitting on my knees feels heavier and kinder.

***

Later, the donga goes quiet in the way shared houses do, showers thunk off, a kettle clicks, someone laughs on FaceTime in a distant room, and then the place breathes. I sit at the tiny table with a lukewarm tea, strong, black, two sugars because right isn't always about me being right, and then I open the notebook.

'A Star to Remember' - DonateLife have pencilled me in for October. Today sealed it. If an Elder can name me nooba, friend, then I can sit with my own history long enough to speak. And if he can make us laugh with munya, bottom, then maybe I can find the plain, human words for what Lionel gave, and for the men and boys who breathe because he can't anymore.

I uncap my pen and write: *We used to have our own idea of grief…* I stare at the line until it blurs and stab a line through it. Too neat. Too many other people's words.

New page. *This isn't about a good death. It's about the lives that kept going.* I delete that too, the way you delete a text you don't want to send because it isn't true enough yet.

I try again, smaller, plainer: *My husband's name was Lionel. He loved too loudly for one body. When he died, three families got to keep someone. That is the whole story and also not close to enough.*

I close the book before I can be mean to myself. Some things just need time to sit.

On the shelf above the tiny sink is the photo I let myself bring north this time of Lionel on the beach, sun in his eyelashes, that forehead groove I used to kiss like a promise. I touch the air in front of it, not the frame, and I don't ask for a sign because he's already given so many I don't have pockets big enough left to hold them.

Before I sleep I write three lines in the back of the red-dirt notebook where I keep the day's small truths:

- Quinsy gone; dignity stayed.

- *Nooba* from the Elder; *munya* from the family.

- Gym boys learned to breathe.

Lights out. The donga sighs. Somewhere out past the staff village, ships queue like punctuation. I promise myself I'll check them in the morning. And if the horizon is clean, I'll take that as the only sign I need.

"Night, Lionel," I whisper to the dark.

"Night, Indi," the room doesn't say back, and that's okay.

Chapter Seven

RDO tastes like oranges and dust.

"Up, princess," Robyn sings at my door at five-thirty, knuckles drumming a rhythm that could raise the dead. "Karijini waits for no nurse."

I'm already awake, watching the first bruised light creep across the lino. "I'm up."

We pack the ute the way people who've lived north know how, esky like a Tetris boss - ice on the bottom, then the chicken wings, then the fruit in a solid layer so nothing bruises, and then the cans - camp chairs, two towels each, "one for the water, one for the dust," Peter pronounces like a prophet, hats, fly nets, extra sunscreen, a first-aid kit that could resuscitate a small cow, and the red-dirt notebook because if I don't bring it, something worth catching will happen and run off.

"Fuel?" I ask.

"Full," Peter says, patting the dashboard like it's a horse we're taking over a river. "Tyres checked. Snakes briefed. Everyone got a head torch?"

"Day trip," I remind him.

He grins. "And yet."

We swing out of Hedland while the town is still yawning, the salt piles catching pink, and the long trains sliding iron toward the ships like beads being counted. The highway south finds its rhythm, low scrub, termite mounds like rusted dunce caps, and a hawk riding a thermal with the smugness of an expensive kite.

Music on low, windows cracked enough to let the early cool in, we let the kilometres do the slow work of unwinding.

"Rules," Robyn says, draping one leg onto the dash like a contortionist. "No talking about work for the first hour. Afterwards we may gossip gently about work but only if it's funny, and names changed to protect the incompetent."

"Rule three," Peter adds. "We stop for roadhouse coffee and a suspicious pie at Auski because it's tradition."

"Rule four," I say. "We remember this is someone's country and we behave like invited guests. Hats off at the water. Quiet at the pools."

"Rule five," Robyn says. "Indi has to wear the pink lipstick because the granddads approved."

I fish marshmallow bunny from my bag and paint on a little courage. The land of country changes bit by bit, and then, all at once, the red deepens, the spinifex tilts its crowns to us like it's in on a joke, and the horizon lifts itself into low, dark humps. Karijini is in there, ancient, patient, and older than the shape of our language for it. The signs thin out. The road ripples. The three of us go quieter without deciding to.

At the visitor centre we stretch the drive out of our bones and read the boards like they are liturgy. I touch the map with two fingers, tracing where we'll go, Dales Gorge, Fortescue Falls, Fern Pool. Robyn says the Traditional Owners' names out loud and slow, the way she does with new parents when she wants to get the baby's name right the first time. We promise each other, again, to walk like witnesses, not like owners.

"First dip?" Peter asks.

"Fortescue first," I say. "Then Fern to rinse my brain."

We edge the ute into the carpark between two caravans that look like grey whales at a resting station. The air is softer here, like someone's turned the volume down. Eucalypts make their small whisper, paper leaves rubbing secrets together, and the gorge exhales a cool that walks up to meet the heat and shake its hand. Magpies throw a few clean notes across the car park. Somewhere a kettle clicks off in a van and the smell of instant coffee threads through spinifex and dust. The light goes honey on the red rock. For a beat the whole place feels held, the road behind us, the deep below, and us in the middle, breathing easier than we did ten minutes ago.

The rim track is a generosity, a wide, sandy invitation. Then the steps begin, the stacked ironstone leading us down into another world. Palms appear where they have no right to be, water voice ahead like a secret being told to someone else. Fortescue Falls unthreads itself over the terrace, sunlight breaking into a hundred tiny knives on the water. People step carefully on the slick rock, and even the kids move quieter than kids normally do, instinct knows a cathedral when it finds one.

We slide in. It steals your breath and then gives it back to you cleaner. The water is an argument between cold and red rock warmth, and I let it explain something to my body I can't say out loud. Robyn swears with reverence. Peter floats on his back and counts dragonflies.

"See you at Fern?" I say eventually, pushing hair off my face.

"Go," Robyn says, examining her toes like they might try to escape. "We'll meet you there."

"Take your time," Peter adds. "You only get your first Sunday here once."

The path to Fern Pool narrows around a bend and the world lowers its voice. A small sign asks for quiet - this is a special place - and people obey without being told twice. Gravel softens underfoot. A big old fig leans in like a grandmother offering shade, skirts of root and moss gathered around her ankles. Paperbarks peel in long, careful curls, and dragonflies stitch silver thread through the stillness.

Then the pool appears, water the colour of a deep green question. The falls at the far end pour in thin white threads, unhurried, like someone combing a child's hair. The air smells of leaf and stone and tastes clean on the tongue. You feel your shoulders drop before you notice you were holding them high. Someone's sandals dangle from their fingers. A boy's laugh starts loud, then lands softly, as if even sound knows to tread lightly here. You stand at the edge, and the place does what it has always done, it holds you and asks nothing back in return but your quiet.

I take the long way, up to the rim, around the gorge mouth, and then back down the other side, because my legs want to climb, and my head wants the space. On the rim, the view is pure Pilbara, the land laid out like skin, ironstone ribs showing, and ghost gums spaced like commas. The track slims to a shelf where you have to turn your shoulders to pass another body. My hands feel out the rock and come away iron scented. In the notch ahead, a shadow resolves into a man coming the other way, broad through shoulders, hat brim pulled down, and a movement that is unshowy and sure. For half a second, I think mine-worker silhouette, standard issue. Then he lifts his head, and the world tilts a bit, like someone has put an extra coin on a very delicate scale.

Big Russ.

We reach each other on the narrow ledge where you have to choose hands and eyes over bravado. It's a meeting that isn't really a meeting, just two travellers doing what the track requires.

"Hey," he says, a low whisper, respectful of the sign, the gorge, and the unspoken words that lingered in the air between us. His eyes dangerous and deep, two dark, chocolatey pools that hold me for a breath.

I tip my hat brim back with one finger. "Hey." My voice comes out steadier than I expected.

We passed each other sideways, his hand finding the rock beside my shoulder, my sleeve skimming his forearm in a way that would be accidental if either of us believed in accidents. Heat radiates off him, and also a different kind of warmth. I move past, then look back because I don't trust myself not to. He does the same. Two caught-out glances. Two small, surrendering smiles that don't promise anything and somehow still feel like a new beginning. I carry on, a little lighter on my feet than I was a minute ago.

***

Fern Pool is a hymn sung in green. The platform leads you down into another temperature, another century. Water falls in two fine veils between ferns and rock that feel older than time itself. People perch at the water's edge and, almost at once, sense that silence fits them here.

Someone has left a small bunch of wildflowers on the timber, paper daisies and mulla mulla tied with a scrap of ribbon, a soft flag of colour against the grain. The petals hold their own light. Even the teenagers, glorious, loud creatures everywhere else, seem to understand the note those flowers are playing. They tumble and surface and still manage to leave a circle of quiet between dives, breathless grins pressed flat by reverence. A girl perches with her toes curled over the plank, counting down on her fingers, her mate shushes the world without meaning to. When they hit the water it's with a gentleness that feels like they've been taught by the pool itself. The ripples reach the wildflowers and rock them, a nod, as if the place is accepting the offering.

I slip in slow, my mouth remembering to shut. The shock of cold resets something in me I didn't know had been knocked crooked. I backstroke out into the green and watch paperbarks pattern the sky. A dragonfly parks on my knee like it owns the lease. When I tread water under the fall, the pelt of it on my head feels like absolution.

On the rocks across the pool, a man sits half in, half out, hands braced behind him the way you do when you want to feel the small tremors of the world travel into your bones. Hat off. The line where the tan meets the old scar on his left shoulder. He tips his head under the fall and comes up with his hair darker and his face younger and that same, same weight in it. He wipes water from his mouth with the back of his hand like he's taking an oath he didn't mean to take.

***

Big Russ had told himself coming here was about the cold and the oldness and the way Fern Pool rinses your eyes until they see straight. It wasn't about the woman he'd watched walk into the Finny like she was trying to be smaller than she is. It wasn't about his mate Lionel, and it wasn't about the way the room tilted toward her at The Finny. It was the deeper thing he didn't yet have a name for."

Except it was.

He tried the water trick. He tried the sit-still trick. He tried the "don't think about a pink elephant" trick that never works. He thought of her anyway. He thought of the way she said *copy* with her eyes when a situation needed an adult. He thought about how her mouth had the humour of someone who'd learned it for survival. He thought about the tiny bow of respect she gave Aunty Lila in a hospital corridor he wasn't in and couldn't have seen, and he knew he was making some of this up and also not making it up at all.

He lowered himself into the pool until it took his ribs and then his stubborn heart and then his stupid thoughts. He held onto the timber edge and dunked himself like the old men at the surf club used to, counting to ten because ten was a thing he could do when other numbers felt unruly. When he surfaced, nothing had changed and everything had.

Across the water, she climbed the ladder in one smooth move, pressed her palms to the deck to squeeze the water out of her hair, and never once looked over, which is how he knew she knew he was there. He stayed where he was and learned, again, how to sit with himself.

***

We picnic up on the rim where the wind takes the heat away before it gets other ideas. The chicken wings taste like they've been smoked in an argument between wood and weather. The mango is a small religion. A kite drops low enough to pretend to be casual and then flicks a wicked wing when it sees we're not gullible.

"Out of ten?" Peter asks, licking sauce off his wrist with a clear conscience.

"Ten," I say. "With bonus points for dragonflies and the old fig."

"Minus one for the boy who did a bomb at Fortescue and got a lecture from six different aunties in six different languages," Robyn offers.

"Plus one for the same boy when he apologised to each aunty individually with his hat off," Peter counters.

We lie back and watch the sky con traffic lines between the few clouds. My heart slows in a way that feels like it will stay slow even when emails and pagers try to speed it up again.

After a second swim, we can't not, we do the rim walk proper, stopping at the bits that feel like postcards and at the bits that feel like they're just for us. On one ledge I put my hand down and come away with ironstone glitter. Robyn takes a photo of our boots next to the seam in the rock at the rim, just big enough to notice and feel the land's old fault, and then captions it #nooba, because that's what we are, two friends sitting together, and sharing the quiet.

On the way back to the carpark, we get stuck behind a line of blokes in hi-vis who are all bravado and no hats.

"Your necks," Robyn calls cheerfully. "You'll boil them."

"We're tough," one says, and the others chuckle like a flock of galahs.

"Sun is tougher," I say, passing them a tube of sunscreen as if it's a hot potato. They take it and, to their credit, use it.

***

We roll back into camp golden and tired. Showers have never felt better. Dinner is lazy, cold things, a bit of bread, Robyn's ambrosia salad that shouldn't work but does. Peter pulls out three camp mugs that have been to more sunsets than most people we know and pours the non-alcoholic ginger beer like its champagne.

"To Karijini," he says.

"To Sundays," Robyn adds.

"To this," I say, nowhere near as eloquent.

When the heat leaks out of the ground and the first proper darkness drapes itself over us, we take our camp chairs three metres from the verandah and tip our heads back. The stars here make a fool of your city nights. They crowd in, bossy, particular. The Milky Way is ridiculous, like spilled sugar and smoke, and the long dark river of the Emu in the Sky laid across it like a story someone was clever enough to pin up where we can all see it.

We don't bother with music. The night has its own. The occasional car in the distance is a rumour. Somewhere far off a dog argues with its own shadow.

A plane cuts a slow line across everything, and I wonder about the passengers, what they can see from up there, and what they think the land is down here. The three of us share the same quiet, but our hearts wandered their own paths.

Stargazing is a good place to tell the truth you can't say out loud in daylight. I borrow the dark and make a prayer out of it.

"Help me live," I mutter into the old cold light, and the words surprise me because they are not a plea for proof or for reversing the irreversible. They are a request to make good on what's already been given.

The DonateLife promise sits in my chest like a small lantern. October is a breath away, and also a long walk. I open the red-dirt notebook by phone light and write four words:

Tell the true parts.

Then I shut it again and let it sit. Let what today put in me find its own shape. You can't tug a sprout into a tree, you just give it time and light.

Robyn snores from three metres away, the dignified thrum of someone who has earned her rest. Peter hums the wrong key of something I almost recognise and then gives up in favour of biscuit crumbs and silence.

Breeze on my neck. Dust on my calves. The kind of tired that feels like proof that you have lived.

My phone at my foot lights up once, face-down glow against the leg of the chair. I don't check it. If it's the world, it can wait. There is a difference between not answering from fear and not answering because you're giving the night its due.

"Night, Lionel," I say later, when the cold has found its way into my shirt and my teeth start to get ideas.

A falling star does what clichés do, shows up like it's working to a script and still somehow feels like it was written for you.

I take that as my answer, I think, and stand, and go inside.

Chapter Eight

Nights smell different.

By 20:45 the corridors have cooled, the daytime arguments have gone home to fight over TV remotes, and the building does its low, patient hum. Hand foam, boiled coffee, fresh gowns, and floor polish, that's the night blend. I badge in at 20:59 with the same superstitious press on the scanner I've been doing since my grad year. It still feels like it lets me in a fraction kinder when I do.

"Rotate to nights?" Kerry asks, half sympathy, half wicked delight.

"Three on, one off," I say. "Then back to days. If I start speaking fluent possum, sedate me."

"Handover at the board," she says. "SCU's light, ward's medium, ED will try to gift you a human at 02:00 because it's Wednesday."

Tom "Tomo" Morrison taps the sheet. "You're with me. We've got Mr O'Riley in 5B - pneumonia, grumpy, Mrs Pritchard in 2 - UTI, even grumpier, 10A's aunty is back as visitor not patient - behave. SCU has Uncle Jerry on palliative watch for symptom control - Miriwoong man, quiet. Families in and out. We'll go there together later."

"Copy."

"And Rule Night?" he asks.

"No heroics without calories," I recite.

He grins. "Good. Let's work."

***

Nights start small and wide. Obs, meds, the friendly lies about dreadful television, "Wow, I can't believe they sent that dancer home." Mr O'Riley tells me the air is too thin in here and the pillows are haunted, I add one more pillow and a fan and don't argue with ghosts. Mrs Pritchard prefers her pan warmed (fair) and her water cold (also fair) and her grandchildren to stop wearing torn jeans (not my jurisdiction).

By 22:10 the ward has gone to low beam. The lights dimmed, and the beeps domesticated. Robyn appears at the desk like a caffeinated saint with a tray of tea that tastes better than religion and a plate of biscuits that definitely meet the night-shift nutritional guidelines in some alternate universe. We inhale them and virtue-signal about the carrot sticks we'll eat later.

At 22:37 the first test of the shift decides to be obvious instead of sneaky. 5B's call bell erupts and the monitor throws a sulk. Mr O'Riley, who's been rehearsing for this moment with minor theatrics all evening, has gone from grumpy to grey-green. The chest, tight and not moving enough air. The sats - 86 and diving. The lips a tight line of "I can't."

"On it," I say, and the world goes small and useful.

Airway, breathing, circulation. Nebs, sit him forward, peel the tight things off the body, extra blankets, unnecessary panic. Tomo is there the way he always is when it matters, calm hands, clear voice. "I'm here, Mr O'Riley. Give us your best breath." I prepare salbutamol and ipratropium without looking at my hands, set up the spacer like it's a magic trick, and talk him through every breath because people can do hard things if someone narrates the road.

"Better," he rasps after a minute, surprised.

"Yep," I say, smiling with my eyes because my mouth is busy. "You're doing it."

We keep at it. The numbers climb like a cautious kid on a ladder. 91, 94, 96. His shoulders come down. Somewhere in my sternum, the strings loosen.

"Good save," Tomo says low as we reset the room.

"We saved him together," I say, because truth matters.

"Always," he says, and ghost-signs a cup of tea. "Later."

***

The ward settles into its 02:00 self. The ventilator down the hall hisses to itself. Someone's IV pump beeps and then thinks better of it. The vending machine displays 8.80 like a taunt. I swallow the banana I promised myself in lieu of biscuits, drink the tea Robyn delivers like she can smell when my hands start to shake, and stand the way old nurses taught me, weight off the knees, shoulders down, face kind.

At 02:09, SCU calls.

"Indi," Daniel says from the doorway, eyes soft. "Uncle Jerry's daughter asked if someone can sit. Tomo said you."

I grab the Bluetooth speaker we keep for bad days and better ones and check with Kerry. "Go," she says. "I'll keep your patch warm."

SCU at night is an in-between country. Not ICU's theatre-bright certainty, not the ward's many-small-stories hum. Two rooms, ghosts of old alarms in the air, the curtains breathing with the aircon.

Uncle Jerry is lying on his side, the way people do when they've fought their whole lives against pain and learned what position counts. The bones of his face show like the land here does when the water's gone. His chest takes the careful breaths of someone who still has his pride about it. His daughter, Lena, sits at the head of the bed with a hand where his hair used to be when it was thick enough to braid.

"Evening, Aunty," I say, small bow in the word. "I'm Indi. Tomo asked me to sit a while if you're happy with that."

She looks at me like she can see the truth of things under my scrub top. Then she nods. "He liked the old ones," she says. "Sing 'em if you know 'em. Not too loud. He's listening still."

"Country?" I ask.

She smiles without the top half of her face changing. "Old country. Charley Pride. Slim Dusty. Troy. Missy's too flash for him. Maybe one of them you know."

"I know enough to hum," I say.

She stands, presses her forehead to his briefly, and murmurs something soft I don't catch. Then, gently, "I'll step outside for a bit. He'll wait, he always did." She touches my arm. "You sit. You've got a good quiet." And she's gone, to the smokers' door, to the stars, to the place where daughters let themselves breathe.

I set the speaker low, the volume at barely-there. Charley Pride finds the room. *Kiss an Angel Good Morning* is both too on the nose and exactly right. Uncle's mouth does that thing mouths do in sleep when they remember joy.

I sit and watch the rise and fall. Between songs I talk to him in the way old matrons taught me, name, place, time, weather, who's here, who loves you. This is Port Hedland Hospital, this is the night shift, the ships are in, the winds blowing from the east, your girl is outside getting the stars in her lungs for you. Your feet are warm. Your pain's under manners. We've got you.

He makes a small sound, and I take his hand. It's light and heavy at once, that hand, with work written into it, and a young man's knuckles hiding underneath the old skin. He squeezes like men do when they think a full handhold is too much. I squeeze back with everything I am allowed.

"Old ones," I murmur, scrolling. Slim Dusty's '*Lights on the Hill.*' A station I grew up hearing in other rooms, through other summers. I don't sing because the nurses' station has never asked for that. But I hum, and I remember how Lionel would make up new words to songs, just to catch my smile.

Grief arrives at the hour it likes best. 02:00 to 04.00. The blue hour where the body feels the truth and the brain hasn't put its helmet back on yet. The ICU in my head lights itself up without asking me. The glass, the bright cold, the way the air felt engineered. Lionel's brow with the tiny groove I used to kiss when I wanted to distract him. The machine that says how many breaths per minute, not how much love there was in those breaths. My hand on his hand. The ridiculousness of us telling grown doctors that we would decide to let him go when we were ready and also how right that was. The way the room went quieter than any room has a right to be when the numbers did what numbers do. The beautiful, terrible discipline of staying until your person's heart stops in your hand.

I blink my way back to Uncle Jerry and lay my palm on the old bone of his shoulder.

"Go gentle, Uncle," I say under the song. "We're here."

Lena comes back in, smelling like cold air and tears dried properly. She takes the other side, puts her hand back on his head. The room adjusts. Time does something funny and accurate. Uncle Jerry's chest pauses between two breaths, not a decision so much as a shift in a story's voice. He doesn't fight. He does not forget to be dignified. He lets go like the old river he's from does when it finds the sea.

The monitor offers to make this into a performance. I turn it off. We sit in the generous quiet instead.

After a minute, Lena exhales. "Thank you," she says, and the words are for me and for her father and for the old singers and for the night.

"Thank you," I say back, because being let in is always the gift.

I do the practical things that are also sacred. The wash of the face with warm water. The brush of the beard. The comb through the hair that still remembers to go to the right. I put the sheet in the right place under his chin. I say the words we always say because they are true, "We'll take care. We'll go slow. You tell us what you need."

Lena asks for a cuppa and I make it properly, strong/black/two sugars, and leave it in her hand like a ritual object. She drinks, and the hot goes into the place that just became a room with one less breath in it.

Tomo stands at the door and doesn't enter. "Okay?" he mouths.

"Okay," I mouth back, and it means not okay and also okay enough for now.

***

At 03:10 I step out to the ambulance bay instead of the smokers' door because the breeze is better there and because you can see more sky without the ship lights making the horizon look like a festival. The stars are ridiculous, they come all the way down here and sit on the car park and on my shoulders. I think about Lionel's driver's license card tucked in my wallet like a talisman and how I still touch it sometimes like braille. How the paperwork we signed on the worst day I've known sent parts of him away to live in strangers who are not strangers anymore. How I keep their letters in the soft-paper drawer and open them when I need to remember that grief can be a river and a channel at the same time.

My phone buzzes in my pocket. I check it because I am not brave enough to ignore the world when it calls at 03:10.

It's the local Tracks & Trails WhatsApp where Peter posts sunrises to annoy night shifters. Tonight he's put up a shot from Fern Pool, green dark water, that fig leaning in like old counsel. Beneath it, a reply from a number I don't have saved, Russ N: Looks colder than it is. Watch the ledge above the fig, left side sketchy after the rain.

Peter, the menace, @'s me: @Indi you take this, gorge whisperer.

I type before my frontal lobe votes on it: Indi: Copy. Will walk like a witness, not a tourist. Cheers.

Three dots. Then: Russ N: Copy.

That's all. Just that word. Military-simple, Pilbara-plain, a nod that isn't a promise. I put the phone back like it's made of glass and bones and go back in before I start inventing conversations I can't afford.

***

The rest of the night does what nights do, moves forward because we have not yet figured out how to move backward. We complete the "care-after-death-tasks" with the respect that makes junior nurses stand up straighter without noticing. We make a neat island of Uncle Jerry's bed and draw the curtain in a way that says both "privacy" and "permission to enter if you come correct."

Mr O'Riley sleeps for the first time in three days, mouth open, snoring like someone who owes the world nothing. Mrs Pritchard compromises with the pan and accepts a warm blanket like it was her idea. Robyn finds a packet of decent shortbread at the back of the staffroom cupboard that expired last month and tastes perfectly fine if you dunk it in tea for exactly one and a half seconds. Daniel writes a note to his future self on a Post-it and sticks it to his ID badge: Own it. Fix it. Learn it. Move on. I love him just a little bit more for that.

At 05:40 I fill in the green form for the DonateLife education night the hospital will host in October. 'A Star to Remember' - community, families, recipients, donor families, staff. Kerry's been nudging. Lionel's been nudging louder. I put my name down to speak, then slide the form under the corner of the keyboard so I can't see it and also can't lose it. That's as much bravery as I've got in me before sunrise.

By 06:20 the building is yawning itself awake. Day staff arrive with their hair behaving and their faces hopeful, bless them. Kerry does bed Tetris. Tomo and I parcel people into sentences someone else can carry for a shift. With nights, the handover is shorter, the long story gets turned into a set of instructions and a trust that the day team can read the rest off the faces.

"Uncle Jerry," I say at the end, because endings matter. "Time of death 02:23. Family present. Country music. Peaceful."

There's a small, shared pause. Then, "Thank you," from the room, like a chorus.

On my way out, I stop by SCU. Lena stands with a brother and an aunty I met once last year when I wasn't me yet. There is cry-laughter at a story I'm not supposed to hear, and it fills the room with a light that isn't electric.

"See you, Aunty," I say, hand on the door.

"See you, nurse," she says. "You got a good quiet. Keep it."

I nod because sometimes all the degrees in the world are just a way to earn the right to be told you were quiet in the right way.

Outside, the sky is that thin Pilbara pink that pretends it's delicate while planning to be 38° degrees by lunch. The ships are still there, patient as cattle. I count them because I do.

Back at the quarters, the dog from the next block gives me a look like I owe it money. I shower the smell of the night off me and pull on the t-shirt that feels most like not-work. On the way to bed I open the red-dirt notebook and leave myself three lines where I'll find them when I need them:

- Mr O'Riley found his breath again (as did I).

- Uncle Jerry went to the quiet with old songs and his girl's hand.

- A Star to Remember: I said yes.

My phone lights up face down once. I don't check it. If it's the world, it can wait.

Sleep shows up like a friend I didn't expect to see and sits me down gently.

"Night, Lionel," I say, like a benediction, like a promise. And I go under, not sinking but being held.

Chapter Nine

The email landed at 07:42 with a subject line no nurse trusts: *Quick chat?* My stomach did a small drop just as Kerry leaned on the nurses' station half a minute later - elbows easy, eyes not.

Interface meeting at the Transport Contractors North yard, 10:00. After those two medevacs in the last fortnight, they want hospital eyes on their controls. You're my eyes."

"Me?" I said, my mouth already saying yes.

"You," she said. "You speak human. Take Daniel. Tomo will cover your meds round. Wear boots."

I swapped joggers for steel caps, threw my hi-vis over scrubs, and printed the bare minimum, a redacted timeline of each retrieval, the part of the map where the mine road kisses the highway, and the half-page of notes I keep on what actually bites people out there - falls from ladders, heat stress, and the accidents that happen when people rush, the three 'h's as I like to call them, - height, heat, and hurry.

Daniel drove the pool ute. On the way he practised not swearing in front of management. I practised not rolling my eyes at management. The road out to the yard glared. The clouds built a façade of rain and then wandered off.

"Who's in the room?" I asked.

"TCN maintenance. HSEC lead. Camp paramedic. Two from Kemerton, they lease the laydown where the fall happened."

"Kemerton and TCN in one room," I said. "Bless this mess."

The yard appeared between the saltbush and the sky, dongas, a dusty car park, two haul truck tyres stacked like monuments, and a meeting room with glass that reflected back a woman in pink lipstick and a hi-vis vest trying to look like practice not theatre. Always pushing for authentic, everyday safety and care, you know, procedures that stand up at 03:00, not just during inspections.

Inside was a laminate table, whiteboard ghosts of old acronyms, and a tray of muffins with the personality baked out of them. The HSEC lead introduced herself as Bron, a smile like a warning and a handshake like she meant it. Gav the site medic nodded at me with the secret fraternity of people who've both held a bag-valve mask at 03:00. The Kemerton pair sat with laptops open and shoulders up around their ears.

And Big Russ.

He was at the end of the table, elbows planted, fingers drumming a rhythm that would have annoyed me had it been anyone else. On him it read as thinking out loud with his hands. Hi-vis faded by work, name still readable: Russell Newcombe - Maintenance Superintendent. He looked up once, quick, clocked me without flinch, and went back to the plan view of the laydown, pen tapping the rectangle that had sent a man to my ward with a skull laceration and a story about "just two minutes."

"Thanks for coming," Bron started. "Purpose, to review incidents, agree on controls, and to stop this happening again. Nurse… Indi?"

"Indi's fine," I said.

"Cool. Indi, you were on the retrievals. Can you give the hospital view?"

I kept it to bones. "Case one - heat stress and dehydration after extended task in full sun. Case two - fall from temporary access onto skid, occipital laceration, concussion. Both evacuated by RFDS. Both preventable."

Kemerton Rep - branded polo, confidence for days, says, "Our Safe Work Method Statement already covers working at height."

"Your SWMS also assumes the platform exists," Bron said, mild as a molotov.

"Good," I say. "Let's make sure the SWMS matches the job as built - ladder angle, three points of contact, tie-off points, rescue plan, and who's the spotter."

"We had a scaffold," Kemerton Rep insisted.

"A plank and a prayer," Gav put in.

A small, dangerous quiet settled. Big Russ's fingers stopped drumming.

"Righto," he said, voice like a door eased open. "We can argue the paperwork, or we can fix the bloody thing. Nurse?" He tipped his chin my way. "You saw the aftermath. What would stop you seeing it again?"

Everyone looked at me, which is a kind of silence you can drown in if you let yourself. I put my hand on the map like I was steadying it.

"A proper access platform," I said. "Modular. Bolt-on to the skid frame. Anti-slip, handrails, mid-rails, integrated ladder with gate, fall-arrest anchor rated to something that isn't a guess. Shade if you can't change the roster to early starts. And a rule you actually enforce, no ad-hoc elevation. No milk crates, no pallets, no 'just for a tick.'"

Kemerton Guy Two - younger, worried - "Lead time on fabricated platforms is twelve weeks." We're already behind schedule."

"Fun fact," I said, keeping my voice useful. "We're behind schedule on funerals too. Let's not contribute."

Kemerton Rep bristled. "With respect, Nurse."

"Respect taken," I cut in. "Also, families wait at home. Our job is to send people back to them in exactly the same shape as they left. That includes skulls without extra staples."

Big Russ didn't look at me, but something in his jaw acknowledged what I'd put on the table. I breathed, not quite steady.

Bron flipped her notebook. "So, platform. Russ, you've built half your life. What can you conjure under us while procurement does its tango?"

He scratched a quick sketch with the callused precision of a bloke who can see a structure in his head before the metal arrives. "We've got three surplus platforms off the old filter press. They're not pretty, but they're 450 kilo rated with the right span. We can re-drill to match the skid bolt pattern. Weld-on gussets here, here. Galv touch-up. Temporary shade sails off existing rafter with rated anchors. I want an engineer to bless it before anyone sets foot. And LOTO (lock out/tag out) on the pumps, no one climbs unless it's dead and proven dead."

Kemerton Rep started to object. Big Russ went gentle and harder. "With respect, mate, I'm not losing a man to a plank. You want the job done? You do it from a safe stance, or you don't do it at all." He glanced at me for half a second. "We like our heads the shape they came in."

My pulse misbehaved. I took a sip of air and pretended it was water.

"Okay," Bron said, pen already moving. "Action list. Russ, pull the platforms, weld mods, and book the engineer. Kemerton, raise a variation, and stop work on anything above knee height until the temp platform is signed off. HSEC, issue a Safety Flash with pictures of what not to do. Nurse, can you give us a one-pager on heat illness and ladder logic that a rigger might actually read?"

"Plain language or die," I said. "Got it."

Gav chimed in. "And we trial twenty-minute breaks every hour in full sun, shade, water, and eyes on each other. You burn slower if someone else watches you."

Kemerton Rep sighed, performed a calculation on invisible paper, and surrendered. "Fine. Variations. Platforms. Breaks."

I drew the platform on the whiteboard the way I'd explain it to a patient, three lines, and two truths. "Handrail here because falling sideways is how you fall. Anchor here because humans clip where it's easiest. Ladder gate self-closing because fatigue makes you forget."

Big Russ came to stand beside me at the board, shoulder a safe distance from mine. He added two neat triangles - gussets - and a little square. "Toe-boards," he said. "Because spanners like gravity." His hand brushed the marker out of mine by accident, and I felt the ghost of it three floors down.

Bron capped the pen. "Timeline. Two weeks' for the temp platform. Twelve for the permanent. If procurement can magic faster, I'll bake them a cake and name my next dog after their buyer."

We broke for smoko we didn't take. The room breathed like a held note releasing, hi-vis rustled, boots scuffed, someone remembered a kettle that never quite boils in meeting rooms. Paper cups stood around like undecided witnesses while the whiteboard kept the ghosts of old diagrams. Big Russ stacked chairs as if they were a problem he could solve in threes, clean, precise, and the kind of order you make when the rest of it won't line up.

"Thanks for coming out," he said, low, to me. Close enough that I could see the deep depth of his chocolatey brown eyes. "That line about families…" He didn't finish the sentence.

"It's the only line," I said, steadier than I felt.

He nodded once, sharp. "You'll send the one-pager?"

"Today."

"Spell out the load rating you want on the anchor."

"15 kN - kilonewtons" I said and watched his mouth do the small approval thing.

"Good," he said. And then, because we'd both felt the room tilt at least twice, he put professional back on like a jacket. "Everything in writing. Rigour - detailed, careful, and complete, or it doesn't count."

"Rigor," I echoed.

Daniel found me by the muffins, already texting Kerry the quick wins. "You were… spicy," he whispered, delighted.

"Appropriately seasoned," I corrected.

Outside the meeting room window, a dust devil marched past the laydown area like a lecturer with notes. The sky had gotten that Pilbara colour again, a blue so honest it almost hurt. Heat shivered above the haul tyres, a scrap of shade cloth flapped itself into applause, and the flags on the site fence pointed nowhere in particular, as if even the wind had stopped to listen.

On the way out, Bron pressed the heels of her hands into her eyes like she was resetting them. "Nice work, Indi," she said. "You lot see what we miss because you see the end of our mistakes."

"I see the middle of them," I said. "Let's not make the ends."

"Copy," she said, and I forgave her for stealing Big Russ's word.

We shook the room into a plan. Action items with names against them. Dates. People who said they would and who, today at least, meant it.

As we walked to the ute, Big Russ was standing by the workshop door speaking to a boilermaker about the old platforms. He didn't look my way. He didn't have to. That was the truce, neither of us pretended we hadn't noticed, both of us pretended we could carry on anyway.

***

Back at the hospital, I wrote the one-pager like I was writing to Lionel at twenty, and to the apprentices who think they're bulletproof at twenty-two.

Heat, what it does to a body and how to not be an idiot. Short sentences. What to drink. When to stop. How to look at your mate and see the things the ego hides. Ladders, the lies they tell. Three points of contact means three points of contact. Planks are not platforms. A "just for a tick" is still a law of physics.

I sent it to Bron, cc'd Kerry, Bcc'd no one because we don't do secrets on safety. Then I wrote the line that felt like a prayer and a dare.

We do this because families wait at home.

I printed the line and taped it above my desk, right next to the DonateLife flyer for 'A Star to Remember.' I ran a finger over the little silver star and pictured a lung in a stranger's chest pulling Pilbara air for the first time, iron-rich, salt-edged, and alive. People living because other people said yes on probably the worst day of their lives. Also this, people living because we refused to let "just two minutes" be the last sentence in anyone's story, because ladders get tied-off, spotters stay, heat plans aren't pretend, and a mate's "I'm fine" gets a second question.

The flyer fluttered in the air-con and I thought of Lionel the way I do when the tide comes in, not softer, just steadier. Consent forms and quiet corridors, hands held while a heart wrote its final beat, the paperwork that becomes a pulse somewhere else. A star on a program, a name spoken out loud so that love has somewhere to go.

I looked around the ward, tape, charts, the bruise-blue gloves, and the window with its thin slice of sky, and I let the two truths sit next to each other, safety as a daily discipline, and donation as a last fierce kindness. Both are choices. Both say the same thing in different languages, someone is waiting. Let's do the work so they get to keep waiting for the ordinary, school pick-ups, burnt toast, and bad jokes, the whole small miracle of a Tuesday.

I left the line where I'd see it at stupid o'clock and on the way out of a hard day. We do this because families wait at home. And when I traced the star again, I promised Lionel I'd keep making that true.

At 16:10 my phone buzzed with an unknown number.

R. Newcombe: Engineer can sign Thursday if procurement doesn't faint. What's your preferred harness brand for the anchor spec?

Indi: The one a rigging dog won't side-eye. Send me your shortlist and I'll translate human-to-hospital.

Pause. Then.

R. Newcombe: Copy.

Respect is a quiet thing. It edged in beneath the sparring and settled where the pulse sits when it's not misbehaving. I put the phone face down and went to count the evening ships from the smokers' door. Four and a tug. Honest.

"Good meeting?" Kerry asked later, in the med room, snapping an ampoule like punctuation.

"Truce," I said. "Progress. Platforms. Rigor."

"And the superintendent?" She didn't look at me, which was kind.

"Good at his job," I said carefully. "Stubborn in the right direction."

She smiled into the vial. "We like that."

That night I opened the red-dirt notebook and left myself three lines I might need when the wind turned:

- We drew a safer platform on a whiteboard and then decided to build it.

- Respect is a better drug than adrenaline.

- Families wait at home. Keep saying it.

I turned out the light and lay there listening to the building breathe. Somewhere out there a boilermaker would be measuring a bolt pattern against a platform that had already held other men up. Somewhere in my chest something that wasn't just grief found a place to stand.

"Help me keep them safe," I told Lionel in the dark.

He didn't answer. He didn't have to.

Chapter Ten

The plan was stupid and perfect, leave at 06:00, quick whip down to Karratha, hugs and a coffee with my god children, and Emma, back in time to badge on at 13:00. Hedland to Karratha is two-and-a-bit hours if the wind doesn't lean on you and the road trains behave. I packed it like a ward round, a thermos, muesli bar, spare scrubs, and a lie to myself that said this will be easy.

The sky at first light was Pilbara honest, a blue so clean it made you suspicious. I texted Kerry, back by 12:50 – promise, and she sent back a skull and crossbones and a heart.

The highway unrolled itself. Termite mounds like old men in red jackets. The salt flats throwing back a version of the sky with bad intentions. ABC radio crackling through footy hopes and cyclone warnings that never quite commit. I counted the small, good things, roos minding their own business, a wedge-tail on a fencepost looking like judgement, and coffee hot enough to make my tongue remember it was alive.

Roebourne slid by in the rear-vision, red dirt dust glinting, and old stone like a memory you're not sure you're allowed to touch. Past the turn for Point Samson. Karratha in that improbable way it has, city shouldered up against scrub, cranes against sky, and the damp heat like an announcement.

Emma was on the front verandah with bare feet and a toddler on her hip. My goddaughter Olive barrelled into me with the force of all five years and none of the brakes. "Nurse Indi! You smell like hospital and lollies."

"Both accurate," I said, scooping her up. "Where's my Jack-man?"

"Here," said Jack solemnly, holding out a beetle like a trophy. "He's sleeping."

Emma grinned at me over their heads. "You're mad, you know. Karratha, here and back just for a cuppa."

"I'm efficient," I said, kissing her cheek. "And it's not a cuppa. It's two cuppas and a slice."

We made the most aggressive small talk in the world with life updates thrown across the kitchen like we were batting off flies, her mum's knee, my roster, the price of tomatoes, and the last time someone stole a trolley from the shopping centre. Olive braided my hair with wet hands and professional seriousness, while Jack lined his cars along the skirting boards and gave me a lecture about gravity.

Emma slid a plate my way. "You look better," she said in that voice that makes you believe her.

"Training's good," I said. "Work is… good in the way that hurts to get to. The mine mob are behaving this week."

"And you," she said, eyebrows up. "Are you behaving?"

"I am drinking water and wearing sunscreen and counting ships," I said, which was true and avoided the part of the answer that had a name.

"Proud of you," she said, and for thirty minutes my chest felt like a room with all the windows open.

Time does that thing where it lies and then refuses to apologise. I left at 10:20 with a lunchbox of cut mango and a promise to come back on an actual day off, not this mad dash. Olive yelled "BYE NURSE INDI" from the gate, and Jack saluted like a tiny admiral with beetle dirt on his face.

The first fat drops hit the windscreen just past Roebourne.

You can smell Pilbara rain before you can see it. Hot dirt takes a breath. The wind checks the hinges. The world goes a fraction quieter and then decides not to.

The squall came in sideways with sheet rain, gusting crosswind, and window-wipers performing at their personal best and still not making a dent. The car in front of me softened into a suggestion. My knuckles went white on the wheel and then remembered they had other colours. I flicked the hazards on and eased onto the gravel shoulder before the highway could make a fool of the both of us.

The cab filled with that wet dog, hot-metal, first-rain-of-the-season smell, even though I don't have a dog up here. I sat and did nothing in a very intentional way. Breath in, breath out. Never alone, I told the storm, and the storm ignored me and did its job.

A ute slowed in the mirror, indicator blinking, red mud freckles on the guards. He stopped a car length back and to the right, safe angle, both of us a triangle and not an accident.

He hopped down and jogged forward with his cap pulled low. I knew it was him before my brain reached for the name. Big Russ. Hi-vis dark with rain, eyes ridiculous under a brim that didn't stand a chance.

I didn't wind the window down more than a finger's width. Rain found the gap like it had been waiting all year, a cool tongue along my knuckles.

"Good?" he called, voice low through the crack.

"Good," I said, though the wind shouldered the glass like it wanted in properly. Out on the bitumen the puddles stitched themselves together until the highway was one sheet of tin-coloured sky. Lightning did a quick white signature over the flats.

"Get in," I said, gesturing to the passenger seat.

Big Russ slid in and shut the door. "You can smell the iron," he said.

"You can," I answered. Wet metal, hot dust turning to clay, that first-rain smell that makes even old arguments go quiet. We sat with the storm doing its maths around us, count, count, crack, and the kind of quiet you only get in the middle of noise settled between our two little islands of light.

"You right?" he asked, "and it wasn't a question about competence, it was a check on you, the person, in this weather, in this minute."

"Pulled over," I said, pointing out the obvious like a champion. "Vision's cooked."

He nodded once. "Good call." He looked past me toward the river you could hear before you could see. "Localised. Give it five."

We sat in companionable stupidity, him damp from the dash, and me sitting in the driver's seat, and both of us pretending the universe hadn't just organised a cliché with excellent production values. He tipped his chin at the row of Akubra's rattling on the back seat like polite ghosts.

"You on a millinery run?" he asked.

"God children," I said. "and-" I opened my mouth and then shut it. "- and a patient who keeps melting in the sun."

His mouth did the almost-smile. "Good memorial, a hat is," he said, glancing at the water whipping off the bonnet.

Memorial. The word settled between us, understood, nothing explained.

The rain slackened. The world sharpened. He pushed the brim of his cap back with two fingers. "I'll go first," he said. "You sit on my tail till it's clear, then pass when you want. Road's greasy around the bend."

"Copy," I said, because apparently, we're that now.

He jogged back to his ute, hopped in, pulled a clean merge that would make a driving instructor cry, and we did a small convoy through the last tantrum of the squall. At the straight he lifted his right hand off the wheel in a half wave and then was gone. The highway took him like it knew where he lived.

I said a few choice words into the empty car and then laughed at myself, because there's only so long you can hold a pose against weather and fate.

Hedland coat-hangered itself back into view at 12:36. The puddles in the car park had ambitions and the wind wanted to have an argument. I badged in at 12:52 with wet cuffs and a face colour that would make an WHS poster smile.

"Cutting it fine," Kerry said, pretending not to be pleased I'd made it.

"Road taught me manners," I said, hanging my hi-vis and swapping out to dry scrubs I'd had the foresight to pack.

This afternoon belonged to 'Outpatients', and 'Whoever the Universe Sent.' The universe sent a little of everything and an Elder I'd met once on nights who had a seated appointment because he likes to do what he calls "hunting shade" between departments. Mr J - Wirru man with a laugh like a pack of cards being shuffled and a hat that had given up trying to be a hat.

He arrived with the brim sitting crooked, right side low, and announced, "Too much rain for dry jokes."

"Good," I said. "My wet ones are better."

We did meds, sugars, a wound review that had me humming Aunty's tune under my breath without noticing. He winced once, then told me a story about a goanna that was probably true and probably not, and in either case, exactly what I needed.

On the way out he paused, weighing the strip of hard sun between the sliding doors and the taxi rank like it might have teeth. We weren't late. "Two secs," I said, and slipped to my locker. The Akubra I'd picked up at the Roebourne servo, because I'm a sucker, and because that rain had made me sentimental, was right where I'd tucked it.

I came back without ceremony, holding it brim-first. "Mind if I fuss?"

He tilted his head, and I set it on gently, thumb and forefinger easing the crown down, a small push to angle the brim. The brightness softened at once.

"There," I said. "Better."

He took it like you take a thing that isn't yours yet and he put it on like he'd been born with it. The hat made sense of him in a way some things just do.

'Steal from you?' he said, eyes a little sly.

'Borrow indefinitely,' I said. 'Pay me in yarns.'

He tipped the brim. 'I'll pay you in yarns and good company.' 'Deal.'"

Outside, the sun still had jaws, but they didn't reach him now. He walked into the light like a man carrying shade.

***

After he'd gone, Kerry walked past, glancing outside as she did. "New look?"

"New home," I said. "Shade belongs outside."

She gave me that side-eye that can crack stone. "DonateLife thing," she said softly, and it landed not as a question.

"I'm going to speak at 'A Star to Remember'," I said, the words out before I'd given them permission. "Later this year." My throat did the threatened close and then decided to be useful.

Kerry rested her hip against the desk. "Good," she said. "You'll be hard and soft in the right order."

I huffed a laugh that sounded like relief. "That's the hope."

"You'll write it here," she decided, tapping the bench like it was a piano. "Between obs and phone calls. Best speeches are written with the ward breathing around them." She nodded toward the little meeting room. "When you want quiet, book it. I'll bully whoever needs bullying."

"Roster?"

"I'll make the grid behave," she said. "Give me two preferred days to protect. And when it gets heavy, come find me. We'll walk to the smokers' door and count ships until you remember your lungs."

I swallowed, grateful landing cleanly. "Thanks, Kerry."

She straightened, already half back in motion. "Also, practice it with us. Staff meeting, five minutes at the end. We'll be your tough crowd and your soft landing."

I touched the DonateLife flyer on the pinboard, the paper star catching the air-con. "Deal," I said.

"Good," she replied, already walking. "Go save someone's tea order."

I opened the DonateLife draft on my phone in the tiny gaps, and typed '*We said yes because love isn't an organ you can bury*' and deleted it. Typed '*Grief is a tide*' and deleted that too. Left the cursor blinking like it was listening.

The afternoon didn't care about my essay. Someone's cannula cried wolf. Someone else had a quinsy that looked like fury and needed an ENT, who, inconveniently, was on lunch. A kiddo brought in a lizard in a lunchbox, and the lizard made its opinion about being in a lunchbox very clear. A man asked if Panadol "actually does anything," and I said, "Yes, aren't you lucky." He looked aggrieved and took it anyway.

At 17:45 the sky did that thing where it pretends it's going to be gentle and then isn't. I stuck my head out the smokers' door and checked the ships. Four carriers, one tug wagging its tail like it kept the whole port in line. The air smelled like hot pennies and salt.

Gav texted a photo of the temporary platform mock-up with one of the boilermakers standing on it looking like a dad in thongs on a brand-new deck.

Engineer Thurs. Ropes Friday. Rigor, I replied, and he sent back an eye-roll emoji which is how he says *good work*.

On the way to handover I passed Mr J again, hat tilted just so, sitting by the doors telling a group of kids a story where the main character was either a crocodile or a cousin. He tipped the brim when he saw me, then looked up through the rugs of his eyebrows at the light changing and said, "Rain over Hedland again, girl. You drive careful."

"I will," I said, and meant it.

Nights took my people like carefully wrapped parcels. I signed the last thing that needed signing, wiped the last smear of tape glue off my arm with the very last clean swab in the box, and stepped into a world that had been rinsed and then ironed. The car park smelled of wet dust and hot metal cooling. Puddles held perfect copies of the sodium lights with a breeze rippling the edges like someone smoothing a sheet. Far off, the port cranes made their slow, patient shapes against a sky scrubbed an honest blue. My shoulders dropped a notch I hadn't noticed they were holding. I checked the ships, habit more than need, counted them like beads and let the quiet after-noise settle its hand between my shoulder blades. The drive home was all afterglows. The river ran high without mischief. The road had lost its temper and then apologised. Somewhere between here and the bend where the squall had made its point, I said thank you to no one in particular and everyone who deserved it.

Back in the staff quarters, the kettle did its faithful thing. Robyn was already in pyjamas with her feet against the donga wall, reading a crime novel like it owed her money.

"Did you actually do Karratha and back?" she asked without looking up.

"Stupid and perfect," I said, dropping a mango peel in the bin. "I brought you a lamington from Emma. It saw some things in the rain but it's heroic."

Peter yelled from his cube, "Tell your boyfriend the superintendent to stop parking in my spot," and I threw a dishcloth in the direction of his voice because it's healthy to have traditions.

When the noise settled and the building did its small-ship creak, I opened the red-dirt notebook and left myself three lines so tomorrow wouldn't clutter over them:

- Squall at Roebourne. Pulled over. Lived.
- He stopped. We chatted. I lived.

- A hat found a head. Shade belongs outside.

I slid the DonateLife flyer under the page and tapped the star with my fingertip like you knock on a friend's door. "Help me live," I told Lionel, which is not the same as help me stop loving you. The night didn't answer. It didn't have to.

I turned out the light and let the dark be a place to rest, not to fall. Outside, somewhere between here and the port, the tug kept doing its relentless, unspectacular work, pointing bigger things the right way.

Chapter Eleven

05:00 is a pact I make with myself, if I show up, the day will meet me halfway. The town gym at that hour is usually mine, wall fans ticking, old plates rattling, and the salt-dry smell of sweat that's part iron ore, part eucalyptus wipes. The dawn comes in sideways through the high windows, turning the dust in the air into glitter that doesn't ask for applause.

I badge in at 04:58 with a thermos of black coffee and a face still carrying sleep. Two blokes in hi-vis are already at the cable machine doing curls like their elbows owe them money. Skid boys, the skid-steer crew from the site. I recognise one from last week's platform briefing, he'd taken notes with his tongue sticking out, concentrated as a kid.

Fine. I can share.

I claim the far-left treadmill and jaw the speed up until my lungs have something to do besides remember every wrong thing I've ever said. Sunglasses of sweat start to form. The playlist is yesterday's bangers and two guilty 90s ballads I pretend are iconic.

The door opens on the stroke of five like a cue the world agreed on without telling me. He's taller than the doorway makes him look. Big Russ. Cap in his hand, towel over his shoulder, and the particular hi-vis fade that says laundry's a suggestion, not a schedule. I feel the brief, ridiculous animal startle of a kangaroo busting itself out of the scrub. He sees me, or he sees the treadmill I'm on, which amounts to the same problem.

He doesn't loom; he never does. He tips his chin hello like a bloke who knows he's a lot, then takes the treadmill beside mine, leaving exactly one polite width of space between his elbows and my not-elbows. Forced proximity is what HR calls it when the roster puts two people in a broom closet with a project. The gym version involves sweat and the occasional accidental eye contact in reflective glass.

We run in parallel for a hundred metres of truce.

"Discipline or penance?" he asks my reflection, voice low enough not to spook the morning.

"Both," I admit. "Trying to quit the cigarettes. Day nine."

He nods like a man who understands numbers that start small and get heavy. "Gave them up after the second relationship breakdown. Picked them back up when I realised mints didn't fix my personality." A beat. "Trying again."

"Group suffering," I say. "My favourite kind."

He huffs, not quite a laugh, but not not a laugh. The display on his treadmill flashes an incline bump and his calves oblige like they're on a roster too. I tell my thumb not to hit down in competitive panic.

Behind us, the skid boys conspire in a whisper you could hear in Newman. One of them props a phone sideways between the dumbbells, lens pointed our way. The other pulls a face, checks the frame, mimes sprinting and thumbs-ups. Influencers of the outback. I roll my eyes at the glass; Big Russ sees the reflection and his jaw goes still.

"Whose phone?" he calls, not loud, just the kind of firm that makes grown men remember they once had mums. He steps off the treadmill, hits the stop on the camera with one dry finger, and passes it back like he's returning a toddler to its owner. "Consent, lads," he says. "And if you're filming for a form check, film your own spine."

They laugh too loudly, toss the towel over the awkward, and pivot into a show-off superset of box jumps and claps that leaves white chalk prints on the rubber floor like kangaroo tracks.

I bring my eyes back to forward. "You always this popular?" I ask.

"Only with people who make terrible choices in the vicinity of equipment," he says, climbing back on. "And a few dogs."

I grin despite myself. He catches the edge of it, and for a second something easy moves across his face. The first real smile I've seen on him, small, and unpractised, like a door opening just to check the weather.

We fall into a quiet that isn't unfriendly. The steady slap of feet. Our twin machine heartbeats making the room feel like some old engine that has decided, kindly, to run.

"You always this early?" he asks eventually.

"I like starting before the world starts deciding for me," I say. "Helps me not… drift."

He nods again. "Starting over takes discipline. Stopping something, too."

We run with that sitting between us, two sentences doing more work than a paragraph. I don't ask what he's starting or stopping. He doesn't ask me the same.

At 05:18, the skid boys escalate. One hops on the treadmill two down from Big Russ and sets it to rabbit, laughing at himself before his legs have been consulted. He goes from zero to fifteen kph with the brash surety of a man whose last good decision involved toast. His foot strikes high, his shoulders chase his hips, and the belt decides he's surplus to requirement. He shoots backwards, lands on a Swiss ball not designed for the catching of adult men, and the ball lets go with a gunshot squeal, dropping him onto his dignity. The chalk, still on his palms billows in a perfect white puff that the fan on the wall blasts immediately back into his face like a cosmic high-five.

There's a beat of silence, the kind that checks for fractures. The other skid boy cackles so hard he has to hold his ribs. The receptionist sticks her head in with the face of a woman who's done a certificate in Disappointment and a diploma in Don't Make Me Write a Report. Big Russ hits the emergency stop on all the empty treads just in case and hands the fallen bloke a towel, which somehow is kinder than a hand.

"You all right?" he asks, the same you he used at the Roebourne squall, not the you that means are you embarrassed.

The kid nods, eyes streaming from chalk and glory. "Absolute epic," he says hoarsely. Cheeky, silly. He scrubs his face, leaves a pale halo in his hairline, and starts laughing at himself too.

I'm already in triage mode without meaning to be. "Any pain in your neck? Head knock? Nausea?" He shakes his head, still grinning. Pupils equal. Colour good. Ego bruised, coccyx negotiating.

Big Russ tips his chin at the control panel. "Rule of treads," he tells him, mild as a warning sign. "You make friends with the belt before you sprint. Machines don't care about your feelings."

"Copy," the kid sniffs, shoulders dropping from bravado to learning. His mate wheezes, "I thought you had it, bro," and then loses the last of his composure when the receptionist silently holds up a laminated PLEASE DO NOT RUN LIKE A CARTOON sign that surely didn't exist until this moment.

I catch Big Russ's eye, he's almost smiling. I mouth, "He's okay." He nods once, the kind of agreement that doubles as a small thank you. The fallen skid boy limps back onto the now-dead treadmill, towel around his shoulders like a prize fighter who has discovered gravity, and presses WALK with the reverence of a convert.

"Start at turtle," Big Russ suggests. "Work up to rabbit next month."

"Next year," the receptionist adds, and the room exhales, fans humming, and plates settling, our little morning church back to liturgy.

We finish our kilometres at an honest pace. My lungs decide they forgive me for yesterday's road and for years of nicotine. His cap sits on the dash of his treadmill like a small bright moon.

He steps down first, towel over his neck like a boxer on a TV ad for mineral water. He leans on the rail, just his forearms, zero theatre. "How's the platform proposal?" he asks, like we've run straight from the gym onto the agenda.

"Engineer Thursday," I say. "Ropes Friday. 'Rigor' is the new word of the week."

"Rigor's a good word," he says. His thumb flicks a silent habit, counting off, or quitting smokes, or both. "You… you were right to push it."

"Families wait at home," I say. The sentence lands in the actual air, heavier than the chalk. He nods once, the gravity in the room tipping around us for a heartbeat.

The skid boys reappear with a mop that has seen better days. "Sorry, miss," one says. "We thought we were funny."

"You were," I say. "And now you can be tidy too. Complex men."

They grin like I'd given them a sticker. One points at my shoes. "Nurse from the hospital, yeah? The one with the pink lipstick? The boys at camp reckon you run like a metronome."

I should want to hide. Weirdly, I don't. "Tell the boys at camp the metronomes off cigarettes and will outlive them all," I say sweetly. "And stop filming women without their consent."

"Yesss, miss," he says, chastened and amused in equal measure.

Outside, the light has the blue-gold that belongs only to decisions made early. We both pretend we're leaving in opposite directions and accidentally walk the same way. The carpark smells like dust deciding whether to be mud, half rain-memory, and half grit.

"You heading out to site?" I ask.

"Day shift," he says. "Bus in ten."

"I'm on from one," I say. "I'll wave to your trucks if they behave in this rain."

He huffs. "Tugs get the ships pointed right," he says, half to himself.

"Unspectacular work," I say. "Relentless."

He nods like he's agreeing with more than the metaphor.

"Doesn't look like much," he adds. "But if the tug's not there, everything drifts."

There's a moment where acknowledging we have each other's numbers would be easy. But we don't. Not yet. It feels like showing respect to something we haven't named to let it take its own time.

"Good run," he says.

"Good run," I echo.

He walks toward the bus stop. The skid boys shuffle past carrying the corpse of a Swiss ball like a fallen comrade. One of them salutes me with his chalky hand, I salute back.

Back in the quarter, the kettle yells its reliable yell. I sit on the edge of the narrow bed and let the sweat evaporate and feel my pulse in my ears like I've swallowed a small drummer. I reach for the red-dirt notebook because that's what I do when I've felt something and don't want to lie to myself about it later.

- Gym at five. He smiled. Real.

- Skid boys learned about gravity and consent.

- Day nine no smokes. Still me.

My pen hovers. The other line is the one I've avoided writing since the ICU room where the machines were louder than God and Lionel's hand was warm until it wasn't.

- I want to be the woman Lionel loved, brave again.

The sentence looks at me. I look back. I don't delete it.

At the hospital doors just before 13:00, the air-conditioning kisses my face in that needy way it has. I catch my reflection in the glass, cheeks bright from effort, ponytail higher than dignity, and eyes clearer than last month. I press my palm to the automatic door and feel it give.

"Let's go, Indi," I tell the version of me that kept the pact this morning. "We're not done starting over."

Chapter Twelve

The road east of Karijini thins the noise out of you. By the time the last bar of phone reception went to sleep, the sky had opened into that big, blunt blue that makes your chest feel both small and right-sized. Red dirt bloomed up behind the Troopy like a flag.

"Clinic is the low buildings by the boabs," the coordinator had said on the phone the day before. "Keys'll be in the meter box. Aboriginal Health Worker will meet you. Janelle. She knows everything that matters."

Janelle was waiting on the verandah when I rolled in, dark braid, sunglasses, and a radio on her hip, the kind of steady you have to grow, not learn. She didn't wave. Just a small chin lift that said *you made it, now we'll see if you can stay.*

"You Indi?" she asked.

"I am," I said. "Thanks for having me."

She hitched the door with a hip and let the clinic air wrap around me, Dettol, sunscreen, and the sweetish undertow of antiseptic wipes and dust. The room was two-thirds practicality, one-third miracle. Photos pinned on a noticeboard of footy teams, school kids with paint on their noses, and a laminated flier for Well Women's Checks that was curling at the corner.

"We orientate first," Janelle said, like a law. "Your way. Then our way."

"My way," I echoed, and set my bag down. "Resus room."

She watched me watch the space. It's my ritual, I'll do it if I've been posted ten minutes or ten months. Crash trolley top to bottom: oxygen *full*, suction *sucks*, defib *charged*, pads *in date*, gel *not fossilised*. Airway: OPAs, NPAs, ETTs, bougie, BVM, PEEP valve. IV/IO: 14s, 16s, drill batteries *green*. Drugs: the green one's *adrenaline*, the blue one's *amiodarone*, the pink one's *magnesium*, the pain *fentanyl/morphine*, the stop *naloxone*, the clot *TXA*. Fluids. Glucometer and spare strips. Two working thermometers because the universe loves irony. I ran PEDPP out loud for Janelle: People, Equipment, Drugs, Patient, Plan.

She didn't nod often, which made the one she gave me feel like a medal. "Good," she said. "Now our way."

We walked the boundary between medicine and country. Radios: *this* channel for clinic, *that* for ranger, *this* for night watch. Sat phone on the charger with the number taped to the back. Spare batteries wrapped like babies. Keys in a shadow board, a hook for everything and a thing on every hook. "Never Alone," she said without me prompting it. "Two-up for every call-out. Eyes on, hands ready."

"#GaylesLaw," I said. She met my eyes. That one doesn't need explaining in a place like this.

"Men's business," Janelle said then, and took me outside. She pointed with her chin, not her finger. A long, low ridge to the west, a creek bend you wouldn't notice if you weren't taught to. "That way and that way - don't look. Don't drive. Don't ask. If you must travel past, you go eyes down until it's behind you. Women's business… I tell you when. You'll know. We walk soft here."

"I'll follow your lead," I said. It wasn't performance. It was relief to be told which way to place my eyes.

"Words," she said as we walked. "Nooba - friend." She grinned. "Munya - bottom. As in, 'put your munya on the bed, nanna.'"

"Sorry business," she added quietly, the two words heavier than the air. "We stop. We move different. We tell you who speaks. You don't say names of the person who passed. You ask before you touch a house, a photo, a thing. People make smoke. They wail. It is right. We make space for spirit."

I thought of the laminated sign in the staffroom back in Hedland - *Be the nurse you would want at your child's bedside* - and of how here, the bedside wasn't a bed but a community, a law older than mine.

Inside again, we sorted my call-out grab pack like packing for a country you respect, head torch, small torch with teeth grip, bandages, steri-strips, suture kit, trauma shears, Vick's under-nose (museum piece I still believe in today), bug spray, water, two protein bars that taste like regret but save your life, spare radio battery, sat phone, a "Dazer" in the outside pouch - dog deterrent, not a toy - because community dogs run the fence line at night like security with their own agenda. A pocketknife. Notebook, pen. A handful of lollies for scared kids and bigger kids pretending not to be scared. And a printed map, even though the tracks change after every wet.

"You a shit magnet?" Janelle asked, bone dry.

"Famous for it," I said.

"Then we'll get a plane in here by noon," she said, but the corner of her mouth gave the truth away.

We walked the medicine cupboard together. The manual with the dog-eared pages sat where you could reach it in a hurry, not locked away like a trophy. The fridge hummed the quiet, important hum of cold chain doing its one job. Janelle's hand paused on the shelf with baby Panadol. "Lots," she said. "Always lots."

I checked the Troopy like it was a patient - lights, tyres, spare, bull bar, fuel, the way the radio spoke when I asked it to. There's reassurance in rubber and repeatable checks when you live at the end of a very long driveway.

At lunch we shared a sandwich, and she told me who held the clinic together when the clinic pretended to hold itself together. Aunty Dot who scares lads into blood pressure checks with a look. Uncle Len whose feet I'd be dressing by Wednesday. Maya from Women's Centre who can get a teenager to laugh when the world has given her reasons not to. The school principal who calls early. The ranger who hears hoons before the police do. The RFDS doc on the end of the line who says, "What do you need?" instead of "Why did you…?"

The first walk-in of the afternoon was a toddler with a nose like a faucet and a patience level like a lit fuse. I put a sticker on my own forehead to change the power dynamic, classic trick, still works. He called me 'her' and laughed until the hurt let go." His mum watched me from behind her sunglasses, and I could feel the algebra of trust doing its sums. I explained the antibiotics, asked permission before the otoscope, didn't pretend I knew what to say about the sleep she wasn't getting. "We'll see you tomorrow," I said. "Same time. I'll be the one with the silly sticker."

Janelle made a note on the whiteboard: *Indi - ok*. The simplest report card, the only one that matters.

Mid-afternoon, she walked me to the edge of town and showed me the road you never take after rain and the tree that always drops a branch when the wind lies. She pointed at the long hill again, and we both put our eyes to the ground until it was behind us. It wasn't theatrical, it was practical magic.

The satellite phone chirped once on the way back - a test. I flicked the antenna up, sent a *'we're here'* ping to the number taped to the case, heard the click-back reply. Little faithful beeps that say the world can still hear you when you're small in it.

Before we closed, we did the thing I have never, ever skipped: ran a mock. Adult collapse on the verandah, call-out tone in the radio, Janelle on compressions like a metronome, me on airway and drugs, swapping at two-minute marks so no one goes soft. We spoke out loud what we'd call the RFDS doc for: shockable rhythm? Adrenaline on the three-minute? Airway difficult? Do we have eyes and hands? Who's guarding the door, whose job is to say *breathe* to the family? We finished flushed and sweating and grinning because practice is a spell you cast to keep the bad things from finding you easy.

"You're ready," Janelle said. "As ready as anyone gets."

"And you're stuck with me," I said.

She snorted. "We'll see."

***

Shift change at camp is its own weather. The mine bus disgorged a wave of yellow and blue and a mood like static. Big Russ slung his bag down in the donga doorway, rubbed the grit out of his eye with a knuckle that had more scars than story.

"Pink lipstick nurse heading bush," Tiny said from the doorway, mouth full of whatever passes for dinner when you don't cook it yourself. "Old Mick's missus heard it at Hedland Woolies. Two weeks' city, ten weeks' outback."

Big Russ didn't look up. He opened his locker like it had opinions, took out the dog-eared paperback he pretended was to rest his eyes and the hands-free that didn't fit his right ear properly since the time he split it.

He scrolled to her contact number in his phone and typed with his thumb like a teenager.

Take a sat phone. Don't drive past the western ridge - eyes down. Don't go alone. #NeverAlone. If you need a head torch that won't die, I've got one. It's not creepy to say that, is it? It sounds creepy. Delete that bit. Just...

He stopped. The cursor stood there, patient. He breathed like a man who knows breathing is a muscle you can pull if you try to make it do more than one job at once.

He deleted the lot. Closed the message app. Opened it again and typed three words he knew he'd never send.

Check the sky.

He thumbed the phone dark, put his back against the cool of the donga wall, and watched the ceiling fan make its old, faithful wobble. He tried to think about the bolt on loader twenty-seven. He thought about a woman in a dress in a pub and a hill you lower your eyes for.

***

The first evening alone in the nurse's house is the opposite of glamorous. The door sticks. The fridge hums a song it learned in 1998. The dog from community I've already made the mistake of feeding lies across the threshold like he owns it. (And I suppose he does.)

I rang Mum on the sat phone just because it felt wicked. "You sound like you're calling from space," she said. "Are you eating properly?"

"Yes," I lied, looking at the universe that is two-minute noodles.

I wrote the clinic landline on a sticky note and stuck it to the inside of the front door because in the dark you forget even numbers you know like your own name.

I showered the day off, dust down the plughole is a weird kind of sermon, and then I did the thing Lionel would have called me soppy for and loved me for anyway: I made a little place. Not an altar, no one gets to accuse me of stealing someone else's language, but a *place*. The windowsill where the ochre dust settles. A small jar of spring water Janelle said was safe. A smooth river stone I asked about out loud, Janelle smiled and said it was fine. I set Lionel's driver's license card there, the corner that's gone soft from my wallet, and beneath it a scrap of paper where I'd written the promise I made back in Hedland when I said yes to the '*A Star to Remember*' night later this year.

When they ask, I'll say: Families wait at home. Choices ripple. Grief is a tide. Donation gives it somewhere to go.

I sat with it a while, hands around a mug of tea strong/black/two sugars because right isn't always about being right, sometimes it's about being with.

From the verandah, the night smelled like spinifex and something sweet I couldn't name. A group of boys hooned a bit and then didn't. Somewhere someone laughed, and somewhere else a baby found the exact note all babies find when they decide sleep is a conspiracy.

I wrote in the red-dirt notebook by head torch because that's how habits get married to context:

- Resus room speaks when you listen.

- Janelle's our way sits right in my bones. Men's business: eyes down.

- First ritual of the contract (sticker on my forehead, still works).

- Promise for *A Star to Remember*: say the thing I needed to hear.

- Sat phone works. I'm small and heard.

When the dark went from blue to proper black, a chorus lifted from a house down the track, low and steady and full of a name they didn't say. Sorry business moving through the night like weather. Janelle had told me what to do. I did it. Lights off. Phone face-down. Shoes by the door. We walk soft here.

I lay on the narrow bed with the dog against the door and the Troopy keys where my hand could reach them, and I pressed my palm into the air where Lionel's forehead would be if miles and time and the business of staying couldn't defeat the ordinary magic of love.

"Help me honour right," I whispered. "Help me live."

Outside, the wind changed its mind and settled. Inside, the little place on the sill held the smallest glow with the moon on stone, reflection in water, and a driver's license card that once fit in a young man's wallet and now fits in the space I make for it wherever I go.

Chapter Thirteen

Janelle shoved the Troopy keys into my palm at lunch and flicked her chin toward the highway.

"Go breathe salt," she said, pressing the ward phone into her own pocket like proof she meant it. "You'll need it later. I'll cover tonight and tomorrow, the roster's fine. Don't argue. Head for Pretty Pool, let the wind rinse the clinic out of your hair. Eyes down past the ridge, you know the rules. Walk the line, don't look up into country that isn't ours. Come back when your shoulders have dropped two inches."

I did. I lowered my gaze where the country asked me to, then drove west until the red gave way to mangroves and the air turned briny and clean. Port Hedland on a Friday was half postcard, half union meeting, fishermen in sun-faded polos, sparkies in hi-vis who never learned how to whisper, aunties in their best shirts, and, threaded through it all, the hum of people who've been hot all week and are finally letting their shoulders drop. The jetty boards knocked under thongs, kids wove past with ice cream already losing the argument with gravity, pelicans loitered like old uncles pretending not to beg. You could smell prawn shells and lime, sunscreen and battered snapper from the pub window where the chalkboard promised reef-and-beef, cash only. Someone tuned a guitar out back, two bright notes testing the air, while esky lids thudded and bottle caps pinged into palms. The breeze came off the water with a clean edge, flattening the heat and lifting the hair at my neck, the bay lay out like hammered tin catching a slow spill of gold. People laughed in that low, end-of-week way, and the caravan park smoke drifted up to join the sunset. I stood a minute, let the place do what it does, salt in, noise out, and felt my own shoulders remember how to drop.

Inside the tavern, the floorboards knew the steps by heart. The bandstand was a pair of milk crates and an amp, the bar a bright stripe of taps and gossip. Festoon lights ran the length of the verandah like a soft runway for tired eyes. It was technically a pub night, everyone called it "team bonding" so they felt more wholesome about chips.

Sharon barrelled in behind me, all bangles and bravado, the OT locum from Hedland who could tape a wrist while convincing a man to take up tai chi.

"You made it!" she sang, kissing my cheek. "I was worried the clinic would eat you up alive. Robyn's parking. Peter's already ordering calamari like we're related to a trawler."

Gavin arrived with the same breeze as the bar door, a scaffold supervisor from a site up the coast, shoulders like scaff joints and a laugh that hit the back wall. He and Sharon sparked on contact, the *you're trouble - so are you* crackle that makes everyone else lean back to avoid getting caught in the arcs.

"What do you even do with your hands all day?" she teased, eyeing his palms.

"Keep people from falling," he said, looking at her like she was a height he wouldn't mind respecting.

"Then buy me a drink," she shot back. "I'm a risk."

They disappeared toward the bar, leaving a tail of electricity and two empty stools behind them.

I took the corner table that sees everything, back to the wall like the hospital taught me. Peter slid a pale ale over and nodded toward the ocean.

"Count the boats," he said, a Hedland habit exported to the coast. Four tinny silhouettes and, further out, a supply ship sitting patient. Numbers to stand on.

The mine bus must've got in at the same time as the tide. A wave of hi-vis washed across the beer garden. In among them, a familiar stillness, like the eye of something you're not afraid of but also don't turn your back on.

Big Russ posted up near the edge of the crowd, hands around a middy he wasn't rushing. His crew made noise enough for ten with the sounds of boots knocking stool rungs, and laughter that started in the chest and rolled. He did that listening thing he does, body still, eyes moving, like he could track six conversations and himself all at once.

"Your friend," Sharon breathed in my ear on a fly-by, tray balanced like a halo. Her grin was shameless. "The one you pretend you're not looking at. He's here."

"Everyone's here," I said, which wasn't untrue. I kept my water glass between my palms like it was a job.

Tiny clocked the moment I noticed. He tipped his glass in that way men do when they're being cheeky and generous at the same time, a permission with a wink. I lifted my water back, cheers without the dare. The temperature in the circle eased a notch. Someone elbowed someone else, someone shushed a story that didn't need telling yet. Big Russ's mouth did its almost-smile and then undecided itself. He looked away first, courteous as a door being held open. The band thumped a chord out the back, the kind that lands between ribs and says, later, maybe.

The band attempted 'Flame Trees', butchered the bridge, and got applauded anyway. The table filled with bowls that claimed to be salad and were mostly chips. Robyn told a story about a delirious farmer who'd tried to pay his bill with a goat and an apology. Peter did the laugh where his shoulders go first. It was easy.

Until it wasn't.

Because the air outside the festoon lights was softer than the air under them, and because the habit of checking the edges is a muscle now - I slipped out for five minutes to look at the dark. The night had its own inventory, salt and spilled beer, the sweet ghost of mango sauce, old timber holding other people's summers. Fryers sighed inside, out here the generator hummed like a distant beehive. Ropes creaked against cleats. The tide took pebbles and gave them back. A gull heckled the bins and lost interest. Moths worked the bulbs like they had a union. Laughter thinned to a blur you could lean away from. I stood where the gravel gives up to boards, breathing the kind of air that makes your chest stop arguing with itself, and let my eyes adjust to the line where sea becomes sky, edges first, always.

He was already out there, in that pool of half-light by the rail. Big men shouldn't be able to move that quietly. He stared at the sea like it had answers written in it small enough to require his squint.

"Evening, Indi," he said without turning, like we'd arranged it. His voice was low enough to be private and clean enough to be kind.

"Evening," I said, taking the stretch of rail two arm-lengths away. "I'm exercising my right to count boats in a different postcode."

"That's legal," he said. His mouth considered a smile and then shelved it. "How's the bush?"

"Good. Big," I said. "Resus room ready. Janelle is smarter than God. I learned the right way to look at the wrong hill."

"Men's business," he said, respectful. "Eyes down."

We stood in a silence that worked like a well-fitted socket, no give, no grind.

He drummed his fingers once on the rail, a rhythm I'd already learned was what he did with nerves he refused to admit to. "I heard you were heading out," he said. "Told myself not to… say anything useless like 'take care.'"

"Sometimes 'take care' is exactly right," I said. "Sometimes it's all you can do."

He nodded, as if he'd been granted permission to breathe.

He didn't look at me when he said, "I did the marriage thing once. Did the long thing after that. Both of them ended. Clean as I could make it. Messy as it had to be."

The plural that wasn't plural. A story compressed to a sentence that said, I won't waste your time pretending I'm undamaged.

"Same here," I said, tasting lie and truth in the same mouthful. "Not the marriages. The… endings." The one that wasn't a choice. The way a life can be divorced from you by physics and fate instead of papers.

He nodded into the night, and I could feel him decide not to reach for me with words he wasn't entitled to. Gentle restraint is a discipline. Some men lift it like a weight at the gym and put it down loudly. Big Russ wore it like a uniform and didn't mention it.

"I speak sometimes," I said, because if I was going to be honest with anyone, it might as well be the man who looked at the horizon the way I do. "For DonateLife. Families, hospital people, sometimes schools. The first time, my throat didn't work. Now it… mostly does."

He turned then, fully, and his eyes were brown, deep and steady, the colour the river gets before it decides to rise. No flash, just intent.

"I'd come," he said, simply.

I laughed, surprised by the sting in the back of my eyes. "I haven't even written the speech yet. I start and delete. Start and delete."

"Start again," he said. "You'll get it. You'll say the thing someone needs to hear and hate you for and thank you for in the same week."

"Maybe," I said, and let the maybe be hope instead of hedging.

Behind us, Sharon squealed, Gavin had produced some ludicrous card trick and turned two coasters into a date. The band found the key they'd lost earlier. Someone at the big table started a round of 'Aussie Aussie Aussie' that died after the third 'oi' because we'd all grown up a little.

Big Russ finished his beer and set the glass down square.

"I'm going to go back in," he said, gentle like you'd speak to a skittish horse. "Not because I want to. Because I should. We do this tidy or we don't do it at all."

"Tidy," I echoed, and my pulse answered in a way I didn't take personally. Bodies respect boundaries when you speak them out loud.

He stepped away, then paused long enough to tilt his head at the sky.

"Check the weather tomorrow before you head back," he said. "There's a squall line that plays silly buggers between here and Karijini."

"Copy," I said. "And you…"

"I'll get the boys back on the bus," he said, his mouth finally letting the smile out. "We're better over a distance."

He walked in first. Gentle restraint. A gift disguised as a goodnight.

When I followed, Sharon and Gavin were leaning into a corner of the room like a new constellation. Robyn raised both eyebrows at me across the table. I shook my head and mouthed 'tidy.' She grinned and mouthed back 'for now.'

We ate what chips we could catch before the avalanche of hands reached them. We made stories with names we won't remember in ten years. We paid up and said the kind of goodnights that are really promises to look after each other's people on the road.

Outside, the festoon lights made halos on the gravel. I stood at the edge of that small, warm world and texted Janelle: *Salt breathed. Finished by nine. Weather looks grumpy.* She sent back a thumbs-up and a seashell.

Robyn and Peter rolled up beside me. "Troopy's out front," Peter said, patting his pockets like keys might hide from him. "Shotgun calls DJ."

"Already called," Robyn grinned, wicked, and unapologetic.

We piled in. The radio checked in like an old friend, windows down, night warm. The tide chewed the rocks and put them back. As we pulled away, I glanced once toward the tavern, somewhere behind those lights, a man who has learned to walk away before he runs sat down with his crew and did not look at the door. Laughter rose, fell, and braided itself back into the music.

Robyn queued something shameless, we sang badly on purpose. Between choruses I did the two-eyes-down thing for the country that deserves it, then lifted my gaze to a sky thick with stars.

Lionel, I said inside the kind of quiet you can carry in a noisy car, *I'm going to try. Help me keep it tidy, grief where it belongs, hope where it can breathe.*

The night held still for a heartbeat, as if it were listening. The road out was combed flat by a passing squall, a sheen like a fresh idea. Mangroves breathed that clean, briny smell that makes old arguments sit down. Peter told a story, mixed up the ending, and the "wrong" version was actually funnier than what really happened, Robyn snorted, we all laughed the kind of laugh that makes corners easier.

We stopped at the servo for ice creams we didn't need and a bag of ice we did, then bumped the last few streets to staff quarters with the Troopy ticking itself cool.

"Spare room's made," Robyn said, pressing a giant borrowed T-shirt into my hands. "No arguing."

"Copy," I said. I showered off the night and slid into cotton, falling asleep to my friends discussing whether the kettle whistles or sings, and to a sky outside doing its reliable work without needing me to watch it.

Chapter Fourteen

Saturdays in Hedland have a different gravity. The air sits heavy but the day floats, half-rostered, half-holiday, and all dust and salt. I woke before my alarm to gulls arguing over nothing, and the smell of heat already pushing at the flyscreen, testing the mesh like a visitor who won't wait to be invited. Somewhere a ute idled, somewhere a sprinkler stitched a crooked circle, and the light slid under the blinds in that Pilbara way, gold first, then white, then the kind of blue that dares you to waste it. It felt like a day that would forgive you for being slow, as long as you showed up.

For once there was no shift to sprint toward, no sedations or stats to thread. Just two texts:

Robyn: Jetty feed? 11? Bring appetite & banter.

Sharon: Gav's driving, I call choosing the playlist. No country.

"Monster," I sent back, and threw a towel, a stubby holder, and dignity into my bag in that order.

By ten to eleven, the staff-quarters kitchen had turned into a communal esky-packing ceremony. Peter, who treats ice like religion, stood up to his wrists in a bag of cubes, chanting, "Cold on top, colder on bottom. That's the rule." Robyn pinballed between cupboards.

"Chips from the kiosk," she recited. "Fish from the shop. Sauce from the glove box. Who's got cash?"

"Who uses cash?" Peter scoffed, and then patted his pockets like a man who'd just remembered he does.

We're not a family the way families are on paper, but we are something close enough to borrow each other's sunscreen and stories.

Kerry, the Nurse Unit Manager, was already in the car park when we pulled in, wedging folding chairs into the back of her ute between a box of talc and three rogue pool noodles.

"Occupational hazard," she said when I raised an eyebrow at the noodles. "Everything gets turned into manual-handling training where I'm concerned."

She tapped the talc. "Friction lesson, sprinkle this on a slide sheet and people finally feel why we don't drag." Then the noodles. "Edge protectors, lever demos, makeshift barriers for 'don't lift that with your back, Trevor.' Also handy if a gull gets ideas."

Only a NUM would bring a picnic and a pop-up toolbox for safe lifting to the same outing. It made perfect sense in Hedland.

We convoyed to the water like migrating birds who'd forgotten how to arrow but remembered the way. The jetty sat long and patient against the glitter, ore ships waited like great beasts, bellies sleepy and full of someone else's future. The river mouth did that Hedland trick, brown water and blue sky marrying into a colour no crayon has tried.

I stepped out and the heat clapped hands around my face. The kind of day that makes every thought slow down and every laugh faster. Pelicans lined the pylons like fat judges. Kids chucked lines over the railings with religious fervour. The kiosk had a queue as long as a night shift.

Kerry and I commandeered a table. Robyn sourced vinegar like a wartime quartermaster. Sharon and Gavin arrived mid-argument about the merits of eighties power ballads, their hands flying, and grins barely suppressed.

"Bonnie Tyler is a lifestyle," Sharon declared, balancing two sauces and a pile of napkins like a waitress in a film clip. "Key change, thunderclap, feelings. That's music."

Gavin shook his head, already laughing. "Feelings are fine, but you can't deadlift to 'Total Eclipse.' Journey or nothing. Maybe a bit of Roxette, plural, Sharon, plural."

They stood a fraction too close for people who are "just mates," hips angling toward each other and then away as if they'd practised not being a pair and kept failing in charming, neon-lit ways. She nudged his shoulder with the back of her hand when he teased her, he remembered how she takes her chips without asking. Trying not to look like a thing and absolutely giving themselves away.

"Don't even start with me," Sharon said, pointing a chip at Gavin. "You thought Roxette was a solo artist."

"Technically," he parried, grinning, "I was thinking of the spirit of Roxette, one woman, one microphone, and the Lord's work."

I opened my mouth to play referee and then the day made a decision for us.

The noise arrived before the roo, a collective inhale, three people yelling "Whoa, mate!" at the same time, the slap-thump of big back feet on timber. Heads turned like choreography. Past the bait boards and the crab pots and the dads in faded fishing shirts, a big red kangaroo barrelled along the jetty with the manic certainty of something that had chosen chaos and found speed.

He was a beauty, lank, clean, and eyes wild with the kind of plan that leaves no room for revision. He shot between a pram and a tackle box like mercury, cleared a low esky in one bound, and kept coming.

"Roo!" someone shrieked unnecessarily, and then the jetty became an old-phone video, shaky, joyful, and ridiculous.

The pelicans lifted like slow bags of laundry. A man in double-pluggers did a high step that would have made the Dockers proud, lost one thong to gravity, and began composing barefoot poetry. A teen with a mullet you could set your watch by yelled "Send it!" because he couldn't think of what else to contribute. A toddler pointed and announced, "Dog!" with ferocious confidence.

I don't remember standing. I remember my body moving without filing paperwork with my brain, toward the problem, then off to the side, then toward the people making it worse. Tomo's voice from a different day ran in my head, *You don't run unless you're on fire.* Walk fast. Make eye contact. People watch your face to find out if they're dying.

No one was dying. A few were about to make regrettable videos. Two were angling to "help" by turning the roo toward the railings, the kind of help that ends with a splash and a story no one wants.

"Hey! Hey!" I called, using my hospital voice, the one that gets obeyed by people who think they're immune. "Give him space. Back up. Let him choose the way out."

It sort of worked. The crowd wobbled and made a lane out of its own breath. The roo used it. He did that flat-out two-beat gallop that turns a kangaroo into a physics lecture, tail, legs, air, and hope. He thundered past us and then, because the universe enjoys punchlines, he hesitated at the kiosk end where the jetty narrowed, straight through someone's legs, left into the picnic area, right toward the marina, or up steps he did not trust? He chose panic.

He skittered, slipped, corrected, and swung right. The crowd swung with him. Fish and chips swivelled. A box of calamari committed to the floor with a greasy sigh. People narrate chaos when they can't control it, so the air filled with, "Watch his tail!" "He'll jump!" "Don't spook him!" "Mate, he's already spooked!"

He nearly overbalanced, hind feet too close to the edge, tail lashed like a question mark, forepaws windmilling, and my stomach dropped. A warm, steady hand landed at my elbow.

"Careful," said the voice my cells already knew.

Big Russ stood half a step behind me, half a shield, half a laugh. Weekend Russ, sleeves rolled, cap low, sunglasses shoved up so his eyes could do the work. Presence like a fencepost that won't give.

"Don't run at him," he said, low, like a suggestion the day might take. "We'll shepherd."

"We'll… what?" I managed, high on adrenaline and deep in the ridiculous.

"Give him a corridor," he chin-pointed. "Make the shape he needs."

We did. Nobody handed me a whistle, but somehow my body knew. I swung Sharon left, Kerry turned into the adult in the room and was instantly obeyed, Gavin spread those long arms and became a human guardrail, Robyn, five-foot-nothing on tiptoe, planted and became a bollard.

"Nice and easy!" someone yelled, helping exactly no one.

The roo saw the new path, took it like a prayer, and barrelled toward the low beach where the mangroves start. For a sick second I thought he'd jump. He didn't. He juked like a half-back, skidded down the slope like a skateboarder who doesn't know despair, and hit the shallows with a splash broad enough to baptise the front row.

"Jesus," breathed the thongless man, watching his footwear sail away on a personal journey.

"Oi!" yelled three teens, but the roo was already chest-deep, swimming with the strong ungainly grace of a creature doing what life insists. He crossed the channel, launched up the opposite bank in one miracle bound, shook himself like a dog with opinions, and vanished into mangroves with a haughty flick of tail.

Silence fell like a laugh that had to catch its breath. Then the jetty exhaled, cheers, claps, holy sh-ts, and would-you-look-at-that's, a dozen stories being born at once to be retold for a decade.

Only then did I notice his hand was still at my elbow. He noticed too. We both went still, then he lifted it away like you move a sleeping child's arm, slow, careful, and regret hidden in respect.

"You alright?" he asked, scanning my face not for pretty but for okay.

"I don't know what that was," I said, breathless and grinning in a way that felt like breaking and mending at once. "But I'd pay to see it again."

"Don't say that," he deadpanned, "someone'll start charging."

We stood stupid-close in the aftershock of silly danger, and something quiet and complicated moved like weather between us. Laughter did the breaking-for-us part. He chuckled first, low, surprised, his head tipping back just enough to show the fine scar along his jaw. My chest tightened in a way very little had for a long time.

"Right," Kerry announced, clapping like a PE teacher. "Action review. What went well?"

"Indi didn't yell," Sharon offered.

"I yelled internally," I confessed.

"Roo did not kill Sharon when she called him 'the big dog'," Gavin added, straight-faced.

"I maintain he was a big dog," Sharon said, unabashed.

"Even better," Kerry concluded, "no one in hi-vis attempted to rugby-tackle a native animal, so no WorkCover paperwork for me." She beamed like Santa without the beard. "Chips?"

***

We fed half the town. Paper parcels split open, steam and vinegar fogged the air like a weather event we'd ordered on purpose. Sharon invented a taxonomy of chips, golden, nearly golden, and courageously underdone, while Gavin insisted the burnt ones tasted like character. Peter salted like a man blessing a boat. Kerry confiscated our napkins one by one and redistributed them according to need and maturity level.

"You hear that?" Sharon asked, pausing mid-munch.

"What?"

"The sound of me not thinking about the ward."

I heard it, the slack in the rope, the quiet between gull raids, and the human hum you only get when no one's checking obs in their head. A pelican blinked like royalty. The river licked the pylons and pretended it had always meant calm.

Big Russ's lot sprawled two benches down, satisfied in the way of people who'd been present for a story they could improve upon later. Tiny reenacted his dignified sidestep, the others threatened to enter him in ballet. Big Russ didn't join the pantomime. He watched the water like he trusted it to be water and not trouble. Every so often his glance skimmed our table and went elsewhere as if it had meant to all along. Mine did the same. Peter noticed. He always does.

"Alright, Romeo and Julienne fries," he murmured. "Focus."

"Reunite that thong with its destiny," I murmured back. "Hero's journey."

He tried. He failed. The thong sailed off to legend.

Teenagers presented themselves for debrief. "Came for mullet," one said, smoothing his own with reverence, "got a roo. Ten outta ten."

"Hydrate," Kerry ordered, because the town is safer when she's bossy. They obeyed like conscripts.

Shadows slid down the ore carriers' ribs. Someone's Bluetooth speaker died and resurrected itself twice. The kiosk recovered from calamari-gate. Gavin wandered over with the last perfect chip - crisp, salt sugared - and split it fair between Sharon and me like Solomon with sense.

He looked at me, then at Sharon. "Friday? Jetty Lights, Friday Nights. Not a date."

"Team thing," Sharon said, failing to keep the smile out of her voice.

"I'm rostered out bush," I said. "I'll see if Janelle can cover."

The words landed between me and Big Russ like a coin, no promise, some direction.

He drifted to the rail when I did, both of us performing the ancient ritual of checking water colour for science.

"Adrenaline tax hit yet?" he asked, not looking, looking.

"Immediate," I said. "Dose, sociopath-level chocolate."

"Noted," he said, approving of correct medicine.

We stood in that easy not-speaking that feels like competence. Close enough to borrow steadiness, far enough to be good.

Kerry clapped us into a group selfie because joy needs evidence. "Say roo!"

"Roo!" We were all teeth and sun and salt on our cheeks from spray-that-wasn't-spray. It would print terribly and live forever on someone's fridge.

And then the simple miracle, I laughed hard enough to hiccup and didn't reach for guilt. Joy landed without asking permission from sorrow. It didn't move Lionel further away, it just made more room around him.

We packed in that end-of-day choreography, folding chairs that pretend not to understand, towels shaken like declarations, and children lured with the ancient promise of ice cream. Kerry made us police our rubbish because a NUM remains a NUM even off duty. Robyn borrowed my lip balm for the seventeenth time and called it community property. Peter discovered he'd sunburned an exact triangle behind his ear and named it 'Art.'

Big Russ came by on his way out, hat brim tipped. "See you round," he said, which in Pilbara is both greeting and hope.

"Round," I echoed.

We again didn't acknowledge already having each other's numbers. We didn't need to, this town hands you the same people until you figure it out.

Back at the quarters, a dog I don't own scolded me for living. We rinsed the day off. Robyn made tea - strong, black, two sugars - because right isn't always about being right, sometimes it's about a hand on your shoulder in a mug. Peter produced chocolate with the solemnity of ceremony.

"Review! Roo, perfect ten." Robyn said, cross-legged, towel draped over her shoulders like a cape.

"Thong! Gone too soon. Indi?" Peter said.

"Joy without guilt," I said, and didn't cry.

I sent two texts right then and there before I could overthink it.

To Sharon: You pick the playlist. Don't let him near Roxette. Friday.

To DonateLife WA: Hi, it's Indianna. I'm in for 'A Star to Remember.' Outline next fortnight.

The second hovered, daring me to unsend. I didn't. It flew, taking with it the small, stubborn belief that speaking would break me. It won't. It'll bend me into a shape strangers can lean on for a minute. That's the work.

We slept like people who'd been laughing in sun. The fan ticked time. Somewhere a ute did ceremonial laps.

Morning wore a clean edge. Coffee steam wrote its own weather in the kitchen. Peter stacked the Troopy with that priestly efficiency of men who have known loss and learned lists. Robyn pressed a foil-wrapped breakfast roll into my hand.

"Cold on top, colder on bottom," Peter intoned, placing frozen bottles under the esky lid.

"That's the rule," I smiled.

"You heading back?" Robyn asked.

"Janelle'll be waiting," I said. Country has its own clock, the clinic does too.

Hugs, quick, then proper. Promises.

"Text when you hit the turnoff."

"Bring back that lip balm, it's mine now."

On the edge of town I did the two-eyes-down where the place asked me to, then lifted my gaze when the road let me. Mangroves gave to red. The radio decided on a station and stuck. I drove like praying, steady hands, and soft eyes, just slow enough to see what matters, a goanna considering the verge, a shimmer that's heat not water, and quick enough to beat the sun to the clinic.

I pulled over once, between salt and spinifex, to catch the day so it wouldn't run off:

- Roo ran the jetty; we made a corridor; he chose it.

- Laughed and didn't ask the sky first.

- Said yes: speech (and maybe something else).

Then, because it felt right, I drew the shape of the jetty and put a tiny stick-figure roo on it mid-leap. The drawing was terrible. It pleased me, and then the red-dirt notebook went back onto the passenger seat with the red dust caught in its spine. I checked the ships in the rear-view, tiny and certain, took a breath that tasted like brine and iron and sugar, and then headed east. The road unspooled, red shouldered and honest. Somewhere a wedge-tail made circles like a pencil testing its lead. I let the radio wander through static until it found a song that didn't ask anything of me.

Janelle had texted a thumbs-up an hour back. She'd have the good tea ready, the verandah already cooler than the day, and the kind of gossip that's just her caring out loud about everyone. By the time the bitumen gave way to corrugations, I could feel the clinic waiting the way a dog waits - impatient, loving, practical.

I rolled in late afternoon. Janelle was on the verandah, mug in hand, and a smile that went all the way.

"Made it," she said, like a blessing.

"Made it," I echoed, climbing the steps.

We did the fast debrief that would sound like idle chat to anyone else, who's healing, who's hiding, which truck needs coaxing, which aunty is cross and why (and what biscuits will fix it). She slid a steaming mug into my palm - strong, black, two sugars without asking - and I sat long enough for my bones to remember where they belong.

"Tomorrow's book," she said, tapping the clinic diary. "Dressings, two medication reviews, a new bub check, and old Mr. P- says he'll only let you look at that foot if I make the tea."

"Then you make the tea," I said. "I'll brave the foot."

Her laugh was a small storm breaking and passing. "Go sleep. You've got the jetty still in your cheeks."

***

I dropped my bag at the quarters, fan already wobbling the air into cooperation, and did the simple chores that turn a place back into a home, rinsed a cup, straightened a pillow, and lined my boots by the door like they might behave if they saw an example. The shower pulled the salt from my hair and the sun from my skin. I stood a minute wrapped in a towel, watching the last light lift off the spinifex, and let the weekend slide into its spot, a soft landing stowed where it wouldn't bruise, ready to be unpacked tomorrow where it mattered.

***

In bed, the fan wobbled its way through warm air. Somewhere in town a ute did a lap because that's what utes do when there's nowhere to be and everywhere to go. I lay on my back and counted the day back to myself, chips, heat, elbow touch, pelicans, and laughter ringing off timber like a bell.

On the desk, Lionel's photo kept doing what it does, not looking at me and still seeing me. I put my hand up to the air where his forehead would be, lined up with the familiar groove. "Help me live." I whispered because I always will. The universe is a practical nurse, sometimes it helps with morphine, sometimes it helps with kangaroos.

Sleep came without a fight. The tide moved in my chest and out again like something I could live with. Out on the water, the ships waited, and the tugs rested, and the jetty held exactly as much story as it needed to. Tomorrow there would be wards and wounds and paperwork, and the kind of courage that hides inside routine. Tonight there was only this, I was alive, and it did not feel like a betrayal.

Chapter Fifteen

By breakfast the horizon had a bruise.

You learn the colours here the way you learn a clinic's alarms, by feel first, then by name. Today the sky wore that Pilbara purple-grey that means the sea is thinking in circles and the wind has opinions. The gulf lay flat in the distance like it was holding its breath.

DFES pinged my phone at 07:06: BLUE ALERT - Tropical low tracking WSW. Prepare for cyclonic weather in the next 48 hours. The Standard Emergency Warning Signal tone made the kettle sound suddenly frivolous.

I was halfway through pouring when Janelle tapped the flyscreen with her knuckle. "Morning, sister," she said, already in a clinic polo and old runners. "You see it?"

"Blue Alert," I nodded, handing her my phone.

She scanned, lips pressed, then gave me the list that lives in her bones. "Alright. Clinic first. Generator test. Fuel level. Freeze bottles. Sharps in the safe. Ring the Elders and check who's staying, and who's got a niece in town. We pull the loose gear in, bins, benches, and that one stubborn wheelbarrow. You do meds top-up and scripts. I do the rounds. Then school, safe room key. Troopy full tank. Sat phone check." She grinned without humour. "Think like the wind."

We live in the clinic house, two fibro boxes stitched together by a verandah and good intentions, where donga rules double as etiquette, share your power board, put your boots outside, knock twice before you borrow someone's talc. Cyclone rules layer on top, full tank, cash out, freeze water, move the furniture that wants to become a missile. And the secret rule the old people taught me on day one, be nice to each other. Provisioning kindness makes everything else behave.

By 07:45 I'd thrown my go-bag together - stethoscope, head-torch, spare scrub top, joggers, phone brick, red-dirt notebook, jelly snakes (for morale), and the talismans nobody teaches you to carry - gaffer tape, a black Sharpie, two teabags in a snap-lock. On a Post-it I wrote 'tea - strong/black/two sugars', Aunty's order turned ritual, rituals are architecture in bad weather.

The clinic smelled like wipes and weather. The concrete out front already had that darkened look it gets before rain actually falls. Inside, the whiteboard held yesterday's neatness, by 08:00 it had been turned into the day's spine.

CYCLONE PREP - BLUE → YELLOW (likely PM)

- Generator: test 10:00 / fuel ¾ full (order top-up)
- O2: cylinders 3× full, concentrator tested
- Suction: checked, tubings bagged
- Meds: 72-hour top-up (abx, salbutamol nebules, steroids, analgesia, antiemetics)
- Lines/Fluids: ugly abundance (Janelle's words)
- Dressings: burns, trauma, IDC kits, Thomas packs restocked
- Comms: sat phone, UHF ch.15, clinic mobiles charged, power bricks charging
- Evac/Stay: RFDS threshold winds, school safe room cleared, list of high-risk patients updated
- Loose items: in store (literally and metaphorically)

"Alright," Janelle said, drawing boxes beside each line. "You do meds and lines. I'll ring round and make eyes on houses. Call Store, tell them aunties need batteries now, not tomorrow. Ask old mate to pull in those milk crates before they fly to Broome."

I started with the drug cupboard, hands doing the maths. Prednisone. Salbutamol. Amox/Clav. Metoclopramide. Paracetamol, ibuprofen. Extra Ventolin inhalers for the kids who always become 'wheezy kids' when the pressure drops. I wrote '72h' on the shelf lip with the Sharpie like a blessing. Fluids next - one litre bags stacked in a ridiculous pyramid because experience says one request turns into four when the wind starts talking.

Janelle's voice moved through the building like a metronome, soft, then firm, then soft again. "Morning, Aunty. You got someone staying? Good… You need me bring the chairs in?… Alright, I come."

A beat later, "Uncle, I see that trampoline in your yard pretending it's a helicopter. Tie him down, eh." Then, in the doorway to me, "School's fine. Principal got the keys and the big mop. We good."

We walked the rooms the way you do before night shift, with eyes on corners. We tied curtains back, taped a small 'X' over glass louvres because someone's nan always asks if you did it, coiled extension cords up off floors, pushed any bed that could roll in away from windows. I made the crash trolley behave (because it likes to wander) and topped the suction jar so future-me would thank present-me when the lights go disco.

"Troopy," Janelle said, tossing keys. "Fuel."

The servo felt like a rumour when I pulled in - two utes, the dog that belongs to everyone and no one, the wind practising.

Store owner stuck his head out from behind a stack of SPAM tins. "You mob right?"

"Blue," I said. "Batteries? Gas? Water?"

He nodded to the pile by the till. "Already doing up the aunties' boxes. Tell Janelle I got the baby formula aside for her list."

"Legend." I filled the tank, paid cash (EFTPOS doesn't like low pressure days), and then drove back past the yards where the kids were already chasing wayward buckets around, and the men were performing the ancient art of tying things to other things with rope that looks too thin until it isn't.

By 09:20 we ran our drill in the treatment room - no power, no lights, half a team - because practice in the light is how you behave in the dark. We walked PEDPP out loud - People, Equipment, Drugs, Patient, Plan - like a secular psalm. Who's doing airway if RFDS can't come? Where's the head-torch live? Which aunties know where the spare keys are? What do we do if the satellite coughs? We timed ourselves to find what stuck and what slipped.

A Toyota pulled up out front and two little boys pressed their noses to the clinic glass to watch us tape the last of the cupboards shut. Their mum called, "You mob open?" and Janelle answered without turning around, "Always."

Then the calls kept coming, on the clinic line, on Janelle's mobile, and shouted from the gate.

"Janelle, my nephew's dog, he dug a hole under the fence, he'll fly to Port if I don't-"

"Uncle's generator is coughing like a smoker-"

"The little one got that cough again with the weather-"

We triaged worries and people at the same time. I ran two nebs, and a pep talk for a six-year-old who swore the mask smelled like the moon. I wrote a script for antibiotics for a cellulitis that was trying it on. I rang the visiting midwife to confirm she was already south of the river and then called the woman due next week and said the words that matter, "We know your name. We have a plan." Janelle talked three men out of staying to drink at the river bend, "Go home. Tie stuff down. Drink water. Say sorry to your wives for being a headache." They laughed and did exactly what she said.

We put our names on the whiteboard beside 'On-call if phones die.' Janelle wrote hers like a signature, I printed mine like a promise. Then she pointed at the verandah. "Break," she ordered. "Eat your banana like a raccoon. Text your people. Then we keep going."

I sat on the top step with my lunch in two bites and counted my breathing back to normal. The wind had picked up to that hiss that lives under everything. Two crows argued about a chip wrapper that wouldn't cooperate. Somewhere a tarp flapped like a stubborn flag.

"Ready?" Janelle asked, coming out with a roll of tape stuck to her wrist the way bracelets are meant to be.

"Ready," I said, and meant it.

Back inside, the afternoon's work stacked itself, a dressings clinic that turned into a community meeting because women will gather wherever there's chairs and shade, a granddad who turned up "just to suss it out" and left with his blood pressure checked, his meds topped up, and strict instructions to charge his radio, a young bloke with a sprained wrist from trying to out-wrestle a sheet of roofing tin that had delusions of flight, my eyes met his embarrassment, and we settled on a compromise.

"Smokers' door?" I asked out of habit.

Janelle smirked. "We check the windmills from the step." And we did, just for a minute, two ore carriers now, not four. The tug had tucked itself somewhere sensible. The purple-grey on the horizon had edged closer, like a bruise remembering why it started.

"Yellow tonight," Janelle said softly. "We sleep with shoes near the door."

"Copy," I said, and wrote it in the corner of my brain where the important small things go.

When the sun slid toward the wrong colour for comfort, we ran our list again, ticking boxes we'd already ticked because that's how you keep nerves from chewing the furniture.

GENERATOR (runs sweet)

O2 (full)

SUCTION (set)

MEDS (enough)

FLUIDS (ridiculous)

COMMS (charged)

TROOPY (full)

SCHOOL SAFE ROOM (key on hook, mats aired, buckets ready)

ELDERS (rung, visited, rung again)

"Last stop, Aunty May," Janelle said, grabbing her hat. "She'll pretend she's fine and then you'll make her feel seen and she'll cry and then you'll feel like a thief. Bring the good tea."

We walked the red street together, the wind pushing our words ahead of us. Dogs announced us. Kids called "Nurse!" like it was a game. A man on a ladder shouted down, "You mob want this shade cloth?" and Janelle yelled back, "After the wind, not before!"

At Aunty May's, the kitchen table smelled like soap and old stories. We brought the chairs in, rolled the fridge forward off its dodgy wheel, taped the window in a token that meant, 'We've been here.' Aunty May told us about the big one, the one with the name she still won't say, and where she hid her grandkids under the bed because the hallway felt too far.

"Home got a sound," she said, tapping the table. "You listen. You know when she's alright."

"We'll listen," I said, pouring tea - strong, black, two sugars - because right isn't always about being right, sometimes it's about doing the thing that feels like a hand on a shoulder.

Back at the clinic house, we made one more map on the whiteboard, the kind that is mostly names arranged like comfort.

CHECKS - MORNING (if safe):
- Aunty May
- Uncle Harry
- Shirley & the twins
- Old man in the blue donga
- Teacher flats
- Store
- Dogs by the oval (water)

Janelle capped the marker, leaned the back of her head against the cool wall for a second, then opened her eyes and smiled at me in a way that put steel in my knees. "Good work," she said. "We got this."

"Together," I said, and meant that, too.

When I finally lay down, I could feel the house think. The fan worked the warm air like a patient. Somewhere a loose tin tap-tapped a confession against a post. I put my hand up into the dark of the night to where Lionel's forehead would be and lined it up with the familiar groove I remembered all to well.

"Help me live tidy," I whispered to the weather and the memory. "Grief where it belongs, hope where it can breathe."

Sleep came without a fight. The tide moved into my chest and out again, like something I could live with. Out there, the wind rehearsed its lines. In here, the plan waited, folded and ready. Tomorrow there would be check-ins and dressings, and stories told on verandahs while we watched the trees talk. Tonight there was only this, we had prepared, and it did not feel like pretending.

***

"People, me and you," Janelle said, ticking boxes on the whiteboard with her thumbnail against the marker. "Backup. Principal on the school safe room, Shire works on sandbags, Store on batteries, and security is every aunty with a broom."

She pointed down the list and made me say it with her.

"Equipment, manual sphyg, penlight, bag-valve mask, suction set and spares, oxygen - wall first if we keep power, cylinders second if we don't. Torches, head-torches on hooks, hand torches by the treatment bed - left side, not right, so we find 'em by feel. Drugs, adrenaline ampoule where my hand already knows, nebules, steroids, pain, antibiotics, glucose gel for that one uncle who 'forgets' lunch. Patient, Aunty May if her chest decides to scare her again, the little fella with wheeze when weather drops. Plan, keep heads, keep hands, keep talking."

We timed it. We talked it. We discovered the torch lives better 'here' not 'there', and that gaffer tape solves everything except heartbreak. We practiced where to stand if a louvre lets go. We said, out loud, I'm scared in the right way.

By late morning the community channel crackled faster, and the sky grew the kind of belly a cyclone uses to store bad ideas. Yellow Alert hit at 11:32, the phones lit with, 'you mob need anything?,' from the sort of people you keep on purpose. I sent Mollie, Aliviya, and Luna a photo of the little tape crosses on the clinic windows, then the follow-up because I could hear their lecture already: 'We know tape doesn't stop glass. It just keeps the shards polite. Promise.'

Out the front, Shire crew built low walls of sandbags and swore affectionately at the wind. The teacher rolled up with a trolley of readers and said, "If the kids get bored in the safe room, we're doing times tables." The store kept a stack of batteries and baby formula aside "for clinic mob", and passed out the last of the muffins so they wouldn't turn into missiles or go stale waiting for tomorrow's weather. Someone suggested we name the generator, we did, because it helps to humanise the thing that will keep your people breathing.

"The Beast," Janelle decided, patting the metal like a good dog. "Don't look at me like that, she likes a name."

After a quick lunch that tasted like adrenaline and Vegemite, I took five at the doorway we had not boarded and checked the horizon. Two ore carriers sat out there like stubborn punctuation, a tug nosed along as if it had someone to mind. I counted them because numbers are the handrail in moving stairwells.

"Count 'em for me," Janelle said, stepping into the lean of shade beside me. "I like it when you say it."

"Two carriers, one tug," I reported. "They're staying put."

"Stubborn mob," she said with affection. "We'll do the same."

By mid-afternoon we moved from tidy to deliberate. We pulled anything soft away from glass, rolled the treatment bed in against an interior wall, negotiated with independence the way diplomats do. Aunty May wandered through on her way home, eyeing our sandbag line.

"Where you gonna put that big fella?" she asked, nodding toward the portable oxygen concentrator.

"Inside corner," I said. "Less wind, more wall."

"Mmm." Approval, small and bright. "You got brains when you use 'em."

At 15:10 the enamel mug on the counter trembled exactly once, the building took a deep breath like a horse narrowing its belly for the girth, and the first proper gust found our door and tugged it like a kid who wants in. Somewhere a siren practiced a wail and half the dogs in town considered their options.

We nested the clinic the way birds do. Soft things here, breakables there. Chargers in any socket that said yes. Long cords taped down. A bucket under the temperamental drip that insists on relevance regardless of weather. I labelled the last of the water bottles like a librarian drunk on power, Janelle came back from tying down the wheelbarrow looking like she'd argued with the wind and won on points.

"Generator test at sixteen-hundred," she called. "Place your bets."

The Beast coughed, rumbled, then settled into that steady industrial purr that can be comfort or dread depending on your history. To me it sounded like a very large, very serious cat sitting on our chests and promising to keep us warm.

At 16:40 we got the RFDS final call. The pilot's voice over the landline had that clipped, practical kindness I love. "Wheels down by seventeen hundred. Last run until All Clear."

"Copy," Janelle said. "We'll send your two and wave like fools."

I walked Mr S and his daughter to the strip with the Troopy lights on low. He was stoic in the way men get before the weather and funerals, straight spine, and jokes that don't quite land. She clutched his bag like it had a passport to a country she didn't want to travel to.

"You'll be right," he lied gently.

"We'll be here," I told them both, and the plane took a piece of the day with it that made the place feel hollow for ten minutes.

By 18:00 we were officially 'Yellow Alert' shading toward 'Red.' The port shut its mouth. The community went from hot hustle to held breath. People did the last-minute mistake run, the one where you buy three loaves of bread and forget the batteries, and then retreated to bathrooms, mattresses, and the places your body remembers as safe.

We moved from prep to presence. Which is the real work.

It's funny what keeps you steady. For me, tasks with edges, the click of the torch cap, the scratch of Sharpie on a label, knowing the suction pulls even when the world gets bored of us. For Janelle, a ponytail so tight it would have survived the Hindenburg, and the way she rests one hand on the bench when the building talks so her body remembers gravity.

At 19:12 the phone bars started that slow blink of 'maybe.' We tried not to stare. We failed. Everyone micro-prayed to their own small gods. I texted all good to Robyn and Peter back in Hedland and got three thumbs-up and a photo of Peter's impromptu candle shrine to electricity as a concept.

And then my phone rang.

Unknown did that swoop in my stomach birds do when they change direction.

"Indi," said the voice I could find in a blackout.

"Big Russ."

The line had molasses in it. We talked like two people on opposite sides of a river shouting the one word that matters so the water will carry it.

"You good?" he said.

"Yeah," I said. "You?"

"Yeah. Camp's locked. Machines parked nose-to-tail. Containers chained. She's coming in egg-shaped."

"Egg-shaped," I repeated, because the right metaphors matter. "We've pulled everyone off glass. The Beast is purring."

He let out a short breath. "Course it is."

From his end, the sound of a building trying not to have an opinion. Voices in the background - low, practical, pretending the weather's the only thing they fear. The line crackled.

"Listen," he said, and the way he said it made me face the wall on instinct, as if privacy can be built with bricks. "If the towers die-"

"I know," I said softly. "We'll wait."

"Check the horizon," he said, half a joke, half something else.

"Always," I said.

The line dropped like a curtain.

I stood for a second with the phone still against my ear, then slid it into my scrub pocket like a talisman. The room had changed shape around me while I was listening. Janelle raised one eyebrow. I shook my head a fraction. Not now. Later. Maybe.

Outside, a palm frond clapped once like approval. Inside, the Beast kept breathing for us. We finished taping the last cord, moved the last chair, and sat on the step for exactly sixty seconds to drink the kind of tea that tastes like a plan.

"Red next," Janelle murmured.

"Copy," I said and checked the sky like it had answers. Two carriers. One tug. Us.

***

Red Alert landed like a gavel at 20:03. Stay indoors. Shelter now.

The building took another breath, and this time let it out through its teeth. Rain arrived not as drops but as a sheet, like someone had tilted the ocean and we were standing under the lip of it. Gusts slapped, then punched, then laid on with purpose. Somewhere a bin turned into a drum. Somewhere else a loose sign changed careers and tried to be a kite.

We did what you do, we did the rounds. We walked the clinic and the school safe room with our good faces on - the ones no one pays for but that hold a room in place. We joked like professionals. We documented like poets - lines so spare only clinic people hear the lyric, *O2 stable. Sat 96% RA. Nil new pain. Family on-site.* We handed out washcloths warmed in the last of the good water. We turned the restless and listened to the stubborn. We pretended the thunder was kids dropping bowling balls upstairs.

Old Mr G asked if this counted as light exercise, I told him yes if he could keep his oxygen above 94 and he called me a tyrant with love. An aunty, eyes on the ceiling like it could answer back, asked whether the building knew the difference between mucking around and meaning it, I told her The Beast did, and she barked a laugh that made the room sit up straighter.

At 22:30, the lights did that long blink that feels like a countdown and then gave up. The Beast took the soundstage, the emergency strips glowed orange down the clinic hallway like a budget runway. The place became a cave with machines in it. We put our head-torches on, and the world splintered into circles of usefulness.

"Tea?" Janelle asked, materialising with a thermos she'd charmed from somewhere.

"Strong. Black. Two sugars," came a voice from a doorway without looking.

"Yes, Aunty," we chorused, and the day remembered itself.

Midnight. The eye was still offshore, the wind still making its mind known in all directions. Somewhere, the port wrote a swear word with spray. The world shrank to the length of a corridor and widened to include everything we loved. I sent a quick 'still here' to nobody in particular and got no reply from everyone, which is how storms talk.

And then, because I contain multitudes and some of them are extremely type-A, I took my head-torch, my red-dirt notebook, and my courage to the little staff room that smelt like instant coffee and disinfectant, and I wrote the speech I'd been avoiding for months.

A Star to Remember. DonateLife. The night I'd promised to stand up and be the person who speaks when everyone else is holding their breath.

I put the date at the top and then the words arrived like a weather system, a little drizzle, then a wall of rain, then a clearing.

I am not here because I am brave. I am here because someone I loved died, and his driver's license said he wanted to make sure someone else didn't. We talk about grief like a tide, and we use that word like it's gentle. It is not gentle. It is a rip. It will take you sideways.

DonateLife gave my rip a channel - papers I did not want to sign turned part of that water into three separate rivers, a lung for a thirty-year-old dad, a kidney for a man who'd run out of jokes but not years, a kidney for a boy who had to choose between lessons and dialysis and can now choose both.

I keep their letters in a drawer with my softest paper. Some days I touch them like braille, some days I pretend I've lost the key.

Both are true.

If you are a family standing in the hallway outside ICU right now in some other town staring at a machine that will not look back, I am not going to tell you what to decide. That is yours. But I am going to tell you what it felt like when the waves stopped hitting from all directions and started to run in one.

My husband Lionel had a groove in his forehead my palm still knows. I used to kiss that groove when the world went sideways. The night he died I put my hand there and said, "Help me live." Saying yes to donation was one way he did.

Here is what consent sounds like on a Tuesday you didn't plan, it sounds like a nurse with a good face and a pen that works, it sounds like a coordinator who does not hurry you, it sounds like the word choice being offered without a push.

Here is what it felt like afterwards, a letter I could hold that said his name mattered to strangers, a grief that kept its weight but changed its direction, a star I could check instead of a ship.

If you are here tonight because someone you loved said yes, I am not going to tell you to be proud instead of broken. You are allowed to be both.

Some days I can laugh without asking the sky's permission now, some days I cry in a Coles carpark because Meteora plays on the radio. Both are honest.

Thank you for making a corridor with your grief so someone else could run. Thank you for choosing a shape another family could step into. Thank you for the ordinary miracles hidden in paperwork.

If you are wondering if your yes matters - it does, it did, it will.

I stopped, pen hovering, the torch making a white coin of the page. The words felt like they belonged to the room and the storm, and the woman I am when I buy vinegar for chips and tell men to breathe.

I added a small story I'd been hoarding.

Once, in a clinic far from here, we lost the grid and the generator took over. The hallway glowed orange and we kept moving because that's what we do. Grief and love are like that, the main power goes and something older hums on.

When I finished, the building did one of those deep creaks old timber makes when it remembers longer than we do. The wind stepped sideways. The rain decided it had made its point for a minute. The safe room hissed with sleeping and small snores and the relief of quiet that might last five breaths. I put my pen down and touched the page like it might run off if I didn't.

"Indi," Janelle said softly from the doorway, head-torch making her look like a miner who'd found something she wanted to keep. "You good?"

"Yeah," I said, and meant it. "You?"

She nodded. "Yeah." She flicked her eyes to the notebook. "You write the thing?"

"I wrote the thing," I said.

"Good," she said, simple as bread. "Tea?"

"Please."

We drank from paper cups by head-torch in a tiny room that smelt like clinic and rain, and it felt a little like church.

Around 02:00 the wind turned on its heel. The building flexed, then relaxed. Red softened to stay put and don't be an idiot, which is not an official status but should be. The phones woke in little bursts, one bar, two bars, none. A photo came from the quarters chat, Roof intact. Peter had married the esky. Another of Robyn with two torches crossed over her chest like a librarian-turned-warrior. A single dot from a once unknown number resolved into a window, smear of dark sky, rain, a line of light like a promise.

You good? the caption read.

Yeah, I typed back. *You?*

Yeah. And then the bars fled. Good enough.

By 04:30 the worst had walked past us, kicking bins and sulking. The building let our breath go back to us. We loosened ponytails a notch, took the head-torches off our foreheads, and returned them to pockets so they could remember being useful. We woke the people who needed waking gently and pretended the sun would be on time.

The 'All Clear' would come later, after the SES did their rounds, after the port counted its beasts, and after the fences had their say. For now, there was the damp silence of a place coming back to itself.

I took five and went to the window. The glass was stippled with salt and high-speed regret. The horizon was a smudge about to be a line again. The ships had done what ships do when we need them to, they stayed. The tugs rested like dogs under the table.

"Four and two," I told the glass, just to hear the count out loud.

In the safe room, Aunty was awake, eyes on the space where the weather had been. She didn't look at me when she spoke.

"You did it quiet," she said.

"We tried," I said.

She grunted. "That big fella ring you?"

Heat went to my face in a way that would've embarrassed me six months ago and did not now. "The towers let him through," I said. "He asked if I'm good."

"Mmm." Verdict delivered. "Make sure he good to you."

"I will," I said - too quickly, too honest.

She finally looked at me, clocked the notebook riding my pocket like it was on the outside, and nodded. "You write," she said. "Good. You tell 'em. You tell 'em right."

"I will," I promised, feeling the weight of the page like a hand on my back.

Dawn put its shoes on. We handed the night back to the day like careful midwives - oxygen steady, lines patent, wound dry, family slept, generator purring. My body was ninety per cent tea and ten per cent responsibility. The storm had turned me inside out and left the necessary bits on top.

***

Back at the quarters, the path glittered with leaves and the kind of debris that looks dramatic but is really just the weather shedding. Peter had built a shrine to his esky out of tea lights and sarcasm. Robyn opened the fridge like it was treasure. We did the quiet laugh of people who don't want to wake the edges of a fragile morning.

I showered the storm off, salt, tape residue, and the fine grit that lives inside Pilbara wind, and then sat in my little room with the fan deciding to wobble and texted two people.

To Russ: All good. Ships stayed.

To DonateLife coordinator: Draft done. Will email as soon as I can.

Big Russ replied three minutes later, a rarity that felt like a gift. "Good." Then, after a beat, "Sleep if you can." (The most romantic thing a man can say to a nurse if we're writing definitions.)

I left the torch off and the red-dirt notebook open to the page that begins *I am not here because I am brave.* The room could be brave enough for both of us.

Before I closed my eyes, I lifted my hand to the air where Lionel's forehead would be and lined my palm to the familiar groove. The storm had taken the shape of a hallway and let us walk through. It had reminded me of the law that saves us and keeps us honest, never alone, eyes and hands. We make the corridor, the kangaroo chooses it. We lay the sandbags, the water honours them or doesn't. We sign the papers, and the tide finds a channel.

"Help me live," I whispered to the man I married at the age of twenty-one and still carry everywhere I go.

The building exhaled. The ships waited. Out past the last of the cloud, the first star shouldered through and winked like it knew a thing. I slept without asking permission.

Chapter Sixteen

The Friday woke up rinsed. The cyclone had argued itself hoarse overnight, and the country wore that washed look, sky wider, air lighter, and everything edged in salt. The clinic yard was a scatter of leaves and sensible gossip.

Janelle stood on the verandah with a thermos and a verdict. "Road's open," she said, passing me the mug like a blessing. "Roster says you're off. Go breathe salt. I'll keep an eye on our mob. Eyes down past the ridge, you know the rules."

I did. I signed the day-book, checked the radio, and packed light, fresh tee, stubby holder, pink lipstick, the red-dirt notebook with its head-torch draft folded inside. The Troopy coughed once and forgave me. As I rolled out, the ridge asked for respect, I lowered my gaze where country asked and only lifted it when spinifex gave way to mangrove green.

Reception blinked to life near the highway turn-off and the town began texting like it had been holding its breath.

Robyn: Jetty Lights, Friday Nights. 6?

Sharon: Gav's on pickup. I'm on playlist. Don't test me with country. Not a date.

Hedland gathered itself on the horizon, ore ships sitting stubborn, puddles flashing tin-bright in the sun, and palms doing the limp applause of survivors. It felt like the town and I had made the same decision, show up, gently.

By late arvo the Hedland streets wore that after-weather sheen, bitumen dark as wet slate, palm fronds doing the limp applause of survivors, and powerlines humming like they'd learned a new note. I swung by staff quarters first. Robyn and Peter had the place mid-chaos, an esky open like a treasure chest, towels half-folded, someone's rogue thongs accusing the hallway.

"Community royalty!" Peter crowed, arms up like a referee. "Ice on top, colder on bottom. That's the rule."

"My love language is logistics," Robyn said, lining the folding chairs up like Tetris pieces.

The quarters smelled like detergent and relief. I dumped my bag, kicked off my dusty flats, and headed straight for the shower. The first hit of water knocked cyclone grit out of my hair and off my shoulders, and the second found muscles I hadn't admitted were braced. I stood there until the day stopped buzzing in my bones. Rituals, then moisturiser, a quick tidy of the braid, mascara steady enough to prove I wasn't shaking anymore. I hesitated over the pink lipstick - the one the skid boys had named me for - and then put it on anyway. Some things you claim on purpose.

I pulled on a dress that remembers how to be light after long weeks in scrubs, slid my feet into sandals, and looped a bow in my hair because I'm still that woman, and I don't mind being seen. The red-dirt notebook went into my bag, the DonateLife draft folded inside like a small brave thing. I took a breath that tasted faintly of eucalyptus and laundry powder, smiled at the mirror version of me who's trying, and went to find my people.

Peter wolf-whistled when I came out. "Nurse with the pink lipstick hits the town."

"Settle," Robyn told him, though she'd chosen gold hoops and was in no position to judge. We locked up and stepped into an evening the colour of apricots and old bruises.

***

The Finny had all its lights on, like the building itself was glad to be open. Kids cartwheeled in the beer garden. Every second person wore hi-vis or wet hair. Somebody's uncle coaxed songs from a speaker everyone pretended not to know the words to.

"Indi!" Daniel waved us over, Sharon and Gavin were already lining up the saltshakers like tiny traffic cones.

Alison, big hair, bigger laugh, caught my hand in both of hers and gave it a squeeze that said more than any speech. "We made it," she said, eyes bright, voice a little rough from two nights of generator air. She lifted her middy toward the ceiling fans. Around us glasses tapped tabletops, elbows, knuckles - anything handy. No formal toast, just the shared relief of people who'd checked on neighbours, bailed verandahs, and slept in their boots. We made it. First sip of cold beer tasted like permission.

"To roofs that stayed on," Sharon said.

"To RFDS pilots who threaded that sky," Gavin added.

"To the generator that coughed back," someone from maintenance called.

"To the one we had to kick," Daniel said, and everyone snorted like people who've met generators.

Who lost fences, who gained swimming pools, which street turned river, which turned lake, stories spiralled. Laughter skimmed like swallows. Every few minutes somebody looked at the door like waiting was a sport.

He came in with the tide.

Big Russ slid in behind Tiny and Cam, sun-browned, hi-vis darker at the collar, the set of a man who'd done long hours with heavy things and was pretending his back didn't know. He took the room's measure, the room took his. Our eyes caught the way magnets do when you hold them just this side of touch.

I looked away first. I am careful with sharp things.

"Don't," Robyn murmured, not unkind. "He's trouble of the slow kind."

"Is there a safe kind?"

"Only in books," she said, and went to steal the best chips before Sharon did.

***

Big Russ had told himself he wasn't coming. Told Tiny on the bus, told the mirror in the ablutions block, told the bit of him that knows how to barricade a heart and stack sandbags across a thought. But the donga felt too small after a week of weather, tin roof ticking like a metronome for nerves he refused to name, and four walls echoing with everyone else's snoring and his own. The radio was too quiet, even the ads sounded lonely. He put on a clean-enough shirt and drove in with the volume low enough that his head-noise could hear itself think. Headlights skimmed puddles that had decided to be lakes. He told himself he was there for the boys, to debrief the storm with beer and bad jokes. He did not admit he was there for the maybe of her.

The Finny was all shoulder-claps and relief, damp hi-vis and hair still carrying rain. He clocked exits because he always does, clocked the jukebox because men like him don't trust silence, clocked the faces he knows by shape not surname. Then he clocked her. She laughed at something the dietitian said, pink mouth, braid like a rope, a dress that had remembered how to be light, and the speech he'd prepared about not believing in signs forgot its lines and left the stage.

Tiny elbowed him with bricklayer delicacy. "Don't. You two together, you'll set the joint on fire."

"Town'd get a second insurance payout," Big Russ said, dry, eyes not leaving her. A muscle in his jaw tried to remember a softer job.

The jukebox picked a slow one. Too slow for cyclone adrenaline, exactly right for a town remembering itself. Indi set her beer down. She stood. She didn't look at him. She did.

His feet went before the committee could vote. He stopped at her table like a bloke visiting a front porch, hat in the hands he didn't have. "Would you-" His voice did a seventeen-year-old thing he hadn't ordered. "Do you want to-"

"Yes," she said, saving them both, and the room obligingly made space where two people might try being braver than they felt.

***

We stepped into a space made by other people's elbows and history. The crowd gave us a little clearing, the kind you don't ask for but everyone understands. His hand found the back of my shoulder blade like it had trained there, warm through cotton, steady without claiming. My left hand slid into his right - callused, clean, the sort of grip that listens first - like a handshake with different rules.

We didn't speak for the first eight counts. Slow songs have a grammar that doesn't need words, set the frame, test the sway, negotiate a breath. Be the weight you'll need, agree to carry only what fits between you. His palm at my back said I've got you, mine at his wrist said I know.

The floor had that old-pub spring to it, soft from stories. Somebody's laugh ricocheted off the tin roof and then remembered to behave. The singer drew out a line everyone knew and the whole room swallowed it up like medicine. I could hear his breathing settle to the tempo - four-beat, practical - and feel the tiny corrections he made to keep us in the pocket. He smelt like soap, machine oil, a hint of rain, and the part of a jacket that's seen a fire once and kept the memory.

"You okay?" he said, pitched for me alone, more check than question.

"Yes," I said. Then, because storms and lying don't mix, "Now."

We swayed. Our feet found the compromise between swing and square - half a turn, a side step, the smallest rock back. His shoulder felt like the kind of place you could rest a question and know it wouldn't roll off the edge.

"You got hammered out there?" he asked, voice low, eyes not leaving mine but not trapping them either.

"Mostly prep," I said. "Lists did what they could. The rain did what it wanted."

"Doesn't it always," he said, mouth tipping, and we both pretended we were still talking weather.

The chorus folded over us. I felt his pulse under my fingers, steady as a metronome. Mine answered, unhelpfully, learning his beat like it had homework.

"Still off the smokes?" he asked, men who've quit can spot other people's battles even in dim light.

"Long enough to be cranky," I said. "Not long enough to brag. Give or take a cyclone."

"Not bad," he said, approving without turning it into a ceremony. "You'll feel mean for a bit. Then better. Then mean again. Then you'll forget you ever did it."

"You have a very comforting style."

He huffed a laugh that nudged my forehead with warm air. "I tell the truth for a living. Or bolts don't hold."

The song thinned to a bridge, and we turned in a slow circle that gave us the same room from a kinder angle. His thumb adjusted once on my shoulder blade, no pressure, just presence. My cheek almost brushed his chest, and I let the almost be enough.

Around us, survival paired with survival. The doctor who'd rolled up his sleeves did an awkward sway with the cleaner who'd kept the loos from becoming crimes against humanity for three straight days, their shoes squeaked, their grins didn't. A foreman stood in the doorway and rocked side to side, a toddler dead-asleep on his shoulder, hardhat hanging from two fingers like a truce. Two ambos who swear they're "just mates" counted the beat on their thumbs and forgot to pretend. At the chorus, even the sceptics, the blokes who say weddings are for fools and wishes are for kids, closed their eyes on the same line, not because they believed in the song, exactly, but because relief has a religion of its own.

"Indi," Big Russ said, too soft to be warning, too honest not to be. "I don't push. I'm not that bloke."

"I know," I said. And I did.

The song ended the way slow songs do, embarrassed to be caught still going. We stepped back a degree. The room remembered how to roar.

"Fresh air?" I heard myself say.

He nodded and opened the door.

***

Outside, the rain had chosen insistence over drama, warm, fine, the kind that sits on your arms and reminds you that you have skin. Port lights blinked in ship language, and the car park shone like a new coin.

We didn't pretend to be looking at anything.

"Thanks for the call," he said, eyes on the rain like it was a person. "During."

"It was nothing," I tried.

"It wasn't." He didn't let me off. "Being checked on matters."

"Okay," I said. "Then - okay."

A ute went by with an esky rattling like a drum. The rain ticked the awning, the concrete replied in tiny cheers.

"I'm not good at this," I told him so he didn't have to guess. "The thing after the thing. The-" I made a shape with my hands as if the outline would help.

"I'm worse," he said. "I have a certificate."

It startled the good kind of laugh, the kind that takes the tight out of a throat. He looked at me properly then. Not like a man trying to decide. Like a man who'd decided he didn't get to decide and was doing the better thing instead, be present. His eyes were that deep, steady brown, iron-rich in the half-light.

My star kicked in my pocket like a small animal. The part of me that had written Lionel a letter by torchlight last night pressed a hand up from underneath and said carefully, live.

I kissed him.

It was the wrong step in a right dance, and it didn't matter. Slow, a bit awkward, perfect. Rain. Soap. Machine oil. His hand stayed at the safe place between my shoulder blades. Mine stayed at his jaw. We leaned exactly as far as two people can lean and still be ready to step back.

We stepped back.

Tears gusted, mortifying, immediate. "I'm-" I threw a hand at the rain, blaming weather for my face. "I feel- like I'm- "

"Betraying," he offered, presenting the blade handle-first.

The relief of being seen was its own undoing. I nodded too hard. "He was good," I said. "And I loved – love - him. I don't know how to do both."

Big Russ put both hands in his pockets like he'd tied them there. "You don't have to know," he said quietly. "Just be kind to yourself while you find out."

A sound escaped, half laugh, half admission. I covered my mouth like I could keep the weather in.

"You're not doing a wrong thing," he added. "You're doing a human thing."

I looked at the wet concrete and saw, for a second, an ICU floor. "The night he went," I heard myself say, "I held his hand until-" I let the sentence end where it ends. "After, there was this, this tide. DonateLife gave it a channel. It was still a tide."

He didn't look away. "I know something about water that goes where it will."

We stood with that. The rain loved the awning, hated the edge. We stayed on the safe side.

"Do you want me to walk you in?" he asked at last.

"I can walk," I said, and he nodded like that was the right answer.

He didn't reach. I didn't either. We let the space be kind instead of a test.

"Goodnight, Indi," he said, making my name sound like a promise to behave.

"Goodnight, Big Russ," I said, making his sound like a promise to try.

***

The Finny was louder or quieter, hard to tell with pubs. Robyn looked at my face and did not ask, which is why she's allowed to borrow my favourite cardigan. Peter was teaching Daniel to cheat at pool using only charm.

I made excuses and left before the second slow song, hug for Robyn, a salute at Sharon and Gavin mid–shoulder sway, a nod that meant thanks to Daniel. Outside, drizzle had chosen mercy. It slicked my arms and took the heat down a notch. The car park shone like new coins tipped out on black velvet, and the sodium lights did their halo trick on every puddle.

I sat in the driver's seat and let the fan push damp air over my face. Head back on the headrest, I counted five long breaths, then five more, until my hands forgot the exact geography of his jaw and remembered the steering wheel instead. Someone in a nearby ute whooped at a goal no one could see. The pub door opened and shut, opened and shut, each swing letting out a brief burst of laughter like a heartbeat.

The streets home were quiet in that post-storm way, dogs taking their owners for a tow, tyres whispering through shallow water, and the port lights talking to no one in particular. The road laid itself out and let me through. At the last roundabout I did the small, old habit, looked right, and said thank you to nothing out loud, and felt silly and steadier for it.

Back at quarters the stairwell smelt of detergent and someone else's dinner pretending to be Italian. I kicked off my sandals by muscle memory, put the kettle on - strong, black, two sugars, because ritual steadies even when you don't need the drink - and watched steam lift like a veil. I didn't pour it. I stood with the soft boil in my ears and let the room catch up to me, towel over the chair, lip balm by the sink, the red-dirt grit still in the zipper of my bag. When the kettle clicked off, the quiet that followed felt like a hand on my shoulder saying, alright then.

The red-dirt notebook slid from my bag, the folded head-torch draft fell into my lap. The first line stared up, *When love moves through a body, it keeps moving.*

I thought about the lung, the two kidneys, the shaky signatures from people who think they owe me anything and who'd given me a raft instead. I thought about an ICU monitor that had fought with itself until it learned a new song. I thought about a kiss in warm rain and a gentle man who kept his hands in his pockets and made the world safer by inches.

I wrote three lines I could live with:
- Town made a circle and called it dancing.
- Warm rain, safe hands, careful mouth.
- Love is not a pie.

I tucked the DonateLife draft back into the notebook and slid it under the bed the way you do with things you're scared will vanish if you put them on a shelf. Window cracked for the scent of wet iron and eucalyptus, and the fan wobbled through warm air.

Somewhere to the north, five ships waited for a tug that knew exactly when to push and when to hold. Somewhere in my chest, two truths made a kind of room.

"Help me live," I told the ceiling, which wasn't who I meant. "I'm trying." Rain ticked yes on tin. I slept without bravery or shame.

Tomorrow before first light, I'd point the Troopy east - eyes down past the ridge - back to Janelle's verandah and the clinic's small brave work. Salt borrowed, country returned.

Chapter Seventeen

Morning came in sticky; the kind of heat that makes last night feel like a rumour you invented. I packed the Troopy slow and methodical with the head-torch back in the glovebox, red-dirt notebook on the passenger seat where it won't curl, and a wrapped slice of Robyn's "cyclone cake" wedged beside the first-aid tin. Peter saluted the esky like a fallen comrade. Robyn checked my tyres and my face with the same seriousness.

"Back roads open," she said. "Text when the bitumen turns to gravel."

"Copy," I smiled.

On my way out of town I ducked by the hospital to sign for a box of discharge meds heading out bush, and to drop off two coils of gaffer someone in Facilities swore they weren't counting. The building had that post-storm hangover, damp air, lino sweating, and a soft mildew tang rising like an old joke. In the waiting area, Aunty sat with a tea and the remote, the footy panel arguing at a respectable volume. She lifted her chin by way of hello. I lifted mine back.

"You go now," she said, not looking away from the screen. "Country quiet there."

"That's the plan."

Aunty still didn't look over. "Camp radio busy today. You don't listen that one."

I opened my mouth to ask which camp. She saved me from the question.

"Rumour wind blow stronger than cyclone," she added, and clicked the sound up one notch, as if to drown out anything that might try and climb in.

"Copy," I said, and meant it.

Back in the car park, my phone buzzed once with a message that didn't ask anything of me: Keep your wheels under you -R

I typed back: You too.

Then I turned the key, pointed the Troopy east, and let town slide into the rear-view - ships small and certain - while the long red road began again under my tyres.

***

The heat stacked early, the sky white at the edges, and bitumen dark as wet slate in the low spots where last night still clung. Past the ridge I did the eyes-down thing Janelle had taught me, greeted the country properly, then let myself look up when the flats opened, spinifex standing to attention, floodplain holding its shine, wedge-tails riding whatever lift the world could offer after a storm.

The UHF crackled to life the way it does when people forget it's public. Bits of site talk stitched themselves together out of static, crib time, a loader sulking, someone's roster swap, laughter that had too much edge for a Monday. Every now and then a phrase would make a shape you could recognise, *the girl from the hospital… nah, mate, different mob… heard she,* and then static would eat the tail.

Aunty's line from the waiting area sat up in the passenger seat like a passenger with opinions. *Rumour wind blow stronger than cyclone.*

"Noted," I told the empty cab, and thumbed the UHF down to quiet.

By the time the clinic fence came into view, a corrugated tank throwing back a shy sparkle, and flag rope ticking against the pole like a clock, Janelle was on the verandah with a thermos and the look that meant both welcome and wash your hands before you touch anything.

"You made it," she said, passing me a mug that could hold its own in a fight. "Community slept. Small ones woke early. Old ones watched. Wind talked then shut up. You ready?"

"As I'll ever be," I said, and put my bag down where it always goes.

"Good," she said, and tipped her chin toward the day. "Clinic first. Then we listen what wind tries. We don't let it in."

I thought of Aunty's tea. I thought of a slow song and hands that knew where to stop. I thought of the way a story changes shape when too many mouths chew it.

"Deal," I said. "Clinic first."

Janelle's smile was the whole chapter title, "Good. Rumour mill can run out there," she nodded at the horizon, "but in here, only truth."

And we began.

***

It started in stupid little ways, like these things always do. A hush on the verandah that didn't belong to the weather. Janelle's "Mmm" at her screen that meant 'I saw a thing and I'm deciding if it deserves oxygen.' Two teenagers at the water cooler went silent mid-giggle and then laughed too loud about nothing.

My phone buzzed on the med trolley: Robyn: Have you seen Camp Facebook?

Before I could answer, a screenshot arrived. A grainy pic from The Finny: Big Russ half in frame behind Tiny, captioned "two-time Big Russ 😉". Underneath, a comment thread doing what comment threads do when bored. At the top: Jess (Stores) with a paragraph that thought it was a novel.

I typed: Context?

Robyn: Jess from stores. Tall, tat sleeves. On/off with half the site, him once last year. She's… implying he's not as single as advertised.

Gav: Reported as trash. Will burn hot for a day, then the mill will eat something else.

Sharon: Deep breath, Indi. It's Camp Facebook, not Hansard.

I kept my face calm for the clinic. "BP cuffs are in the blue tub," I told Damo, because saying a true thing often helps with the untrue ones. Then I stepped off the verandah into the glare.

No ships out here to count. So I counted what I had, one dust devil marching the road like it had a schedule, two crows arguing the minutes, the tank tick-tick-ticking like a metronome trying to teach my chest a slower song. I breathed. Camp radio, I told myself. Not gospel. Not even good country.

Then, traitor brain, why does it sting?

Because warm rain isn't neutral. Because careful hands had felt like permission to try. Because after the kiss he'd put those hands in his pockets and said the gentlest words anyone had said to me in years. Because I'm still learning how not to drown in a teaspoon. I rubbed my thumb across the stopwatch face of my nurse's fob, listened to the tank keep time, and went back in. "Next," I called, voice steady enough to pass inspection.

***

Russ heard it on the bus before he saw it on a screen. The pre-start coach growled over corrugations; men settled into their dents.

Tiny dropped into the seat beside him, with his knees braced against the rail the way long-haul blokes do without thinking.

"Camp radio's rotten," Tiny said, more disgusted than amused. "Jess has been busy with her thumbs."

Something old, part guard dog, part scar, lifted its head inside Russ. "What now."

"She's resurrected herself as a cautionary tale," Tiny said. "Posting like you promised her the moon and… other celestial bodies."

"I didn't promise her anything." He kept his voice even. "We had a few beers months back. She wanted more. I didn't. I said so."

"I know," Tiny said. "Half the camp knows. The other half prefers a story to a timeline."

The bus took the bend that shows the flats, a country raked like a giant had dragged comb-teeth through it. Russ watched salt haze make its own weather. He thought of warm rain under an awning, of a careful mouth and steady hands that had stayed exactly where they should, of a woman who'd said yes to a dance after a storm and then, later, yes to the truth about tides. It put a new weight in his chest, nothing heavy, just present.

"Don't go near Facebook," Tiny added, scratching his neck. "Bad for your back."

"My back?"

"From carrying other people's nonsense."

Russ huffed a laugh he didn't feel. The bus hissed into the laydown, machines stood in rows like cattle at a trough. He could already hear the site speakers clearing their throat for toolbox.

"Toolbox in ten," he said, standing, shoulders finding the set that means work-only. "We've got ladders to un-stupid."

Tiny grinned. "That's a category now?"

"Has been for years." Russ slung his gloves into his back pocket. "We'll fix what's ours to fix and let the wind deal with the rest."

He didn't look at his phone. He looked at bolts, pitch, tie-off points, the honest grammar of things that either hold or don't, and let the day save him the way days often do.

***

By lunchtime, the heat had the texture of wet felt. Janelle and I worked the list that never shrinks, dressings that wanted dignity, sugars that wanted shepherding, a granddad who would only take his tablets if we both promised not to call them tablets.

"Sit," Janelle told him, all authority, all care. "Water first. Then the blue, then the white. Don't be clever, be alive."

The radio crackled in that way that means the world just hiccupped. *SITE 14 - STOP WORK. ALL HANDS TO SHADE. MEDIC TO LAYDOWN.* The words arranged themselves in my spine.

"Go," Janelle said, already grabbing the orange kit. "I'll lock the clinic. Damo - ute."

We banged down the track, iron smell up off the road like breath. Laydown was a quilt of shade cloth and opinions, two riggers pale around the mouth, a sampler swearing he didn't faint, and a supervisor counting heads with the panic hidden just under his hi-vis.

"What happened?" I asked, already kneeling.

"Heat and hurry had a baby," the supervisor said grimly. "New ladder on the gantry, wrong pitch. A bloke tried to be a bloke. Nearly wore the deck. He's over there, Jase."

Jase looked like he'd tried to wrestle a fridge and lost, grazes along the forearm, pupils a fraction too wide, skin too hot.

"Look at me," I said, cool cloth on his neck, shade first, talk second. "Breathe. Slow. We're not brave, we're smart."

He tried for a grin. "Lucky my mum's not here."

"Unlucky for all of us, I'm a close second," I said, and his pulse found a saner tempo under my fingers.

I heard Russ before I saw him, the particular clatter of a man putting things back where they should have been in the first place. He came up out of the gantry like the ladder had offended his bloodline, jaw tight, eyes the dark brown of iron in water.

"Pitch was wrong," he told the supervisor, voice flat. "Tie-off point's a rumour. We're downing tools until the platform's in and a spotter's named. Get Kemerton to sign the SWMS again, as built, not as imagined."

He clocked me then. The flicker. The held breath. A pause long enough to be a hello, short enough to be nothing anyone could screenshot.

"You right?" he asked, same question as the rain, different weather.

"I'm good," I said. Work voice. "He's cooling. Fluids now, review in twenty."

He nodded. "I'll be at the container."

I didn't say I saw the thing online. He didn't say it's rubbish. A man from Stores wandered past and stage-whispered "two-time" like he wanted to be part of something. Russ threw him a look that could sand timber. The whisperer devolved into a cable tie.

We packed the kit. Jase swore to drink more water and to stop trying to impress physics. I wrote shade + sips + sit on his forearm in Sharpie like homework.

Back at the clinic, Janelle made tea strong enough to argue. "You don't bring camp radio in here," she said mildly, watching me not look at my phone. "Let it blow past."

I put the phone face down anyway and felt thirteen. "Copy."

Late afternoon sagged into that fly-buzz quiet. I wiped benchtops that didn't need wiping. I lined the obs trolley from tallest to shortest like it mattered. When I finally checked my screen there was one message from Robyn: It's already dying. Meme about someone's wet swag has taken the lead. Breathe.

Nothing from him. Which was not a crime. Which still felt like a bruise you only notice when you roll onto it. So I did the thing that makes sense when other things don't, I sat at the tiny staffroom table with the head torch looped ready and opened the red-dirt notebook. The DonateLife draft waited where I'd left it, steady as a handrail.

I added a line under *Thank you for making a corridor with your grief so someone else could run. And when the world gets loud with the wrong story, remember yours. The one with a forehead groove your palm still knows, the one with machines you could not negotiate with, the one with a signature that turned rip-tide into river.*

Janelle leaned on the doorframe, reading without pretending not to. "Good," she said. "True."

"Rumours make me feel thirteen again," I admitted, closing the book. "I hate that."

"Then don't be thirteen," she shrugged. "Be thirty-and-brave. Work. Sleep. Tomorrow's got a long list."

***

Evening slid in, softer than it had any right to be after a day like that, edges rounded, and heat loosening its fist. The clinic eaves let down a little cool air like a welcome relief. I stepped outside and let the first stars declare themselves one by one, pricking the sky where the light still hadn't made up its mind. No ships to count out here tonight, so I counted crickets instead, seven loud, three shy, one determined soloist near the tap. Two community dogs staged an argument about nothing and resolved it with a mutual huff, the treaty signed in dust.

My phone sat a quiet weight in my pocket. No pings, no blue dots, no little hooks dressed up as news. Somehow that was the answer I needed. I typed a message and didn't send it. Boundary for now. Big week. Be well. I watched the unsent words sit there like a fence I could actually see, then slid the phone away and chose the thing that would hold, work.

Inside, the clinic had its evening face on, a small lamps, big shadows, and the hum of a fridge earning its keep. The lights pooled gold on red dirt tracked in by a hundred useful steps. Janelle moved through the space with that no-spill grace she has, humming the kind of tune that keeps walls upright and nerves steady. I washed the last cup, lined up the obs trolley so the small things would be where morning hands could find them, and breathed where my feet were.

At the tea shelf I flipped the lid and taped three little words to the inside where only I'd see them on the shift that tries it - Own it. Fix it. Breathe. I pressed the tape down like it was a promise. Then I clicked off the big lights, left the lamp by the door to make its small circle of welcome, and stepped back into the night.

Out there the air smelled like iron cooling and spinifex sighing. A breeze fussed with the shade-cloth and moved on. Above the clinic, the Milky Way had pulled its blanket tight, generous, and ordinary at the same time. I stood until my shoulders dropped, until the day let go of my jaw. Then I locked up, pocketed the keys, and let the dark be a kind thing.

***

Near miss at 09:20 on the east laydown. A dogman took a hand signal from the wrong bloke and the sheet pile swung like a drunk. The spotter caught his boot in a rat's nest of leads, and the load kissed a scaffold upright. No damage to person, just pride. Blessed be.

Russ didn't raise his voice. He never needs to.

"Full stop. Eyes up. Reset," he said, quiet, absolute, and the whole crew came in like iron filings to a magnet. He walked them through the choreography step by step, no hurry, no heat, who calls, who echoes, who points, who watches the watcher. He made the dogman run it again with his eyes closed, head-torch on, hands doing the talking until muscle memory replaced the leftover panic. When they had it, he nodded once. "Again." They did it until it was boring, which is where safety lives.

Back at the ute tray he wrote the incident report like scripture, precise, unadorned, and built for a courtroom he prays never convenes. Between paragraphs, phones came out. Thumbs scrolled. Faces changed.

The post had grown mould overnight. New comments, "Did you kiss her under the cyclone?" And, somewhere in the mess, one stubborn line: "Shut up. He's not like that."

Big Russ didn't look. Tiny did, flinched, and pocketed his phone like it had burned him. "Set radios to channel eight," he told the boys, deadpan. "If you want drama, listen to the geos argue with dirt."

Big Russ went back to verbs and timestamps. Words behaved. People didn't. He kept writing.

Smoko. His phone buzzed with an unknown number. He stepped away from the shade tent and answered because hope makes fools of careful men.

"Is this Big Russ?" a woman asked, a voice he didn't know. Jess's cousin. You should apologise. She's upset."

"I'm not discussing private stuff with a stranger," he said, even.

"She says you led her on."

"I said no," he answered, tired of whispering his own version. "More than once."

"She said-"

He ended the call and turned the phone off properly, the old-fashioned way - press, hold, dark. Then he stood at the edge of the laydown and counted to twenty like a man who knows about pulse and control. He hit seventeen.

"Head!"

The suspended load had twitched while no one was looking. It touched nothing, hurt no one, but the air changed, the way it does when you remember gravity has no favourites.

"Everyone out," Russ said, already moving. "Reset. Again."

And they did. Radios quiet, hands steady, pride checked, procedure in front. Rumour could have the internet. He'd take the work.

***

I didn't see Russ, which is almost the same as seeing him, because out here not seeing is how a small place makes seeing complicated. Every ute that rumbled past the clinic sounded like a maybe and then wasn't. I finished the list with that behind-the-eyes tired that refuses to leave, handed my careful little parcels of people to the night notes, and walked slow so my brain could chew without me.

Janelle was on the verandah with two mugs and the look of someone who's been keeping the evening steady. "You want the five-minute rundown," she asked, "or the don't-ask, eat, and talk about anything else?"

"Rundown," I said, and sat on the step so the community dog could accuse me of everything at once.

She kept it kind. "Jess been busy on that camp Facebook. Likes a yarn more than the truth. Mob here know. People who matter know." A small shrug. "Wind blows, settles."

"Does he know?" I asked, voice tight around something that kept changing shape.

"Boys always know," she said, not unkind. Then, gentler, "You want to walk the oval?"

"Later," I said, standing. "I'll check the evening."

The community had that post-heat hush where the eucalypts breathe again. No ships again, so I counted the crickets instead, the thrum of the gen shed, one kid on a scooter doing laps, two dogs arguing and then agreeing. The water tower threw a long shadow over the clinic roof. Somewhere a windmill clicked like a metronome trying to help. Smoke from someone's dinner drifted across with the soft, good smell of onions and fat, the kind of smell that says, you're safe enough to be hungry.

I took out my phone and opened a blank message. Are you okay? I didn't send it. We should talk. I didn't send that either. Then, because I've learned small is better when you're not sure, I wrote: Hope you're safe. Big day here. I'm going to focus on my speech prep for a bit. Take care.

I signed it the way he says it when he's careful with me: Indi. Send - before I could rescue myself from being human.

No dots. No reply. A galah heckled the sunset and flapped off like it had somewhere more dignified to be. I stood there until the sky changed to the colour that makes everyone quiet, then went back to the verandah where Janelle had left the good tea cooling and the chair beside her empty on purpose.

"Write?" she said, not pushing.

"Try," I said. "My brain's… windy."

"Then write three heavy things," she said. "True ones. They hold the paper down."

So I opened the red-dirt notebook and let the page be smarter than me. I wrote:

- He breathed because we said yes.

- Grief didn't shrink, love got bigger around it.

- Families wait at home; we work like that's true.

Janelle read them upside down and nodded once, the way people do when something lands right. "Good. That's enough for tonight. Tomorrow you add the soft bits."

We ate on the steps, bowls balanced on knees, watching the oval lights come on in a slow ribbon. Someone tuned a guitar three houses over, someone else told a joke you could hear the rhythm of but not the words. The clinic cat made its inspection of our ankles and decided we passed. When the mozzies started writing their own names in the air, we moved inside.

I washed two mugs and a day out of my hands and set out the morning obs kit the way future-me likes it, lined up tallest to shortest, blood-pressure cuff folded the right way, spare pen that actually writes. I checked my phone once more, quiet, which somehow was the answer I needed, and then put it face-down on the shelf.

Before lights out I stepped into the yard and let the stars take attendance. No ships to count, so I counted satellites and the small, steady beat of my own chest. The phone stayed still in my pocket. I chose my work. The clinic lights pooled gold on the red dirt, behind me, Janelle hummed the kind of tune that keeps walls upright.

"Alright," I told the night, and meant it. Then I went in, left the little lamp on, and let sleep come like a good nurse, quiet, timely, and kind.

*****

Gym at five, because when the ground shifts I keep my habits. The community rec shed woke the way country does, slow, sideways, and then all at once. Corrugated walls sighed. The rattly pedestal fan clicked through its moods. A single fluorescent bar thought about flickering, then decided against it. The radio only found one station, last night's footy calls dissolving into ads for fencing wire and the butcher's special.

Janelle lapped the basketball court outside, thongs slapping soft, coffee in one hand like it had grown there. "Fifteen minutes," she called through the open roller door. "Then stretch, then breathe. That's the medicine."

I climbed onto the nearer treadmill and let the belt take the argument out of my legs. Dust and eucalyptus sweated out of the rubber mat. Through the mesh screen I could see the town shaking awake, two camp dogs negotiating territory, a granddad on a Postie bike puttering past like a clock that runs on stories, and kids in school shirts doing that last-minute tuck that never quite takes.

Two FIFO lads had colonised the squat rack as if it had their names on it. One wore socks to his calves like ambition, the other had a mullet that believed in itself.

"You seen it?" the socks one cackled. "Jess's post? Poor girl."

"Poor Jess," mullet echoed, turning poor into a barb. "Poor anyone who believes her."

I slid my headphones on and didn't press play. Sometimes the theatre of not-listening is enough.

"Oi, nurse," socks called, because boundaries mean nothing to men who treat every shed like their lounge room. "You know the diesel boys?"

"Only the clean ones," I said, eyes forward, pace up a click.

Robbed of an audience, they deflated into the bench, all volume and no voltage. The fan threw a faint blessing across my face, the treadmill found its rhythm, my pulse remembered it had other jobs besides worry.

Janelle wandered in and leaned her elbows on the treadmill rail like it was a fence. "Count your breaths in fours," she said, not looking at the lads. "That's where the good blood lives."

"In…two…three…four," I obeyed, and the world stopped jangling quite so loud.

By the ten-minute mark, the shed had gathered its regulars. Aunty doing her gentle hip circles near the wall mirror, a teenage girl practising netball shots against the roller door, catching her own rebounds with the neatness of someone who didn't need praise to know. The boys tried a deadlift PB (personal best), the bar didn't care for their optimism and strolled back to earth. Nobody got hurt. Mercy.

I hit cool-down. The radio segued into an announcer who sounded like he'd slept under the desk. Someone requested a dedication for their "nanna doing chemo," and the whole shed softened a degree like fabric in warm water.

Outside, the sky went from tin to pearl. Galahs did their ridiculous pink parade. The dogs, argument concluded, shared a shady patch like diplomats after a treaty.

"Stretch," Janelle ordered, handing me a resistance band. "Calves, hammies, shoulders. That's three debts paid."

We stood in the doorway, pulling breath through our ribs like new laundry. "You good?" she asked without turning her head.

"I'm choosing to be," I said. "Choosing boundaries."

She nodded once. "Good choice."

"And I'm choosing to write instead of spiral."

"Best choice," she said, flicking sweat from her wrist like a little blessing. "Words tidy the paddock."

I laughed, and the laugh sounded like mine. I rolled my shoulders, felt the heat loosen its grip, and glanced at the clinic across the road with its tin roof, tidy ramp, and shade sails that looked like they believed in holding.

"Tea," Janelle decreed. "Strong. Black. Two sugars. Then wound round at nine."

"Copy," I said.

Back at the clinic, I propped the red-dirt notebook on the staffroom table, head torch coiled beside it out of habit. I wrote a line before the day could steal it. 'When the world gets loud with the wrong story, remember yours.' Outside, the rec shed door thumped shut, the dogs sighed in chorus, and morning finally made up its mind.

***

The speech draft waited where I'd left it, its first line a doorway I kept almost walking through. When love moves through a body, it keeps moving. I made tea - strong, black, two sugars - part ritual, part superstition, then set the red-dirt notebook on the table. Beside it I laid the small reliquary of this life, a photo of Lionel squint-smiling in Karratha light, and the three letters with careful, shaky signatures from people who live because he didn't.

I wrote - I used to think grief was a place you leave. It turned out to be a tide. It comes. It goes. Some days it knocks you off your feet. Some days it lifts you. On the worst night of my life - antiseptic in the air, endings in the corners - someone asked a question I never believed would be mine, 'Would you consider donation?'

I kept some things off the page. Not the monitor blue that made my eyes ache. Not the exact way the neurosurgeon's mouth shaped 'there's nothing else.' Not the moment I bent and kissed the small groove in Lionel's forehead - my hand's home for a decade - and whispered I know, I know, I know. Some parts you keep, so they don't shred.

I wrote, 'Saying yes didn't make anything easier. It made one thing possible. Love did not stop in that room, it kept moving. A lung to a thirty-year-old dad. A kidney to a forty-year-old man. A kidney to a boy still on his L-plates. I get cards, and letters on soft paper that live in a drawer, where I touch them like braille.'

I paused and let the tide rise. I did not fight it. I breathed until the swell gentled enough to pick up the pen again.

I wrote what I want the room to know, 'You don't have to be fine. You don't have to be brave. But ask each other now, while the light is good, before a stranger in a bad room asks you later. Talk now so later isn't harder.'

I read it aloud to the kettle and to the dog that isn't mine, and then struck out a paragraph that sounded like I was trying to be wise. I am not wise. I am a woman who counts ships when the world tilts.

I added, 'Months or years on, you might find yourself laughing in a pub you swore you'd skip, and the laugh may feel like betrayal for a minute. It isn't. It's human. Love is not a pie. It doesn't run out, it multiplies.'

I stopped. I set the pen down and pressed my palm into the air where Lionel's forehead would be if love worked that way. "Help me live," I said, the only prayer I seem to know.

My phone stayed face-down on the table. I didn't look at it. I let the quiet be both boundary and balm, and I let the tea go cold because the words, for once, were warm enough.

***

On site, Big Russ ran the near miss meeting twice, because repetition is how you turn chaos into muscle. He made the youngest bloke talk through the signal plan until the blotches on his neck faded. He handed the whiteboard pen to the old dogman and had him teach it back - men that age relax when you give them authority they recognise.

At lunch, Tiny balanced a sandwich the size of a newborn on his knee. "What's your plan?" he asked, tone casual enough to have been rehearsed.

"Work." Big Russ said.

"Outside of that." Tiny nudged, gentler than he looked.

Big Russ thought of the message: Hope you're safe. Big day here. I'm going to focus on my speech prep for a bit. Take care. He heard the boundary in it, and the kindness too, and decided to respect both.

"Let her breathe," he said. "Let it pass."

Tiny nodded like that was the answer he'd hoped for, and also the one he knew would cost. "You're a good man, Russell."

Big Russ grimaced, praise itches. "Don't tell anyone."

Tiny laughed the big, stupid, blessed laugh that keeps a camp alive on a day the wind's wrong.

***

Work stacked on work. The clinic did what clinics do, filled, breathed, fussed, and forgave. I did what I do, wrote names small and careful, got tea wrong then right, earned Aunty's ten minutes and lost it by being too quick with a joke, and then earned it back again by apologising for being too quick with a joke.

By late arvo the camp radio had moved on to serious business, which roadhouse does the best chips between Hedland and Newman. (Nan's at Whim Creek, obviously, don't @ me.) People stopped glancing at me like I was a headline. Daniel texted a meme of two ships passing in the night and wrote "check them" underneath. I sent a photo of five ship lights pricking the horizon, he replied with a gold star.

I went back to the house before the little gym got loud, reheated Aunty's stew again, and sat cross-legged on the lino with the red-dirt notebook open. The speech looked less like a dare, more like a thing I might be allowed to say.

I did not open Facebook. I did not Google Jess. I did not drive to camp and knock on a donga door like a woman in a song. I held my own hand, made tea, and wrote, 'If you have been loved, say so. If you can love again, say yes.'

Simple, maybe too simple - but simplicity is ballast when you feel like a paper boat.

***

At 21:12, one bar flickered to life. My phone buzzed once.

Long day. Will call when the tower behaves. Stay safe - R

I looked at it until the meaning settled. Then I put the phone face-down and slid the notebook under the bed, the way you hide the one thing no thief gets.

Lights out. The house softened by degrees. The tide came, as it does, sure-footed and uninterested in my schedule. I let it move through. I named what I could, sadness, anger, embarrassment, longing. Somewhere in there, gratitude - annoying and true. Who asks to be grateful for complication? And yet.

No ships to count this far inland, so I counted crickets. Somewhere a tug out there would be pushing just enough and then holding off, which is its own art.

"Not alone," I told the dark, making it law, and vow, and reminder. #GaylesLaw. Never alone.

***

Across town, a man who tells truth for a living took his boots off, stared at a metal shelf like it owed him rent, and chose not to call. He let the rumour wind pass, the way you let grit blow past your eyes and don't rub. He slept hard and set his alarm ten minutes earlier, which is how men like him make peace.

We were both right. It still hurt.

Morning would come. I'd go to work. I'd tape the next small future, sign the next careful form, rehearse the speech until the words knew where to sit in my mouth. I'd be the nurse I'd want at a child's bedside, even if I didn't have one. I'd be the woman Lionel loved, not by freezing, but by learning to move again without shame.

For now, I breathed. The rumour mill turned. Country settled after storms the way it does - one ear open, one eye on the horizon.

"Indi," I whispered to myself. "Hold."

Chapter Eighteen

The road out breathes me back to myself.

I leave before dawn, thermos on the passenger seat, windows cracked for warm iron and spinifex. The Troopy smells like eucalyptus wipes and old sun. First the stars thin, then the horizon unzips, by Yandeyarra the sky is a bruised peach and the highway a pencil line someone forgot to lift. I drive the way you pray when you're out of words - steady, listening. The engine hums its plain hymn. Road trains ghost past in twos and threes, lights softened by dust, each one shouldering a little more night away.

Country lifts and breaks - tablelands to ribs, ribs to gullies - the old bones showing through. Kangaroos consider the verge and think better of it. A wedge-tail writes slow cursive on the morning and rides a pocket of air I can't see. Mirage puddles wink and vanish. Cattle grids ring like coins dropped in a bowl. The white posts keep time. I sip the thermos tea that tastes exactly like 04:00 and count the small mercies that lay before me, no stray stock on the bend, no tyre whisper turning into a shout, and no rain but the good kind dried to memory on the windscreen.

By the time the sun lifts clean, everything has edges again like the spinifex lit like wire, the mulga throwing honest little shadows, and the red earth waking up to its own heat. I turn the radio low and let it be static and breath. Country does what country does when you give it room, it settles the noise in your head, one ridge at a time.

***

Karijini does the thing it always does to my chest when the ranges shoulder the horizon, like a hand, open and certain. I pull in at Dales and the day is already a degree louder with galahs heckling scribbly gums, and a family negotiating hats and sunscreen like they invented both. I lace my boots and breathe the baked-clay smell that lives nowhere else.

At the Dales Gorge car park I almost kept going until a familiar laugh bounced off the ironbark. Robyn straightened from the boot of a dusty Prado, a muesli bar in her teeth and a map in her hand, then she did a full body double take.

"You sneaky cow," she muffled around the wrapper, launching across the gravel to hug me. "I thought you were bush side!"

"Was," I said into her shoulder. "Leave pass. Didn't want to jinx it by texting."

Peter popped up from behind an esky like a jack-in-the-box. "Community royalty, in the wild! You could've warned the dress circle."

"What, and miss this face?" I teased. Sharon and Gavin rounded the bonnet with hats and an argument about which trail was "civilised." The argument died mid-step.

"You came," Sharon grinned, relief and sunshine in one syllable. "Right, chips later, water now. We're walking."

I fell in beside them and let their racket wrap around me, Robyn bossing sunscreen, Peter pretending to read the trail notes like scripture, and Sharon bullying everyone into one photo "for the descendants." No one asked why I was here unannounced; they just made space on the path the way friends do.

At the junction we split, Robyn and Peter to Fortescue, Sharon and Gavin toward Circular Pool. I promised a rendezvous at the rim for chips and bragging rights. When we hugged goodbye, Robyn cocked her head at me like she was taking a reading and said only, "Careful feet." I nodded, understood.

I watched them go until the scrub took their colours, then turned back toward the ledge and the quiet that had called me here in the first place.

The first steps into the gorge are always a surprise, even when you know them. Rock steps cut clean into time, water talking to stone in a language you don't need to speak to understand. Fortescue Falls is a staircase of green glass, every pool a different shade of permission. At Fern Pool, steam ghosts off the surface, as if the water has something to say and can't quite bring itself to say it. Two tourists whisper "sacred" like a password. I give the water the bow it deserves and keep walking.

I think I came to count something. Ships, if there were ships. Breath, maybe. The number of times I can think of him and not feel like I'm betraying the forever I promised in a room full of machines. I don't know. I only know my feet wanted red rock and a ledge.

By late morning I'm on the Weano trail, the light gone high and white, heat settling like a shawl. The walls narrow to a slot, the water is shoulder-deep and cold where the sun can't find it. There's the ladder you trust because you've chosen to, and the bit people call the "handrail" even though the rock itself keeps you honest. I move the way Tomo teaches on first days, slow, breath steady, and pride in my pocket. My bag is heavier than planned, my head is, too. Past the squeeze, the path thins to a skerrick. It always does with its boot-wide red rock with air leaning out beyond.

I see it and feel fine, then I move and don't. It's nothing at first, just a small roll of gravel beneath the boot that should've stayed put, a tilt in the ankle, that tiny traitor wobble that arrives not in your legs but in your jaw. One hand goes to the wall, palm searching for a hold that isn't there, fingertips scrabble against heat. The other hand does the useless bird-flap you do when you forget your training and remember only that you don't want to fall. The drop isn't a death, it's a curve into water, bruise, and embarrassment. My gut unbuttons anyway.

A hand closes on my forearm, warm, dry, and certain.

"Got you." A voice says. Not loud. Not dramatic. Enough.

He's braced into the wall behind me like he grew there, one boot canted, hip turned, and a wrist doing the unshowy work of keeping me where I am. My other hand finds rock that is suddenly all purchase.

"Okay," I tell my body because my body listens when told. "Okay."

We stand like that for a slow count of ten, his grip a promise, and my breath a small animal coaxed back into its crate.

"You right to move?" he asks.

"I am now."

"On three," he says. "One." The word is enough. I step the way he's angled me, back onto the trustworthy bit, boot to boot, the kind of small victory your knees celebrate in private. When I'm clear, he lets go the way careful men do, making sure I know he hasn't taken anything but the moment.

Faded cap, brim broken just enough to prove he wears it. Shirt dark with sweat between the shoulder blades. Eyes doing that check men do when they've been scared on your behalf and are pretending they weren't. His eyes are that deep river-brown, iron-rich, and steady in the half-light.

"Hi." I manage.

"Hi." he says back, equal parts relief and something he keeps folded in the pocket with his spares.

"You… what are you…" I laugh at myself. "Are you following me?"

"Not officially," he says, the kind of answer that made me look up at The Finny and think, 'oh, trouble.' He shrugs, honest-casual. "Tiny saw your car at Dales. I was at Auski. Thought I'd make sure you got down safe."

"I usually do."

"Then call it quality assurance," he says, mouth tipping the way it did when he handed me a beer after the cyclone and asked if we were pretending not to be nervous.

He steps back, enough space for what we both need it to mean. The gorge hums, flies in shade, and a wedge-tail drafting sentences on the sky. Heat presses my shoulders like a hand that could be kind or not, depending.

"I'm fine," I say, because I am, and because pride still outruns pulse. "Thank you."

He nods, like he believes both parts. "Walk out?"

"Yeah," I say. "Walk out."

We go single file through the narrow, then side-by-side where the ledge fattens enough to fit a conversation. Our boots make that hollow clack on dry rock, the sound that lives in the bit of your ear only Karijini can reach. He lets me go first over the handrail, down into cold water that erases heat the way good news erases a bad morning. When we climb out onto a ledge with room for two, he sits, forearms on knees, studying the far wall like it's got something worth hearing.

"I didn't look," he says, before I can ask. "At Facebook. Tiny told me the gist. I figured I'd rather see your face than a screen."

I watch a dragonfly pretend to be a leaf and fail delightfully at it. "It was… noise."

"It was mean," he says, and then, choosing to lay down a thing he's carried too long, "and it wasn't true."

I nod. Mean I can absorb. Untrue makes me kick. "I decided not to make your mess my job."

He doesn't flinch. "Good."

"I sent you a message."

"I got it." He rubs the back of his neck with his thumb, the way he does when picking the version of truth that will do the least damage.

I wanted to call. The tower wasn't cooperating."

"Maybe that was kind," I say. "Leaving some air."

"Maybe," he says, low. "Or maybe I was a coward for a minute."

We let the gorge talk. Downstream an English couple argues about whether the map's upside-down. A kid squeals and the sound bounces like a bird that hasn't found the door yet.

He picks a burr of red dust off his knee and flicks it toward the water. "I've been bad at this," he says finally. "Historically. Not because I wanted to be, but because I… panic. I don't want to wreck things, so I tighten everything until nothing can move. Then I call that 'safe' and wonder why I can't breathe."

I make a sound that could be sympathy or recognition. "I panic in all four directions," I admit. "Professional at running away while standing still."

He smiles without teeth. "You scare me," he says, clean as a nailed plank. "Because you matter."

The sandbags in my chest shift, small, startled. Sometimes truth isn't fireworks, sometimes it's exactly that, a simple sentence a man took a decade to learn how to say.

"Ditto," I say, not dressing it in bows. "Also, because I don't know how to do this without feeling like I'm… doing something wrong."

"Wrong to who?" he asks, careful, not fishing.

I look at the water. At the shallow that looks warm and isn't. At my own hands, nicked from tape dispensers, steady around syringes, shaky around this.

"You know who," I say, and the name sits between us like a stone and a blessing both.

He doesn't look away. "Yeah."

The donation letters live behind my ribs like small, soft lights. ICU lives there too, a geography you don't get to exit, you just agree to live around it. Lionel's forehead groove is a map my palm can still trace in the dark. It will always be there.

"I said I'd try," I tell the water. "I said it to him, not you. I said, Help me live."

"And?" Russ says.

"I still don't know if I can." Honesty is the only currency that spends in a gorge like this. "But I want to."

He nods, watching a leaf circle an eddy it can't see. His fingers drum once on his knees, the old rhythm that maddens dogmen and calms the part of him that's never trusted a quiet room.

"I can do careful," he says. "Slow. We don't make it town radio. We don't promise what we can't keep. We don't kiss where it's a dare, we kiss where it's a choice."

I look at him. The cap shadow cuts his face in half, the eye on the lit side is that deep, steady brown, river after rain, iron-rich, unreadable, and kind.

"Show me careful," I say.

He doesn't rush. Doesn't reach first. He waits until I shift, until my knee brushes his, until my hand finds the line where jaw ends and day's stubble begins. He turns into the touch like permission, not theft. Then he leans, slow as policy, and kisses me with his mouth and not his hurry.

Not fireworks. Not rain. Deliberate, built the way we build safe access platforms in breathless meeting rooms - braced where it should be, no clever for clever's sake, everything you need and nothing you don't. He tastes of sun and river and the mint someone hands you at the end of a long meeting because your mouth has said too much and not enough. When he breathes, I feel the part of him that used to wake at three learning it can stop waiting for the bad noise.

We don't make a sound. The gorge keeps talking, unfussed by our small, human choice.

When we separate, he eases back an inch like he's showing his working, See? Slow. See? No one died. We both smile, small, private, the way you smile when you've done something worth doing and no one has to clap.

"Okay," I say. Not a contract, but something.

"Okay," he says, and in that syllable his shoulders drop a fraction.

We sit in the shade until sweat dries cool in our shirts and the rock at our backs makes our own heat visible. We eat the oranges I packed, oiling our hands, pith under nails. He offers chocolate like a cartoon gentleman, I pretend to steal half, he pretends to mind, we don't pretend long.

When we start back, he does the handrail behind me again, no touch, just the promise of it, obvious as a guardrail. At the ladder he waits at the bottom and sets his palm not for holding me, but for showing where to put my boot. A man who's learned usefulness that doesn't tidy me into a box.

Out of the slot, the sun is a drum. We walk the last red-sand stretch companionably, that rare quiet you only get with someone who frightens you in the good ways. At the car park he angles his brim and looks suddenly, stupidly, like every story about men who remember to hold a gate and your gaze.

"Coffee at the roadhouse?" he asks, tone neutral, easy to refuse.

"That'd be nice," I say. "Strong, black, two sugars." The joke lands, we both feel the Aunty-blessing in it.

We sit under a shade sail the colour of an old bruise and drink something that only nods at coffee. He tells the near-miss like a confession, I read him the line from last night that's true even when it hurts, 'Love is not a pie, it multiplies.' He nods. He tells me a dogman once taught him to read men's hands before their mouths. I tell him about a junior doctor who kept his hands in his pockets because helping would've made it worse. We swap these small precisions like charms.

"Text me when you're back in range?" he says at the utes, not a demand, not quite a question.

"Yeah," I say. "You too."

We are careful with the part where we don't hug. The space is its own kind thing; we don't mess with it. He touches two fingers to the broken brim like a man in an old film practising decency because he's decided to become it again. He goes, taillights cough red dust into afternoon.

I drive to the lookout, sit on the metal rail, and do what I came for.

"Lionel," I tell the gorge, because the gorge can carry it. "I'm going to try."

The words don't echo. They soak into rock like water and go somewhere useful. I put my palm into the air where his forehead would be and it doesn't hurt in the fatal way, it hurts in the healing way, announcing itself, then asking if I mean it.

"I'll love you all my life," I say to the red. "And I will love again. I think you'd want both."

A fly tries for religion in my left nostril. I take that as a very Western Australian benediction, laugh, and wipe my eyes with my wrist. The sky is immodestly blue. A spinifex pigeon pretends not to care.

On the drive back I count things, not ships, not today. Road trains. Crows. The number of times I rehearse what I'll tell Robyn when I get home. It's not simple, but it's good. The bars arrive, two, then three, then the buzz. Home safe, I text him.

Good, he replies. Thank you for letting me be careful with you.

I sit on the staff-quarters step with boots unlaced and socks rolled, letting the day sit in my lap. The neighbour's dog noses my knee like I owe him apologies and biscuits. I give him both.

Inside, the air tastes like whatever air tasted like before. I boil the kettle and make tea the way Aunty insists - strong, black, two sugars - and stand at the sink to try the sentence on my mouth.

"You scare me," I tell the empty kitchen. "Because you matter."

It doesn't taste like fear anymore. It tastes chosen.

I open the red-dirt notebook and write the three lines I'll want at 02:00 when the tide comes to test the fences:

- Hand + rock + breath. Okay.

- We kissed like choosing.

- Lionel, I'm going to try.

The room makes the small settling sound rooms make when they approve. Outside, somewhere past hospital and port and the camp radios still arguing about chips, the ranges pink themselves toward quiet. Tomorrow the building will breathe, the alarms will howl, the footy will blare, Aunty will test my tea, and I'll be the nurse I promised my younger self I would become. Somewhere, a man who doesn't like noise will reread a two-line text and let it be enough for a day.

I turn out the light, lie on my side, and lift my palm to where a forehead would be if the world worked the way I sometimes wish it did. The tide lifts and sets me down again. Night is a place to rest, not a place to fall.

"Indi," I whisper, half prayer, half promise. "We'll try."

Chapter Nineteen

Kerry caught me between a stocktake of gauze and a kettle that sulked on the clinic bench.

"Quick check-in," she said - quiet-excited down the line. "A Star to Remember is all locked in for next week in Perth. You're on the program."

"I'm in," I said, because I'd already said yes in my bones weeks ago.

"Good." A tiny exhale. "Travels sorted through staff flights, out Friday arvo, back Sunday evening. Janelle's happy to cover clinic while you're gone."

"Of course she is," I said, already picturing her hand on the doorframe like a guard dog. "I'll leave her a notes avalanche and a tidy meds fridge."

"Do you need anything from us?" Kerry asked, slipping into the voice that has seen people through worse than microphones. "Letters of support, extra data for your slides, a contact at DonateLife, accommodation tweaks?"

"Notes, not slides," I said. "And I've got my DonateLife person. Maybe-" I glanced at the bench, at my red-dirt notebook, "maybe a spare pen that actually works."

"I'll pop two in your pigeonhole at the hospital here for you to pick up before you head to the airport," she said. "And a packet of those ginger bikkies you pretend you don't like. Indi… take the time you need. We're proud of you."

The words landed like clean linen. "Thanks, Kez."

"Break a leg," she added, then gentler, "and if you need to call from a foyer somewhere just to breathe, do it. I'll answer."

I put the kettle back on and laid out my small pilgrimage; red-dirt notebook, the folded program from the last 'A Star to Remember' ceremony, the three soft-paper letters I carry when I'm brave. I added two teabags in a snap-lock labelled 'strong/black/two sugars,' and the pink lipstick. The draft waited where I'd left it, tight in places, loose in others. In the margin I wrote one new line. Speak plain. Say his name. Breathe.

Janelle stuck her head in, clocked the open notebook, and the travel email on the ancient monitor that wheezes in hot weather, and nodded like a woman who knows a thing or two when she sees it. "I'll cover Friday through Monday" she said. "You go do the talking that matters. Bring back stories… and minties." She winked, then added, softer, "We'll be right."

"Thanks," I said, feeling steadier just because she'd said it out loud.

Country breathed that slow-in, slow-out permission it gives when it's letting you go and expects you to come back. I set the cups to dry, flipped the clinic sign to CLOSED, and stood a moment on the verandah to memorise the light. Then I went inside to pack the kind of bag that holds both scrubs and a dress, both work and love, and a notebook that knows the way home.

The little clinic hummed like a tired auntie, the flyscreen kept singing its thin song. I leaned my forehead to the cool cupboard and let my breath catch up to my mouth. Outside, the afternoon was a sheet of white. No ships to count here, so I counted the small constants, the windmill turning its slow yes, the low line of hills proving the earth still curves, and the red dirt holding its nerve. Walk long enough in one direction out here and you don't find a port, you find a tree you know, a family to wave to, a place that lets you sit. Close enough to home for now.

I checked flights on the old computer that forgets its manners in hot weather, texted Robyn a one-liner: Perth next week, star night is on, then packed a zip-lock with the talismans that make me less likely to bolt at the last minute, the pink lipstick, a spare pen that actually works, two teabags in a snap-lock labelled strong/black/two sugars. The clinic clock ticked its practical beat. Country breathed in that slow way it does when it's about to let you go and expects you to come back.

***

Packing for grief looks a lot like packing for health checks; sturdy shoes, a dress that won't fight a microphone lead, spare tights, the pink lipstick that makes me feel marginally braver than I am. I added the red-dirt notebook and the folded program from the last 'A Star to Remember' ceremony I'd attended, where I'd sat in the third row and cried into a tissue that disintegrated like bad news.

Janelle tapped the doorjamb with two knuckles, the knock that says both I'm here and I'm busy. "Kerry told me. Good girl," she said, and passed me a ziplock with tea bags and a note in her tidy capitals: strong/black/2 sugars. "Speak plain. No hurry. Say his name right."

I swallowed. "I will."

Damo honked the Troopy like a wedding car and hauled my bag into the back. "Airport," he declared, as if we were an operation with codes. The road to Hedland shone where the last rain had licked it flat. We didn't talk much. Country did the talking, the spinifex with its helmet on, and the sky pretending it didn't know heat.

At staff travel, Kerry met us in a brisk breeze of lists and kindness. "We've shifted your roster," she said. "Janelle's got clinic, Daniel's on call, Robyn will meet you when you land. Go be excellent and ordinary, in that order."

I nodded because speechless is sometimes the right size.

***

The flight lifted us over stitched salt lakes, over a train so long it looked like a thought you can't finish, over the ghost of a long drive I've done more times than I dare to admit. Somewhere between the drinks trolley and a pocket of turbulence I wrote on a sick-bag with a biro that worked only when it wanted to, 'Grief isn't something you get through. It's something you learn to carry well.' I kept going, on the back of a printout, my hand, the boarding pass.

Little planes on the seatback screen crept along their line like proof.

***

Perth rose up in slick roofs and river blue. The jetway air had the clean-filter smell of someone else's ocean. I put my feet on city and felt the double thud of you left here to survive, and you came back because you can.

Mollie's text pinged as the doors slid. We're parked illegally. Run.

I ran. We screamed. The three-way embrace of people who have hauled each other through exams, and breakups, and house moves, and funerals. A security guard waved us on like we were his nightly entertainment, and we were.

"Home," Luna sighed, meaning the rental that isn't the old share house but still smells like our twenties, and eucalyptus, and stubborn hope. The couch is the same. So is the charred pancake pan nobody will throw away.

My bag thumped the hallway. Aliviya appeared with a tray like a magician, curry, rice, naan, and a glass of wine I nodded at and ignored.

"Speech first," she decreed. "Wine tomorrow."

"I haven't... finished finishing," I confessed.

"Lucky we have a stadium of opinions," Mollie said, lining up shoes with architect fury.

They turned the lounge into a rehearsal corridor and added a lamp for good skin tone, tissues, and water. Luna pressed a smooth stone into my palm, weight for my body when my mind tries to float.

"Breathe into your back ribs," she said. "You forget you've got more lungs than front."

We tried a run-through. My voice climbed onto a shelf and refused to come down. Too fast. Too rehearsed. Too sorry. I stumbled over Lionel's name.

"Again," Mollie said, not unkind. "Like it's our kitchen, first time you've told it."

So I did. I talked about the call and the drive and how a room can be full of machines and still feel empty. The neurosurgeon's quiet voice. Decisions that aren't decisions because you made them years earlier washing dishes, 'If it's ever me.' Lungs and kidneys and letters later from three people whose handwriting I could pick in a police line-up now. Practicalities, the coordinator saying our names right, how I signed forms with a hand that wasn't entirely mine, how I kissed Lionel's temple and tasted saline and shampoo and the end of before.

By the time I'd stopped, we were all crying.

"Okay," said Aliviya, wiping the tears from her eyes. "That's the middle. We need a beginning and an end."

"The beginning is you," Luna said. "The moment you realised the way you'd honour him is the way you're built, by nursing, by speaking plain."

"The end is an ask," Mollie added. "What do you want from them - register, talk, write?"

"Say thank you out loud," I said. "To whoever needs to hear it."

***

We went to bed late, high on purposeful sadness. In the spare room that smells faintly of everyone who ever borrowed it, I wrote lines until my hand cramped and deleted most of them. I practised in a whisper and watched phrases either land or float through the vent. At 02:00 I introduced myself to imposter syndrome by name, she stayed. At 03:00 I texted Sue from DonateLife: Landed. Writing. Might speak from notes - okay?

She sent back a heart and: Your story is the speech. Notes welcome. Mic check 14:00 at State Theatre. You'll be beautiful.

I set the alarm for seven and woke at 6:58 to pretend I'm in charge.

The State Theatre in daylight smells like yesterday's applause. Sue met me at the stage door with a lanyard, a hug, and water. The AV guy adjusted a pack, so it didn't click against my bra with the sly competence of someone who's saved a hundred speeches from sabotage. We walked green room to lectern like it was an evacuation plan.

"You can read. You can look up. You can cry," Sue said. "There's tissues under the lectern. Several, frankly. A whole box."

"I'm not worried about that," I lied.

"We're not worried about you," she said, and for a second, I believed her.

Other speakers came and went; a daughter, a brother, a recipient who still gets breathless on the word running. We nodded in the corridor like weather people who recognise each other's storms. The green room sandwiches were gone in minutes. The cut fruit earned its keep.

Perth outside did its tidy life; teens with gelato plans, a man in the world's most determined suit, a mother hauling a pram up the steps with a face that said she'd do it again tomorrow. I walked the corner and back twice to get the charge out of my legs.

Back at the house, four women yelled tenderly across a narrow bathroom. Bathroom mascara, rejected, re-borrowed. Hair pinned into a bun with exactly the right amount of deliberate mess. The bow, yes. The dress I'd kept for this and only this, deep green,

Karijini at late light. Flats, because grief is already a balancing act, and I refuse to do it in stilettos.

"You look like yourself," Luna said, exactly right.

"Diaphragm," said Aliviya. "If you faint, faint forward. Row two lady will catch you."

"Do not faint," said Mollie. "But if you do, don't take out the AV with your elbow."

My phone buzzed. A number no longer anonymous: Pilbara sky, bruise-in-reverse, horizon a ruler-straight breath line. Save me a star -R

All the noise fell away. The picture was exactly where I'd left the feeling he'd given back - home. I typed, deleted, sent the only thing that wasn't a speech: Always.

I pocketed the stone, put the phone face down, and let the city carry me to the theatre.

***

People came the way they do for brave things, carefully dressed, and carefully held together. DonateLife purple moved like kindness in motion, ushering, steadying, and handing out water before anyone could ask. Names were read, faces shone, a star for each, constellations arranged by time, not by astronomy. The emcee made space around the hard parts so we could step into it.

I was fourth.

My legs took the side stairs. My fingers found a tissue and left it. The lights warmed my face until I couldn't tell if the heat was grief, or nerves, or simply living.

Front row, Mollie's chin set to take on traffic for me, Luna's eyes like breath, and Aliviya already crying to get it out of the way. I let the room arrive. Then I began.

"Hi," I said. "I'm Indianna - Indi. I'm a nurse. I'm here as a donor family member. My husband, Lionel, died five years ago. He was twenty-seven." There. His name, said where he'd hear it.

"We used to talk about big things in small ways," I said. "Driving at night. Washing dishes. 'If it's ever me,' he'd say. 'If it's ever me,' I'd say. Then we'd argue about who makes better tea. We weren't making decisions. We were just being us."

I talked about the morning that split my life into before and after, the phone heavier and lighter than it has any right to be, the corridor that turns into kilometres. A room that hums like a fridge at 3 a.m. The kindness of people whose job is showing up without flinching. The coordinator who said both our names right, every time, and how that anchored me to something human when everything else was beeps.

"People say grief is like a tide," I said. "I live where tides are honest. They come in with a job, take what they can reach, and then go back out without asking. I tried to fight it. DonateLife gave mine channels. Papers I never wanted to sign took some of that water and sent it somewhere useful."

I told them about the lung that went to a young dad, the kidneys to a forty-something bloke and a fifteen-year-old boy who had to learn to be a patient before he learned to drive. I said I keep their letters with my softest paper, birthday cards from Mum, a kid's drawing, the brochure from the first 'A Star to Remember' ceremony I was brave enough to attend. Some days they're prayer beads. Some days I pretend I can't find them. Both are true.

"I'm a nurse," I said, three colleagues in my head rolled their eyes, sermon incoming. "I don't like telling people what to do. I like questions that let you find your own answers. So, I'm not going to tell you to register, or to talk to your family, or to write a letter, though the woman in purple has a pen that makes bureaucracy feel like a hug."

A ripple of laughter. Room exhaled.

"What I will ask," I said, "is that you love your people out loud. If your person is next to you, squeeze their hand now. If they're somewhere else, text them later, something real, not just a meme. If your person isn't in this world, say their name when you get home. The room you say it in will be better for it."

I talked longer than I feared I would and shorter than I thought I could. When the last sentence landed, I let it stay. Then I said thank you and meant it like an action.

After, in the gentle crush where faces find faces, an older woman took my hands and didn't say anything, that's a language too. A young man with a scar under his collarbone said, "I run now," then cried with surprise at his own relief. A teenager asked how to start a first letter to a donor family. "Anything true," I said, and gave her three specifics because I cannot be vague when there's a pen.

Sue hugged me the way a back stops feeling hollow. "You did beautifully," she translated, you didn't bolt, you didn't faint, you made space. I said thank you and surrendered to my friends, who fed me oranges like I'd done sport.

We stepped into a night that glowed from within, the river ribboning the dark. People flowed around us, a ferry cleaved past on its way to somewhere important. My phone remembered me.

How's the sky look from there? -R

I sent a photo of the nearest star (possibly a helicopter), the theatre lights, and the outline of three women pretending not to hover.

We found it together, I typed. One for you, one for me, and one for him.

Three dots. Then: That's plenty.

"Gelato," said Mollie, practical even while tender. "Cry in the car if you need. I'll drive like a nun."

I cried like someone whose body finally found a use for salt. They let me. They fed me by spoon, mocked my lipstick survival rate, cheered when I stopped apologising for needing anything at all.

Back at the house it smelled like eucalyptus, our twenties, and the curry we always swear we won't eat at midnight and always do. I scrubbed my face and put on the Homer Simpson pyjama pants that refuse to die. In the quiet, with soft clatter in the kitchen, I opened the red-dirt notebook and wrote three lines I'll want later:

- Said his name into a room and the room held.

- The tide did its job, I did mine.

- Saved a star, was saved by one.

I slid the teenage boy's thank-you letter behind the page and closed the cover.

Before bed I texted Big Russ a photo of the bow slouched over a chair and the program corner smudged with pink where I'd kissed Lionel's name without thinking.

Tough crowd, I wrote. But I think he liked it.

His answer arrived before I put the phone down: He would've loved it. And you.

The room tilted, not like falling, but like a boat finding the deep line it's meant to follow.

"Night," Luna said from the doorway, question and benediction.

"Night," I said, and switched off the lamp. Dark wrapped without swallowing me like a good blanket, like a good speech that remembers it isn't about perfect sentences. It's about telling the truth and trusting your listeners to carry some.

I slept like someone who didn't have to hold the room up anymore. In the morning I'd fly back north, back to red dirt and practicalities, back to the clinic where tea is strong/black/two sugars and you count crickets and windmills, not ships, to remember your edges. Back to work that was never just work. Back to a man who texts skies like prayers.

For tonight I let myself be only this, a woman in a city that still fits, wearing a bow because she wanted to, with a mouth that tastes of citrus and salt and the last of a speech that finally found her.

Chapter Twenty

The city woke me the way the Pilbara never does, with bins clattering, a bus sighing, and a magpie somewhere doing scales like an overachiever. I lay there long enough to watch the light pull itself along the wall, listening to the old house remember how to be a house, with its plumbing muttering, and its floorboards stretching like the kind of domestic argument that sounds like love in the next room, as Mollie and Aliviya negotiated who had stolen whose Tupperware.

My phone glowed on the chair beside where I'd thrown last night's bow.

R: Can't get leave. Site's down a man and the roster's set. I'll be under the same sky though. Save me one anyway.

For a second the disappointment bit, quick and clean. I let it. Then I texted back the Pilbara answer to everything: Copy. Head up, boots on. Star saved.

He sent a photo of the morning out there, sky wide as ever, camp lights winking like someone had sprinkled sugar, and a red line of dawn sharpening the world. I tucked the phone away like a small heat source and got up.

"Tea?" Luna called from the kitchen, voice soft and stretchy with first words.

"Strong. Black. Two sugars," I said, and heard her smile from three rooms away.

We did the kitchen dance we've been doing since we were nineteen, mugs trading hands, toast dodging elbows, and someone making a list nobody will read. Mollie planted me on a stool and peered at my face like it was a blueprint.

"Raccoon," she diagnosed, and dabbed at the mascara I'd missed with the gentleness of a good architect touching a heritage window. "You're on at eleven?"

"Prep at nine, ceremony at eleven," I said. "They want help with the order. It's mostly families and recipients. Speeches are short, the room is not."

"You'll be good," she said. "You're always good with rooms."

"I'm good at tea," I corrected, and stole a piece of banana bread off her plate because that's what sisters do, even when they're not.

***

DonateLife WA borrowed the Government House ballroom for the morning, all echo and velvet and people trying to make their grief behave. Purple lanyards moved like purpose. Sue caught me by the artist's door again, same hug, different day, and shoved a run sheet into my hands.

"You're wrangling the front row," she said. "Families and recipients turn feral when they're told to sit anywhere else."

"I can herd cats," I assured her. "I work in a hospital."

The run sheet was a choreography of careful. Welcome. Acknowledgement of Country. A choir made entirely of nurses because of course it was. A donor mother reading a letter she'd written three years ago and no longer needed to look at to know by heart. A transplant surgeon who could talk about anastomosis and also, somehow, make it sound like poetry. Time to light candles. Time to let the room breathe.

The purple crowd had turned one corner of the ballroom into a small soft factory; stars cut from thick card, pens in cups, tissues in boxes, bowls of mints because grief dries everything out. On a long table a quilt lay folded like a sleeping animal, each square sewn by someone whose house had been too quiet one winter and who had decided to put their hands to work.

"Indi," Sue said, tugging my elbow. "There's a teenager you'll want to meet. She and her mum are backstage, saw your name on the program last night and asked for you this morning."

Backstage smelled like lilies and furniture polish and the sugar of the muffins nobody wanted yet. A girl stood by the door with her mother's hand threaded through the pocket of her jacket like a second heartbeat. Fourteen, maybe fifteen. Hair braided like someone had done it with love and practice. Hospital pallor only in the way her cheeks went flush, quick and proud, when she saw me.

"Hi," I said, and put my hand out so I wouldn't crush them both. "I'm Indi."

"I know," she said, and then blurted the sentence we both needed her to say before the moment made her too shy. "I got lungs. Last year. From someone like Lionel."

The room tilted the way it does when a boat finds its groove. My hands did their shake, a small internal seismograph reporting honestly, and then they steadied, because I had Luna's stone in my pocket and a job to do.

"What's your name?" I asked.

"Neve," she said. "Like 'never,' but without the r."

"Neve," I said, and tasted it like a blessing. "How are you?"

Her mother's mouth twitched, the laugh of a person who has forgotten how to answer that question honestly in polite company.

"I can run," Neve said, and the words came out like she'd been stretching them secretly in the backyard for months. "Not fast. But I can do two laps of the oval and not… you know."

"I know," I said, because I did. "Two laps is a kingdom. Two laps is everything."

She glanced at my hands like she could see every time they'd held a person who was both here and not. "Can I…?" She fumbled for something in her pocket and produced a business card-sized rectangle of laminated paper with a star drawn in the corner. "We made these for today. My mum said we should write 'thank you' a lot of times and then I thought maybe that's too many 'thank yous' for one card.

I took it like it was glass. On the card she'd written: Thank you for people like Lionel. Thank you for breath. Thank you for hills that are only hills now. Underneath, a wobbly heart, and then her name.

"Neve," I said, and felt my throat do that thing where it narrows then goes wide all at once. "I'll put this with my softest paper. Would it be okay if I told Lionel's mum about you? She likes hearing about hills."

She nodded. Her mother made a noise like relief escaping a teapot.

"We'll put you in the second row," I said, practical like a nurse because that's what steadies people. "So you don't have to crane your neck. And if you need to step out, the balcony doors stick, so you have to push them like they owe you money."

She laughed, and it sounded like breathing.

The ballroom filled the way you fill a fragile thing, one careful hand after another. People arrived carrying themselves in the particular way you do when you are both tender and tired, shoulders square like armour, eyes already swimming. The transplant recipients were easier to spot; they had a bounce impossible to contain. The donors' families were shoulders and hands and the kind of posture only grief can teach.

Somewhere near the middle a man clutched a baseball cap like a passport, a woman smoothed the knees of a dress with a pattern of native flowers until the fabric couldn't take any more smoothing.

"Seats at the front," I murmured, ushering the people who held his photo and the people who wore her perfume. "You're in good company."

A man in purple pressed a program into my hand with a sticky note: Indianna, would you read the donor roll with George?

"Sure," I said, and my stomach did a small, unhelpful loop. Reading names is a kind of sacrament, you have to get each syllable right like it's a GPS coordinate.

Sue did the welcome. The Acknowledgement rolled through the room like it had been waiting there all morning. The choir consisted of nurses in their off-duty dresses, doctors who'd been talked into it, and an allied health student with bangs you could hide a pencil in. They all sang something about stars that wasn't corny because they sang it like a prayer they'd practised in a storage cupboard between shifts.

George took the lectern, a recipient father with a voice made for radio and a face made for someone who has seen his child go blue and then pink again. I stood next to him, and we traded the names like passing a small sleeping child between us, carefully, steadily, and without fuss. We said them and the room breathed and the candles flared. The house lights blurred the front row and then cleared. When I got to a name I'd practised in my kitchen because the vowels had argued with my mouth, I slowed down and met the middle-aged woman in the third row halfway. She mouthed the name with me and nodded like we'd done something together, which we had.

On the balcony, someone was brave or foolish enough to be wrestling a pram. Down the left aisle, two teenagers were trying to stand still in suits that hadn't belonged to them yesterday. On the right, a nurse from Hedland hospital had turned up on her day off and was crying behind a pillar like she needed to not be seen doing it. Aunty would have told her to stop hiding. The thought made me stand taller.

After the names the quilt got unfurled, the whole room leaning forward as the stories spread out. Here a square with a guitar stitched into it, for a boy whose music had to come out somehow. Here a square with a messy aerial view of a country football ground, the grass too green in thread because thread can't do Pilbara dust. Here a square with a pair of work boots, the stitching deliberately loose because the person who sewed it had never threaded a needle before and loved someone who had put those boots on every single morning without complaint.

Between items we turned the lights up a notch, turned the noise down a notch, fetched water like we were ferrying something holy. I moved between rows with tissues the way I've moved between beds with meds, a habitual dignity. On the end seat of row four a boy with a transplant scar that glowed faintly under a too-starched collar nodded at me and I nodded back, and in that nod lived a whole thesis I didn't have to write.

At the interval I followed the tide to the foyer and poured tea like a person who has done it professionally. Strong/black/two sugars first, because Aunty's voice in my head would tolerate nothing else. People queued and told small versions of big stories to whoever was unlucky enough to be holding the milk at the time. A man in hi-vis, someone's uncle who hadn't taken it off since the funeral, told me about his nephew's kidneys and the woman who had written to say her ankles didn't look like footballs anymore. An aunty in a dress that had seen better days and didn't care told me the young one who'd gone had been "a little bugger with the biggest smile" and that he would have wanted his eyes to keep seeing country. I pressed her palm to where the tea was hottest and nodded like a daughter.

Phone buzz. I glanced. Russ again.

R: Signal's rubbish. Power's out in one block. Looks like a storm that didn't get the memo it's meant to be somewhere else. You'll smash it anyway.

My thumbs hovered, decided on simple.

Me: We're okay. I'm reading names. Thinking of the ships.

He sent a single anchor emoji and a star, which was ridiculous and correct.

"Eat this," Sue ordered, appearing at my elbow with something savoury in pastry. "You're white around the edges."

"I'm always white around the edges," I said. "I was born that way."

She snorted. "Then eat two."

***

Backstage again, quieter now, the way rooms go quiet after a good cry. Neve and her mum had claimed a patch of carpet near the wings. The card she'd given me sat in my pocket like a second pulse. I crouched so I wouldn't press large adult energy down on them.

"How's the room?" I asked.

"Big," she said, and for the first time the teenage eye-roll appeared, which felt like health. "But they're nice. That man with the voice made my mum cry."

"George," I said. "He does that. It's his side hustle."

Neve pulled at a loose thread on her sleeve. "Can I… is it okay if I ask you something?"

"Anything true," I said, and meant it.

"Does it ever… stop? Missing?" She said the word like it had sharp corners.

"No," I said, because lying to children is a religion I don't practise. "But it changes shape. It learns some manners. It stops barging into rooms with muddy boots and starts knocking. And some days it sits politely on the arm of your chair and watches you breathe."

She nodded like she'd already suspected that was the answer and just needed an adult to confirm. "I thought… last week, when I ran the second lap… I thought, 'I don't feel bad.' And then I felt bad for not feeling bad."

"Ah," I said. "The classic double-bad. Here's a thing I say on the ward, two things can be true at once. You can be happy and you can be sad, and you can honour both without having to pick. You had a good lap. Have a good lap. Lionel would tell you to stop arguing with your lungs and let them do their job."

She smiled. Her mother's hand tightened in the jacket pocket then loosened, the fist inside unclenching by millimetres.

"Do you want to see the balcony?" I asked. "It's where the speeches go to stretch their legs."

We slipped out through the door that sticks and stood in the small square of air that smelled less like lilies and more like river. Perth did its daytime gleam. Across the gardens people took wedding photos like the city had been invented for them, which, in a way, it had. We leaned on the balustrade and let the room inside keep breathing without us for sixty seconds. Over my shoulder, my friends hovered at the edge of the corridor like a well-intentioned Greek chorus, then wisely retreated.

"I have to go back in," I told Neve, "And find a way to not cry when the choir reappears with that song about hands."

"You will," she said, the kind of certainty I didn't want to argue with. "You're the nurse with the pink lipstick."

I laughed. "Don't tell the doctors. They'll put it in my performance review."

"Come," Sue mouthed from the wings, and pulled me back into the hum.

***

The second half is always where the room does its work, stories have softened the edges, songs have put breath into tight places, and people are brave enough to look up. A surgeon spoke, careful, and technical, and kind. A father stood with his daughter and didn't look at the photo of the son who should have been standing with them, he looked at the room instead, and the room held him as best it could. A recipient described the smell of rain after steroids have stopped ruining your nose, and half the nurses present took notes in their heads because we are nerds and that's how we show love.

When it was my turn again, I didn't talk long. I thanked the families with the kind of thanks that isn't about grammar. I told a small true story about a boy whose letter had said "I can hear the wind now" and how I use that sentence like a handhold on bad days. Then I did what I'd promised myself yesterday to do. I asked for nothing except this, "Say their names out loud when you get home." The room nodded like a field in wind.

After, the foyer became a soft storm of conversations that will keep three people sleeping and keep three others awake. I shook hands until my shoulder threatened to go on strike, held a woman who would never hug me again for as long as she needed, and watched Neve and her mum get cornered by a transplant coordinator who will be a friend by lunchtime.

At some point the room thinned. People left slowly, as if speed would be rude. Cleaners hovered at a respectful distance, proposing the future with their mops. Sue squeezed my elbow, an alert. "You've got someone," she said, and tipped her chin toward the doors.

For a breath I thought she meant one of the donor mothers coming back for a second hug. Then the air shifted in a way my chest recognised before my eyes caught up.

He stood on the steps outside like he'd grown there, wide shoulders folded into a shirt he'd tried to make look like it belonged in a city, boots he hadn't bothered to pretend about. The day wrapped around him like he'd told it to behave. He'd shaved, badly. He was exactly where he shouldn't have been and exactly where I wanted him.

"I thought you couldn't get leave," I said, voice somewhere between accusation and prayer.

"Boss owed me," he said, as if that explained changing a roster the size of a small army and getting on a plane like it was just another bus. "Mate covered a swing. I'll cop night shift next week. Worth it."

He didn't step into me or say anything grand. He just took his cap off like the stairs were a church, and let the city, and the day, and the job I'd just done keep their dignity.

"How was it?" he asked.

"Big," I said. "True." And because he would ask for the weather report he cared about, "I didn't faint."

He smiled with half his face. "Knew you wouldn't."

We stood there with the river doing its ribbon thing and the traffic trying to pretend it had places to be more important than this.

Behind us, the choir spilled out in clumps and did the performance debrief common to all choirs since the invention of harmony, the altos explained that the tenors had gone rogue, the sopranos explained that the altos were wrong, the basses found sandwiches. No one looked at us like we were a scene in a movie. We were just two people standing outside a building that had asked a lot of everyone inside it.

"Walk?" he said.

We walked, down the bias-cut path, across the lawn, past a kid in a miniature suit chasing a pigeon and losing. Big Russ kept his hands in his pockets like a man who knows exactly what to do with them and is choosing nothing. I talked about Neve, he listened like a person who knows the difference between fixing and hearing.

"She thanked Lionel," I said. "Not me. Him."

"That's right," he said. "But you carried it in."

We sat on a low wall where we could watch the water forget and remember itself. He looked at my shoes like he was making sure they were the kind you could run in if you needed to, which was ridiculous and sweet.

"I can't stay," he said, apology implied, truth told. "Red-eye back. On the floor at six."

"I know," I said, and meant it. "Thanks for coming anyway."

He shrugged a shoulder. "Couldn't let you do the after on your own."

I let that lodge somewhere useful. He didn't try to make the day about us. He made it about showing up and then leaving clean. The gift of men who understand context is underrated.

We walked back when the shadows started to make the path ask questions of your ankles. At the top of the steps he paused, as if waiting for a signal that I couldn't see but felt.

I took the stone from my pocket and put it in his hand. "For your truck," I said. "So you don't forget to breathe into your back ribs when the world goes feral."

He huffed a quiet laugh. "I'll put it next to the spanner that only fits that one bolt we never see until Friday."

"Good," I said.

He looked at the theatre doors and then at me. "Save me a star?" he asked, less a question this time, more an offering of a line we could both hold.

I nodded. "Always."

He tapped the brim of his cap like we were in a different century, then turned and did the practical thing - left. I watched him fold back into a city he didn't practice in and be fine at it anyway.

Inside, volunteers dismantled a day with the efficiency only people who've held the weight of other people's feelings can muster.

The quilt got folded, the stars gathered, the water bottles rounded up and counted. I hugged Sue and promised to email a sentence for the media release and made good on my promise to the nurse behind the pillar by catching her eye and making the universal face for you cried, me too, and we're both still professionals.

***

At home the house put itself to use again as a nest. Luna handed me tea. Aliviya cut up fruit with the seriousness of a surgeon. Mollie debriefed more gently than her default setting and only bullied me out of one adverb.

"Three lines," Luna reminded me when the kitchen noise went soft.

I took the red-dirt notebook into the yard where the city tries to keep a bit of sky. The ground smelled faintly of basil and last summer. I wrote:

- Neve runs two laps. Hills are only hills now.
- Said Lionel's name in a room full of names, the room held.
- Thought he couldn't come. He came anyway. Left clean.

I tucked Neve's card behind the page with the teenage boy's letter and the program with my lipstick on it. I pressed my palm to the air where Lionel's forehead groove would be and resisted the brief urge to apologise for being alive.

"Help me live," I told the sky, same as I always do when the day has been bigger than my bones. Somewhere a magpie answered back like it thought I was asking for scales again.

Inside, my phone buzzed once more before I turned it face down.

R: You did good. Tell Neve I said two laps is elite. See you on the other side of sunrise.

Me: Copy. Always.

I put the phone under the notebook where it could keep watch. The city made its city noises and the house settled and the dark did the thing it's best at, wrapped me up without swallowing me.

In two days I'd fly back north to the horizon that tells the truth, to ships and smoke breaks I don't take, to wards that hum like fridges and people who need their tea just so. In two days the red dirt would climb into my socks, and the road would remember my car. In two days I'd go back to the place where grief has edges you can walk and work that is never just work.

Tonight, I let myself be the sum of the rooms I'd stood in and the names I'd said and the people who had handed me their thanks like something they'd been carrying too far. I let Big Russ's image of dawn sit behind my eyelids like a light I could borrow. I let myself sleep without rehearsing what I should have said.

The tide, busy and honest, kept its own time. The stars, saved and unsaved alike, did what stars do. They stayed.

Chapter Twenty-One

Dusk took its time the way Perth does in late spring, light going lavender, the river turning itself into ribbon. On the lawn, the Astronomy Society were already in their elegant ballet of tripods unfolded, telescopes aimed, and red cellophane taped over torches so no one's night vision got sent to kingdom come. A DonateLife volunteer in purple with a cardigan cross-stitched in constellations pressed a run sheet into my palm like a secret.

"You're on third, Indi," she smiled. "After the Acknowledgement and before the choir."

"Copy," I said, because some words are the only ones that behave under pressure.

They'd strung warm bulbs between jacarandas, our makeshift galaxy. The stage was a simple riser with a lectern and a microphone that would squeal once and then, if the gods were kind, remember its manners. Back tables wore dark cloths of paper stars, gold and purple pens, tissues stationed like little white sentries, and water bottles with their labels peeled so they wouldn't flash in photos. On a smaller table, the *A Star to Remember* plaque waited under a cloth, weighty, humble. No one here believes in naming rights for the sky. This was just a human way to point up and say, that one, for now, will hold some love while I catch my breath.

Sue appeared at my elbow, hug first, clipboard second. "Good crowd," she said, eyebrows waggling. "Lots of country families. One mob drove four hours with Eskies. Say they don't trust our city pies."

"They're right not to." My stomach did a quick, unhelpful backflip.

Behind the stage there was a crescent of dark where people take their courage off and put it back on. My notes lived on a card I'd cut down from an A4 because I refuse to be a person with A4 at a lectern. The card had gone soft-edged from pockets. At the top I had jotted three block-lettered instructions, steady. simple. true.

Families arrived the way grief always arrives, braced and late and somehow early. A teenage boy in a suit that remembered its hanger stood too straight, a grandmother in a floral dress sat like she was ready for Mass in a windstorm. A man in hi-vis took his cap off when he stepped onto the grass, habit with its own gravity. Kids chased each other until they didn't, tugged back by the undertow of an emotion their bodies were still learning to name. Two nurses I knew stood under a fig and tried to hide, then stopped hiding and lit candles the way we practise in treatment rooms.

The telescopes waited like a small army ready to be kind. One aimed at the Tarantula Nebula. Another lined up on the Pleiades.

"Seven Sisters," a volunteer winked. "Greek count. We've got our own as well."

I tucked the line away. The present, if you let it, gifts you sentences like spare batteries.

In one of my pockets was another of Luna's small stones, thumb-worn from two days of asking it for steadiness. In the other I had tucked a photocopy of Lionel's driver's license card, corner softened by my thumb. In my head, the line that's truer than any neat ending. Grief doesn't shrink; love grows bigger around it.

Uncle Eddie's Acknowledgement moved like a story told for grandchildren, "dark sky is Country too," he reminded us.

The choir consisting of half nurses, two orderlies, a transplant coordinator, and Sue on the end with eyebrows doing their own conducting, all sang without making a meal of it. Thank Christ. I set my hand on the back of the lectern and breathed into my back ribs the way we tell each other to after hard shifts. Aunty's tea-order mantra steadied me, strong/black/two sugars.

"Next," Sue mouthed, tilting her head, the universal sign for your turn now, you've got this whether you think so or not.

The microphone squealed once, considered its life choices, then behaved. The lawn hushed in that particular way groups hush when they choose to. The river did its ribboning. The sky leaned toward velvet. I put my fingertips on the wood to connect to something that wasn't an idea.

"Good evening," I said, and my voice came back lower than I expected, steadier than I felt. "I'm Indianna. Indi will do. I'm a nurse up north, and a woman who loved a man named Lionel."

Something like kindness flocked then. The way you watch someone at the lip of a pool when you can't swim, ready to help if they slip, and ready to clap when they don't.

"I promised Lionel I'd live a big life," I said. "I didn't promise I'd do it neatly."

A rustle of recognition moved through paper leaves.

"I want to say three things," I told them, lifting my small card like it could be read from twenty rows. "Then we'll look up together."

First thing, "If you're here because you signed a form you never wanted to sign, I want to say the smallest, truest words we have, and that is thank you. They aren't big enough, nothing is, and nothing ever will be, but language is what we've got between casseroles and long nights, so we use it. Thank you for being brave at the ugliest hour. Thank you for the second chances walking this lawn with new breath."

Back left, where I knew Neve stood with her mum, both inside one cardigan, "Some of those second chances are fourteen and running two laps now, some are seventy and finally smelling first rain. You did that."

Silence, not absence, deepened. Nurses know the difference.

Second thing, "If you're here as a recipient or their mob and you're wondering how to be joyful while someone beside you is relearning how to hold a photo, here's your permission slip. Be joyful. Please. Carry that joy like work boots. When guilt creeps in, as it does, remember this, our donors didn't leave us so we could be miserable together. Honour them by turning breath into hills climbed, songs sung, grandkids swung round kitchens."

A laugh rose, wet, real, needed.

Third thing, "People told me time heals when I was twenty-seven and learning a silent ICU and a ring that still lived on my hand. I wanted to throw them into the river. Time doesn't heal. Grief doesn't shrink. It stays the right size for what you lost. But love, love grows bigger around it. Your life grows. You get new rooms in a house you thought had run out of walls. One day the grief is still there, on the good cushion, but there's a kitchen where tea is made properly, a backyard where kids shriek about a telescope, a front step where you can sit at dusk and know you will be okay."

A breath caught, released, somewhere past the last row. At the back edge where the lights were worst and the shadows kind, a broad figure slipped in, travel still clinging, mud at the cuffs like a memory of road. He stood out of the way like a good man late to something that matters. Cap off. Eyes bright. My microphone did not get custody of my feelings.

I finished the way I started, steady, simple, true. "Tonight we give ourselves to the sky for an hour. We say their names out loud, and we look at light that left home a long time ago to reach us just when we needed it. We don't own stars. We can't. But we can dedicate one, and we can say, 'That one will do for now. I'll tuck some love up there and look when I forget where I put it.'"

The cloth came off the plaque to reveal a black and silver, uncompromising. *A STAR TO REMEMBER - Dedicated to Donors and Their Families, Whose Love Lights the Way.*

"Thank you," I said, honest. "For letting me tell the truth. For showing up in your good clothes and work boots and shaky hands. For making room for each other under this sky. For Lionel."

Applause hit like rain on tin, sudden, and wholehearted. It tipped to standing before I could tell them they didn't have to. Sue hugged me off the stage. "You gave them the sentence they came for," she murmured.

"I gave me the sentence I came for," I breathed back.

Then ritual took over. Families wrote names on stars and pegged them to a line strung between trees. The line sagged like any good washing line. Stories fell out of mouths and were caught by strangers who had apparently been taught how. The astronomers shepherded small hands up stools and used excellent staffroom voices when a kid said, "I see it! I see it!"

I did rounds with tissues and water, and the particular permission a lanyard gives like names said right, and silences left alone. In the telescope queue, a woman in denim took my hand like an old friend. "I didn't know why I came," she said. "I know now." I didn't ask for details. The squeeze said enough.

At the dark edge of the lawn, Big Russ waited. He'd had a go at his boots with something, probably the inside of his shirt, and failed. A grime line shadowed his jaw and made my heart behave foolishly.

"You're filthy," I told him, because obvious is easier than naming the fifteen seconds on stage when my lungs forgot their job.

"Came straight through," he said. "Airport shower was broken. Bloke called it water-saving. I told him I'd save him if he didn't fix it."

"Did you threaten a stranger on behalf of hygiene?"

"Would I ever," he deadpanned, and my face nearly cost me my lanyard.

"How-" I began, then spared him the roster-swap confession. "Thank you for coming back."

He shrugged, the kind that carried a whole day. "Red-eye up, on site by six. Then I realised I'd hate myself if I missed this. Asked the boss and jumped on the next available flight straight back to Perth."

We stood like people who know how to stare at contained fire. He tipped his chin at the telescopes. "Show me your star."

"Not mine," I corrected. "Ours, the one holding the love we can't keep in our pockets tonight."

We chose the smallest scope, the one with the step stool that makes grown-ups ridiculous, and kids feel royal. The volunteer twitched the focus with the precision I reserve for IO access. "There," she said. "Just above Pleiades if you're Greek, and in a patch where plenty of people have always put story, so you're not alone."

I looked. Pin-bright, utterly unbothered by our ceremony. Light from far back in time arriving right on schedule. It felt less like looking and more like being looked at. I did not cry on the optics. Big Russ took his turn, longer than I expected, and then stepped back with the kind of peace I've only ever heard after a job well done.

"Okay," he said softly, to the star, or me, or Lionel, or the fairness of it all. "Okay."

We didn't kiss. We didn't make a holy thing cheap. He went to help a dad with a stubborn focus wheel. I found Neve and her mum and stood with them while they taped their star beside one that read SIOBHAN in a shaky hand.

Later, at the line, George and I traded the donor roll between us like passing a sleeping child. Carmen. Noah. Siobhan. Patrick. Lionel, my mouth rounding the vowel properly, not a name that broke me anymore, just a name that belonged. George squeezed my shoulder at the end, we made it across.

The choir borrowed someone else's words about light, and then night was allowed to be exactly what it is, a place you can stand without a roof. People left slowly, because speed felt rude. Telescopes folded with surgeonly efficiency. Kids slept crooked in back seats. Nurses coiled cable, negotiated chippy orders. Sue pinched the bridge of her nose. "You'll sleep," she declared.

"Bossy," I said. "Correct."

Big Russ hovered like wildlife. I went to him because pretending not to isn't a strategy that serves me.

"Staying?" I asked. "Or red-eye?"

"Early bird," he grimaced. "Camp's short the only idiot who knows which spanner fits the Friday bolt."

"Of course it is."

He glanced at the pegged stars, the talking clusters, the plaque breathing quietly. "You did good," he said. "You said the thing."

"You came," I answered.

Silence built. He turned the small stone I'd given him once in his palm and pocketed it. "Truck needed it," he said. "So did I."

"I'm glad."

He tapped his cap brim like we were in black-and-white. "Save me the same star?"

"It's not going anywhere," I said. "Light left a long time ago to get to us when we needed it."

"See you under the same sky," he said, and did the kind thing, and left.

Packing up felt like a joy we'd earned. I rolled cloth, stacked programs, rescued a duck-print cardigan for a mother who looked like she could sleep a month. One last indulgent look through the baby telescope. A whisper to the pinprick, grief doesn't shrink, love grows bigger around it.

My phone buzzed: a number I could find blindfolded.

R: Sky out here's ridiculous. Our star's showing off. Stand where you stood and look up for ten. I'll do the same. Copy?

Me: Copy. Always.

I leaned against the cool brick and looked until my neck complained and then gave up. Somewhere, the river shifted its shoulder. Somewhere, streets away, a woman said a name into the night, and the night held it. Above, points of old light kept doing their work. I picked ours, not to own, just to practise, and let love grow bigger around the grief like a muscle when you ask it properly.

"Goodnight, Lionel," I told the sky. "Keep an eye on the apprentices."

And into the same air heading north over red country toward boots with dust at the cuffs: "Goodnight, Big Russ."

The lawn plaque winked under the moon and behaved. The city hummed instead of screamed. I turned off the kitchen light and let dark do what it had learned tonight, wrap without swallowing.

Tomorrow there would be planes and rosters and the long road back to community. Back to crickets and windmills instead of ships, clinic lights pooling gold on red dirt, Janelle's steady humming, tea made right. Back to friends who are family and a man who texts sky like prayer. Tonight, there was this, a sky big enough for all of us, and one sentence that will still hold when the rest don't - Grief doesn't shrink; love grows bigger around it.

***

Home was a nest again. Luna had left tea and a note, *Proud of you. Strong. Black. Two sugars.'* The bow on the chair looked like a joke I was still allowed to tell. In the little yard with our postage-stamp of sky, the basil breathed out green. I opened the red-dirt notebook and wrote:

- Said Lionel's name into a microphone and didn't drown.

- He came-filthy from travel, eyes bright-and left clean.

- We don't own stars. We dedicate them. Love knows the way up.

I tucked the photocopy of Lionel's driver's license behind the page, slipped Neve's *thank you for hills* on top so the words could keep each other warm.

In the morning, I would fly back north.

Chapter Twenty-Two

The house went still but sleep wouldn't come. The speech kept replaying, not the words so much as the hush after, the way a crowd breathes together when something lands. I made tea, stood under the back step's slice of sky, and felt the tug again. Not grief this time. Gravity.

The park would be dark now. The telescopes packed away, the lawn squared, the plaque breathing its own quiet. I put on flats, took a thermos and the little wristband I've carried for years in a folded tissue, white plastic gone the colour of old paper, Lionel's name smudged into familiarity, and drove back.

The river wore the moon like a brooch. Jacarandas had dropped a confetti that made the path look like a party had passed through and forgotten to clean up. A council truck idled two streets over. Otherwise, Perth had remembered how to be silent.

He was there already.

Not a surprise, exactly, more like walking into a room and knowing where the light switch is. Big Russ sat on the tailgate of a battered ute that wasn't his, the Astronomy Society's logo stencilled on the door in peeled vinyl, boots on gravel, elbows on knees, a thermos at his heel. A short Dobsonian telescope waited on the grass like a squat black drum, the kind schoolkids adore because they can point it with their whole body.

He looked up, and I felt it in two places at once, in my throat, and in my ribs.

"Borrowed a toy," he said, nodding at the telescope. "Ken reckons the kids like to find the Sisters themselves."

"You talked your way into the telescope library."

"I offered to carry boxes and not touch anything that looked expensive," he said, deadpan. "Turned out most of it looked expensive. They gave me the heavy stuff."

I climbed onto the tailgate beside him. It rocked, like boats do when they're relieved to be back on water. We sat with our shoulders aligned but not touching, the kind of geometry that felt like good manners.

"You did good," he said after a minute, voice low enough the river could claim it as its own. "It was… exactly what it needed to be."

"Thank you for being there," I said. "I saw you."

"I saw you see me," he admitted. "Felt like… not pardon. Not permission. Something steadier."

We poured each other's tea without asking how we take it. Strong. Black. Two sugars. Some liturgies install themselves and refuse to be uninstalled.

He nodded at the scope. "They left Jupiter fat and flashy. Saturn's showing off. And the Sisters, for Ken."

"The Greek count," I said, thinking of the volunteer's grin. "And everyone else's."

He bumped my shoulder lightly, weather, not argument. "Show me."

We set up the little scope by guess and kindness. He knelt to sight along the tube, easy in his body, that mechanic's economy I'd started to read like a language. I took the focus, feathered it, let Jupiter sharpen until the moons popped into attention, four perfect beads on a wire.

"Your turn." I stepped back. He looked, whistled, then laughed softly the way men do when a machine behaves better than they deserve.

"Okay," he said, voice thinned at the edges. "Okay."

We swung to the Pleiades. The cluster glittered like a spill you don't clean up. A meteor scratched the sky, and I felt twenty-one again, backyard blanket, Lionel's shoulder under my cheek, the future, a thing that would definitely turn up on time.

We moved seriously through showpieces for twenty minutes as if we had a list and a supervisor. The small work of it smoothed our edges, "a quarter turn more," and "hold it there," and "your eyes are better than mine for this bit." When spectacle ran out and we settled into simply looking up, he blew a breath and leaned back on the tailgate, palms flat, making a seeing chair of his spine.

"I ran," he said, to the Southern Cross or to his boots. "From you. The first night. At the gym. In the car park. In my head most of all. Every time something in me reached, the rest of me took a step back."

I didn't rescue him. I didn't "it's okay" the confession smaller.

The river folded the city's hum into something bearable. The jacarandas listened like old aunties.

"My marriage," he said, steadying himself with the word. "We were kids. We made it good until we couldn't. The long one after-" He shook his head the way you dislodge grit from a bearing. "I don't bad-mouth her. We broke a lot of things trying to fix other things. Somewhere in there I learned a stupid lesson, I'm a dangerous man to love."

"Stupid," I said, because it was, and because he needed the name.

"Yeah." He scrubbed his jaw, leaving a clean track through the dust that had defeated his earlier wash. "So I built walls you could anchor a truck to. Made rules. No nurses. No mums with kids still at home. No women who look at the sky like it's telling them secrets I don't speak. I worked. I slept. I didn't go where temptation lived."

"And then?"

"And then," he said, a smile tugging in despite him, "a woman walked into a pub in a dress that made the air stand up, and I thought, ah, hell no. Not because of the dress. Because of the way the room moved around her. Because I knew her grief and respected it and wanted to sit next to it like it was a fire."

Edges of tears made the night look slightly underwater. I blinked them back with the discipline you learn on wards where you don't get to make the family do the comforting.

"I ran," he repeated, "because you matter. Because if I messed this up I couldn't throw a tarp over it and keep working under the weather. Because you're the kind of person a man ought to come correct for or not come at all."

"And now?" I asked, not to test him, but to give him the end of his own rope.

"I don't want to run," he said simply. "I'm tired of being fast the way frightened animals are fast. I want good slow. I'll listen when you say stop. I won't ask you to make me a saint to excuse my human. I'll show up. And if you say no, I'll-" He swallowed. "I'll still show up for myself and for the crew. I'll be grateful I heard you speak under a sky that made sense of me."

The breeze flipped jacaranda leaves to their pale backs. Far off, a fox barked at a bin it couldn't open. I put my thermos down and let my hands be empty so they could be honest.

"I haven't kissed anyone since Lionel," I said, and felt the truth land like a small, clean stone between us. "I was careful not to. It felt like… stealing. Like I'd be taking something from him to give to someone else."

He didn't flinch or reach. He waited.

"DonateLife gave the tide somewhere to go," I went on. "A lung, a kidney, another kidney. But some water stayed. Some always will. I thought if I started again I'd be betraying him." I looked at our practice star. "I think I was wrong about the shape of betrayal."

We sat with that, the way you sit with a child who's stopped shouting and started asking the real question.

"Lionel," I said to the not-quite-blue above us, "I need permission."

The river was kind enough to wait until I was done.

"I'm going to live," I said. "I am. And I'm going to love with the same hands."

The night didn't split with lightning. No owl swivelled unreasonably. The plaque didn't hum. The only sign was the smallest release in my chest, like a door unlatched.

"Okay," I said, to him, to me, and to the man very still beside me on a tailgate like he didn't want to spook a bird. "Okay."

I took the wristband from my pocket. The plastic was thin where my thumb had worried it. His name, the whole of it, the way the ED printer had given it to us, was still there, ghost-sturdy.

"I've carried this too long," I said. "Not to remember him. To punish myself for remembering."

Big Russ slid off the tailgate without a question and walked with me across the sleeping lawn. We stopped at the plaque, black and silver and uncompromising in the moonlight. I knelt. The grass marked my knees. There was a gap at the back between the base and the earth where the volunteers' careful setup had left the smallest invitation.

"Here," he said quietly, and without fanfare put his palm under the base and lifted a fraction, just enough to make space. The kind of help that doesn't need to be seen to be honoured.

I slid the wristband under. Plastic. Paper. A held breath. No bargaining. I tucked it into darkness and felt the ridiculous surety of a child who's placed an important note under a pillow and knows the right magic will find it.

"Permission granted," I whispered. Not from Lionel, who never denied me anything but his continued breath. From myself.

We stayed kneeling a second too long for our joints and exactly long enough for the moment. He eased the base down. We stood and went back to the tailgate like we hadn't just changed the shape of something that swore it wouldn't change.

"Indi," he said, and the i at the end held a world of questions arranged into one. "May I-"

"Yes," I said. "Please."

He didn't lunge. He didn't perform. He lifted a hand, palm open, and I stepped into it. He touched my jaw like he'd been trusted with it, not like a trophy. We kissed like a first and a continuation, like choosing. He tasted of strong tea and the day's road. It was slow because we could afford it, careful because we meant it, whole because we were tired of halves. When we stopped, the world had the grace to keep going.

We looked at each other the way you look at the ocean, with respect and relief, and a little healthy fear.

"I'm scared," I told him, because it would be poor strategy to start with a lie.

"Me too," he said. "For once, that's not a stop sign."

We made rules because I need them and he likes them, and between us a rule can become a kindness:

Slow.

Honest.

Never alone, even when the thing isn't a shift but a feeling.

Work first when the world tilts, work keeps us both sane.

No rumour diets. If the mill grinds, we grind back with truth.

Tea when it's too loud for food.

No saving each other from the work that makes us whole.

No doing it alone.

"And if I run?" he asked, half a dare to himself.

"You'll text me: *Checking ships*," I said. "I'll find you at the smokers' door and we'll count together until your head is yours again."

"Copy," he said, and I heard the smile before I saw it.

We packed the little scope badly and then properly, because even on nights like this, you don't mess with Ken's favourite teaching scope. He wrote a note on his phone, to the boss, to the foreman, and to himself, and then he pocketed it like it had done its job and could be quiet now. We sat side by side again, thermoses empty.

"What time's your flight?" I asked.

"Stupid early," he said. "Enough time to get to site and pretend I slept. You?"

"Tomorrow midday," I said. "I promised Sue I'd help pack boxes. I promised myself the ocean before I leave the city. It's the rules."

"Good rules," he said, thinking. "There's a thing I tell apprentices their first week. Something I keep for me. Want to hear it?"

"Always."

"Torque is trust," he said, not sheepish. "You can strip a thread in one second if you're chasing fast. But if you go slow and pay attention, there's a point where the metal says, 'enough.' Not less. Not more. Exactly this."

"Okay, poet," I teased. "Are we a bolt now?"

"We're a machine that needs both our heads screwed on," he said, unbothered. "We can be funny about it if that keeps us from pretending it's not serious."

We stood. He lifted the telescope like he'd been born to it. I took the thermoses like I earn my keep. At the gate, among the jacaranda mess, he turned me toward the river and kissed me again, brief, and certain.

"I'll see you under the same sky," he said, and I nodded because any other word might have made me cry and I hadn't brought the good tissues.

He drove the Astronomy Society's ute like a man in borrowed shoes, careful, and grateful. I locked the park gate because Sue had the key and I still had the keyring in my pocket from pack-down. On the plaque, silver letters took a sip of moon. In the earth below, a small strip of old plastic began its new job as a bridge between then and now.

Back at home, I sat on the back step and wrote three more clean lines in the red-dirt notebook:

- Left Lionel's wristband under the star. Permission granted.

- He told the truth about running. We chose slow.

- Jupiter fat and flashy; four moons like yeses.

I put the notebook under my pillow like a child and, finally, slept.

Morning found me honest and puffy. The city woke me again the way the Pilbara never does, with bins clattering, a bus sighing, and a magpie running scales. In the kitchen someone had left a note under the mug: *Ocean first. Tea second. Love, the Committee.*

I obeyed. Cottesloe had the gall to be beautiful, flat pewter tipping to green. I walked the hard line where the water keeps its promises and said Lionel's name into the wind; it came back without echo, which is the best you can ask of a big body of water.

After, I helped Sue box programs and fold tablecloths that still smelled of lilies and texta. We stacked stars into archive tubs like stained glass for a quieter church.

"You good?" she asked.

"Now," I said, which was true enough for today.

***

By midday I was at the gate with salt still drying on my skin and a boarding pass I didn't argue with. North, then.

Chapter Twenty-Three

The Pilbara met me at the aircraft door the way only this place knows how, and that is heat with a history in it, the iron tang that gets into your cuticles, and that sudden slackening inside your chest that says, home. The tarmac shimmered and the bus driver didn't hurry, you don't in a town where everyone knows heat is a thing you negotiate, not beat.

At baggage claim I found my kit bag by the scuffed duct-tape cross I'd put on it in a different life. I texted one word before I walked outside.

Landed.

Three dots. Then: Copy. Welcome back, Indi.

The taxi driver asked if I wanted the back roads or the long way and I said, "Ships," without thinking. He grinned and took the coastal loop so I could do the ritual. Out past the salt pans and the mangroves, the port was busy, three iron ore carriers in a neat queue, one tug leaning its shoulder into a hull like a shearer. I counted them under my breath, the way you count rosary beads, not because the numbers change anything but because the counting changes you.

Back at staff quarters in Hedland first, the donga's aircon laboured like a faithful old dog. Someone, Robyn, had left a note and a bowl of mandarins on my bed.

Welcome back, lady of the pink lipstick. xo

I put my bag down, put the kettle on, put my forehead to the cool tin of the window frame and watched the red dust decide whether to settle. On the opposite verandah Peter was mending a pair of shorts at a speed that suggested he'd prefer to be mending a truck. He raised his mug, I raised mine, and that was all the ceremony required.

Tomorrow morning early I will be heading back to the community with Janelle.

***

My first back-on-country shift was the kind that fits you like a glove you've broken in, clinic doors propped with a brick, the whiteboard full of simple lies ("Not Too Busy Today"), the smell of hand foam and eucalyptus, and the sound of kids laughing at a volume that suggests they are not on school grounds. Aunty June was at the desk with her crossword and her verdicts.

"You put weight on," she said cheerfully, eyes twinkling.

"On purpose," I deadpanned. "My Sisters fed me good. Doctor's orders."

"Hmm," she said, which in Aunty means, 'I approve of your cheek.'

The morning ran on rails. A boy with an ear that had lost an argument with a fence. A blood pressure check that turned into a yarn about a nephew's new baby that turned into agreement on the best way to make damper (we did not agree). A man with a cough who needed more than cough syrup, we did the bloods and made the plan and the promise to ring tomorrow because promises are medicine too. A woman who sat quiet for a long time before saying "the sad had come back," and I sat quiet with her the way my Elders taught me, no rush, no fixing, the kind of presence that is its own kind of analgesia.

At 12:10 the RFDS called about a transfer, at 12:12 we were ready. At 12:23 they diverted to someone worse off. We ate banana bread in the staffroom like people reprieved.

Between patients I sent two photos: the ships; and the whiteboard with Aunty's additions ("No fighting in the waiting room, unless you're fighting over who makes tea"). He replied with a photo of a pre-start whiteboard that read: ZERO HARM TODAY. UNDERLINE IT TWICE. Someone had drawn a stick figure with a hard hat too big for its head.

Zero harm, he texted. I like the ambition.

Ambition's good, I wrote. So are naps.

Big Russ stared at the screen in the shade behind the workshop, thumb hovering like a bloke afraid of a detonator. He was twelve days into a two-and-one, the kind of roster that turns men into weather systems. The Nifty had spat a bearing during night shift, and by morning it was logged as first job for Big Russ to strip and rebuild. He could feel the old reflexes starting up, the ones that say, when in doubt, quiet. Hide in the job. Pull the blinds down in your head and call it discipline.

He typed two words, erased them, typed three different words, erased those too. Then he sent the only combination he trusted.

Knock off 18:00. Ships?

I knew better than to say yes immediately, rosters are gods you don't tempt, but the smile arrived without permission. Aunty June clocked it and said nothing, which is her way of blessing a thing she'll interrogate later.

***

We tried a version of ordinary that week. It looked like this, my alarm at 04:30, gym at 05:00, clinic by 06:30, first patient at 07:05 because "only five minutes" is not a unit of time here. His bus at 05:40, pre-start at 06:00, the long hot of men and machines, knock off at 18:00 if the gods were kind. We ran on thermoses and lists. We swapped two-message check-ins like beads on a string.

We had our first proper argument on a Thursday I'd been sure would be gentle. It started as nothing. They always do. A man came in with a snake in a bucket and a story that turned out to be a rash and a bad dream, I smiled my way through adrenaline's hangover. A teenager asked about thrush with the solemnity of a treaty signing and I did not giggle even once. A little girl brought me a drawing of a lady with round hair and a pink mouth, and I loved her fiercely for seeing me at my silliest.

By three, I had my own silliness under control and my list mostly defeated. I texted him a photo of the drawing because I knew he collected the scraps of my day like someone who'd build a house from them if he could. Nothing came back. Fine. He'd be on a job. 16:00, nothing. 17:00, still nothing. The old animal woke.

At 18:30 the ships were four and a tug. I counted, because that is what I do when I am choosing not to panic. At 19:10 he texted a single word.

Alive.

My reply arrived with more heat than sense.

That new code for "I'm not texting you all day"?

Three dots. No dots. Three dots. Then: No service. Incident. I'm clean and safe.

Safe, I typed and then deleted the other words that wanted to follow, you promised to show up / I don't do disappearing men / if you need out just say out. I put the phone in the cupboard with the gauze so I wouldn't answer from the place in me that still believes it is easier to leave first than be left.

He called. I let it ring out. He didn't call again.

At 20:10 someone knocked on the clinic's back door. The light through the frosted glass turned him into a shape I knew even if he hadn't moved. I called out before I opened it to check first though, because Aunty June says cowards never built a good roof and because #NeverAlone doesn't just belong on a ward.

He had two coffees in a cardboard tray, a clean shirt, the kind of face that says the day took a bite but didn't break the skin.

"05:00 was the earliest I could make," he said.

"It's eight," I said, and the fatigue in my voice made it sound like I was accusing him of last Tuesday.

"05:00 tomorrow," he corrected gently, holding the tray like an offering. "I came to book it in person."

I took the coffees because they were hot and because pettiness is a mean god to serve.

"Talk to me," I said when we were sitting on the back steps, elbows almost touching, watching a lawn that refuses to grow pretend it's not losing. "Not like I'm a foreman. Like I'm me."

He nodded. Steady, not abashed. "We had a near-miss. Young bloke, new to site. I'll debrief it with you properly when the report's done and details aren't just hot panic in my head. I went quiet because we shut everything down while we made it right. It wasn't a choice, it was a site-wide. When the phones came back, I called you first. You didn't pick up."

"I know," I said, because honesty is a habit you practise, not a virtue bestowed. "The bit that panicked wasn't current. It was old. And it's mine to take to a smokers' door and shout at the ships. Not yours to fix."

He looked at me for a small forever, then put one big hand palm-up on the step between us. An invitation, not an order. I put my fingers into it because that's the kind of day we were having.

"Okay," I said. "Rules for when rosters and coverage conspire against us."

He smiled, relieved to be handed a tool. "Go."

"If you're locking down and can send a breadcrumb, send a full stop. That's it. I'll know the dot means 'not dead, cannot speak'."

"A dot," he repeated. "I can do a dot."

"And I won't turn dots into doom. I'll count ships. I'll go breathe near a tree. I'll text an Aunty instead of a man at a mine."

"Copy," he said, and didn't make a joke because he knows when jokes are not tools.

We drank the coffee that had gone from hot to perfect while we were talking. A moth battered itself to pieces against the fluorescent tube and then remembered the night. When he stood, he looked less like a tractor idling too high and more like a man who'd adjusted his own choke.

"05:00, then?" he said. "I'll bring better coffee."

"Better than this?"

He tilted the cup toward me. "I know a bloke with beans. Don't tell the roadhouse."

He left like men who have to get up at four leave, efficiently, and grateful to the door for doing what doors do. I did my night checks, locked the drug cupboard like it owed me money, and stood in the dark a long minute longer than usual to feel the clinic breathe. Then I lay on the narrow bed and let the old animal lie down at last.

He was sitting on the clinic steps when the 04:58 kookaburras laughed. Two cups, two pastries in a paper bag greasy in the right way.

"I was early," he said, faux-solemn. "I went and checked the ships."

"How many?"

"Three and a tug," he said, proud of himself. "And the tug looked like it was nagging."

We took the coffees to the oval because the sky was doing that pre-dawn blue that makes you forgive everything. The ground smelled like damp rust and last night's dew. I pointed where pointing makes sense.

"Crux," I said. "Southern Cross. Alpha and Beta Centauri, The Pointers, if you're a lighthouse keeper or a schoolteacher. Carina's there -" I moved my hand, showed him the keel of a ship that no longer existed but left its name. "That bright one low is Achernar, last of the river. Canopus is above the horizon like an old friend who sends good texts. And when the black is blacker than this, that long smear is the River itself - the Milky Way."

He stood with his head tipped back, jaw shadowed, eyes trying to drink more than eyes can. When I traced the outline of the Emu, the dark constellation the Elders had first taught me to see, he didn't say the name out loud. He held a gravity I recognised, the tenderness you bring to a story that isn't yours to retell without permission.

"You'll have to come when Ken does the community talk," I said softly. "He has the words for it that belong."

"I'll be there," he said, and I believed him.

We were getting better at this. Not slick, slick is for people with nothing to lose, but practised. We wrote a mini-roster into our lives, Mondays were for groceries and not The Finny. Tuesdays were for the gym at five, mutual tolerance of skid boys, few words, good sweat. Wednesdays belonged to sleep. Thursdays were anyone's guess. Fridays, when the gods smiled on rosters, we took the long way home and counted kangaroos and didn't make it a metaphor for anything.

The small-town eyes got bored when we refused to give them a show. A woman at the servo called out, "Good on you two" once, and I pretended she was talking about our choice of milk. Aunty June demanded to inspect his hands and declared them "useful," which is her equivalent of an engagement notice.

Purpose needs somewhere to plant itself. Mine asked for a Thursday night.

It started like most good things here, four women at the clinic table with too much tea and not enough printer ink.

"DonateLife night," I said, laying out the pamphlets I'd begged from Perth. "Stories and facts. Not a lecture. Yarn, really. A place to ask the questions you can't Google."

"Can we call it a yarn then," Aunty June said dryly, "and not a 'night', which sounds like someone's going to play guitar?"

"Yarn," I agreed. "With scones. And damper if you're feeling competitive."

She sniffed. "Your damper is cake that lost its way. I will bake."

We made lists. We love lists. Who to invite and how, face to face, not flyers blown down the street. Who would hold space for sorry business when it arrived, because it always does, and how to move gently around names that aren't spoken. Which questions need a doctor, and which need a grandmother. Whether we'd translate the pamphlets or just translate the room. We decided on both. Robyn wrote "KIDS WELCOME" in letters big enough for the shy to believe. Peter volunteered to make tea and then lied about not caring whether it was strong enough to bite.

I asked permission from the people who could give it. The Elders said yes with caveats that made sense and saved us from harm. The hospital sent down a small box of "resource packs" that looked like they'd been designed by a man in a tie who had never seen dust. I added pegs and a handful of tissues to each. The power company lent us a speaker that remembered how to be useful.

***

On the night, the little community clinic hummed the way clinics do when nobody's sick, kids under chairs with scones, aunties on the plastic chairs that we should have replaced a decade ago, uncles doing the winter shuffle at the door, men from the depot standing like trees pretending they're not listening. I wore my softest shirt and my least bossy lipstick. I took a deep breath and told them about Lionel the way I always do, no more than two minutes, no less than the truth.

"A lung went to a dad who's still taking his kid fishing," I said. "A kidney went to a man who got to walk his daughter down an aisle. A kidney went to a boy who learned to swear at the Eagles like a professional."

Laughter is medicine you don't need a script for. It moved around the room and took people's shoulders with it.

We didn't do slides. We did hands. I showed them the donor card in my wallet like it was a holy thing because it is. I said, "You can change your mind" and "You can tell your family" and "You can carry the hope without carrying a date." I said "It's okay if this isn't your way. It would be a terrible world if we all did the same thing the same way." I said "Questions?" and then shut up properly.

They asked the good ones. "If I'm old?" (You're fine to be generous.) "If I was sick?" (So are most of us.) "Who decides?" (You, and the people you tell. Always tell.) "Does it hurt?" (Death is not a thing pain understands.) "What if they're not really gone?" (We do not take from the living. Ever.) "Will they leave him alone? His spirit?" (We do not touch the parts of a person that belong to their family and their old people. We go around, never through.)

An Elder woman stood and spoke about a nephew who'd been saved by a stranger. A young mum said she'd changed her mind because she'd changed who she listens to. A teenager asked if he could put a sticker on his phone case and I said, "Mate, you can put a billboard on your forehead if it helps but tell your nan too." He laughed and took two stickers anyway.

When we were done, Aunty June tapped the mic like it had misbehaved and said, "Scones now. And that tea that thinks it's a soup."

People lingered because good rooms ask you to. I watched them read and not read and tuck pamphlets into back pockets and under babies. I watched them look at the stars as they stepped out the door because once you start looking, you don't stop.

He'd come in the back, the way men who don't want to make a show of themselves come to things, cap in hand, shirt clean. He'd taken a chair outside and let the little kids borrow his torch to make shadow dogs while they waited for the kettle to boil again. When I stepped into the air he stood, not because he's old-fashioned but because he is careful with me.

"You were good," he said softly. "Not a saint. Not a martyr. Just good."

I breathed, and it went all the way down.

We walked to the edge of the oval where the lights couldn't boss the sky. He tilted his head like a man receiving quiet instruction.

"Crux," he said, pointing with two fingers, checking his work.

"Crux," I confirmed.

"Pointers," he said, pleased.

"Alpha and Beta Centauri," I added, because I like that he likes learning the grown-up names too.

He gestured at the smear. "The River."

"The River," I said, and because the night had given me permission, "Milky Way."

We didn't kiss because we didn't need to. We did the kind of leaning that says repair isn't a thunderclap, it's a decking board you sand with your hands and oil with your patience. He handed me a thermos. I handed him a biscuit. A moth made a seen-you before it went to find the single working light by the back door.

***

On the way back into town I checked the ships (three and a tug). Back at the donga, Robyn had left the last of the pumpkin soup on my shelf with a note that said, YOU FED THEM, NOW FEED YOU. I did. Then I wrote my three lines in the red-dirt book so tomorrow wouldn't steal them.

- First real fight. First real repair. Dot = not dead.
- Aunty's scones won a war.

- He knows Crux on sight.

Outside, the dust settled in that particular way it does when the land approves. I turned off the light and let the dark be a room I'd chosen. Somewhere up the highway a man set his alarm and put his phone face down. Somewhere on a kitchen table a young bloke stuck a DonateLife sticker to his clear case and asked his nan where the best place on the fridge was for the pamphlet. Somewhere in the port a tug leaned its shoulder into iron and did a whole day's work in the time it took me to fall asleep.

Chapter Twenty-Four

Karijini does that thing to you on the drive in, like someone pressed a hand to your sternum and whispered, slow. The road narrows to reason, the ranges lift their red shoulders and pretend they've been here forever. Spinifex does its glow-at-the-edges trick, and the sky turns into a dome you could set your tea under. We came in convoy because that's how families do it here when they aren't technically family. Robyn's troopy with the reliable rattle, Peter's ute with a new rattle he refused to acknowledge, Sharon and Gavin arguing about which playlist is scientifically proven to improve road safety (Sharon won), and me behind them with a cake tin tied-down for dear life, and an esky that clunked every time the corrugations asked it a question.

We'd decided on Dales for the evening, Fortescue Falls below us, Fern Pool a slow hymn up the track, sunset at the rim before head-torches and a warm night. Aunty June didn't come, she'd patted my cheek and said, "Tell Country I said thank you," which is both permission and instruction. So, I did, out loud when the ranges showed their faces. Thank you. Thank you for letting me on your back again.

By the time we found a patch away from the crowd, one gum for company, enough flat for a picnic rug, and a view that made your lungs remember the job, Peter had his little gas burner balancing on a rock like a dare. Sharon coaxed the flame with the calm of a woman who can parallel park a troopy in a gale. Robyn unpacked her never-ending hamper of steak sandwiches wrapped in last week's paper, boiled eggs, orange quarters, damper she called a "scrap-bin special" and which tasted like every grandmother you ever missed. I spread my ridiculous floral rug because I refuse to apologise for pink anymore, set down the battered thermos, and sent a text that said simply: Here.

Three dots. It still thrills me, those dots. Then: On my way. Ten.

Gavin's phone became the DJ because his playlist provokes the fewest groans. He started with Troy Cassar-Daley, slid to Kasey, slipped a Paul Kelly in there like a sly wink to the cities. The sound came small and perfect from the phone in a lunchbox, Peter's invention, the acoustics are surprisingly excellent. Sharon click-click-clicked her disposable camera like it was 2002 and insisted on one "nice photo" before the steak, which caused universal distress and then universal giggling. The light went honey. The flies went to vespers.

A diesel pulled in at the end of the track, and something in me settled and sparked at once. He walked across the red striations like he'd been made for this place, an esky in one hand, a paper bag in the other. His hi-vis was clean enough for a christening, which meant the shift hadn't eaten him. His smile was unshowy and aimed at me first, then at the rest of our unruly congregation.

"Who invited management?" Peter called, because he can't help himself.

"Here to do a risk assessment on your sausages," Big Russ said, deadpan. Peter pretended to shield them with his body.

He set the esky by my rug and put the paper bag in my lap. Inside, mango cheeks wrapped in cool cloth and two lemonade cans that had somehow stayed cold. My heart did a small, embarrassing thing. I hid it by making a great fuss over mangos and then immediately failing to cut them without wearing half of one.

"Indi," he said softly, thumb catching juice off my wrist like it was sacrament. "You're supposed to use the hedgehog method."

"I'm using the chaos method," I said. "It's more Pilbara."

We ate with the silence good food deserves, then with the noise good company demands. Stories tasted different in this air, so we told them again, the roo on the jetty day (Peter swears it winked at him), the great soup theft of last winter (Sharon still suspects Gavin), the cyclone that turned camp fridges into slot machines. Robyn reenacted her first remote clinic Monday with props (two bandages, a tea towel, and my lipstick) and had us howling. Big Russ leaned back on his elbows and let laughter un-stiffen him, which is one of my favourite things to watch.

Country music turned to the softer end of itself the way it does when bellies are full. Someone hummed. Someone else couldn't help harmonising. The light made everyone look kind.

We did the rim walk slow, the way we promised, because even in joy there are edges, and Country is older than our strides. Fern Pool below was already a coin of shadow. Children's voices echoed like birds. I touched the rock and said Ken's words in my head, thank you for making me small so I remember where to put my feet.

We settled again as the sun thought about leaving. Sharon produced emergency fairy lights like a magician, Robyn rolled her eyes and strung them anyway. Gavin, as a joke, pulled his hi-vis on over his T-shirt, the joke made itself and we applauded its commitment.

Big Russ caught my eye and tilted his head toward a quiet scrap of rim. "Count the ranges?" he said.

We walked until our friends were background and the world ahead was red, then purple, then bruised-in-reverse. He didn't touch me. He didn't need to. We are better now at holding a space between us that doesn't belong to fear.

"One," I said, pointing at the nearest run of rock, "two, three…" A distant fourth softened into evening. "Four, if you squint. This time of day you can't tell if it's a range or an idea."

He made the little sound he makes when he's storing something for later, a small huff you'd miss if you didn't live inside his weather.

"I did a meeting today," he said, still looking out. "Took the young ones through the near-miss again. Numbers, sequence, how we make it never happen. Then I told them the thing I never used to say."

"What thing?"

"That families wait at home, and I'd like them to not have to answer doors." He glanced at his boots like he was checking they were still tied. "I used to stick to bolts and torque. Felt… safer."

"It's risk management too," I said.

He scuffed a bit of dirt, watched it decide where to go. "I think I know what I'm asking for," he said at last, "and I'm either brave enough or stupid enough to ask."

The ranges waited. The playlist behind us found a slow something about roads and staying anyway. In the blue above us the first stars lit up, familiar as freckles.

"Okay," I said. "Ask."

He exhaled like a man who'd been underwater an inch too long and found air. "Not the big promise yet," he said, and the relief in that honesty made me love him in a new shape. "Not because I don't want it. Because I want to do it right when we do it. But a Pilbara promise. The next season. On purpose."

He ticked it off like a pre-start, which made me laugh and then not laugh at all.

"Roster cards on the fridge," he said. "Yours and mine.

Highlighter for days we overlap, dots for the ones we don't. One proper dinner a week that isn't roadhouse if our gods allow it. One phone photo a day of something that's not a person, ships, ranges, bolts behaving, damper that didn't. One Sunday a month we leave our phones in a glovebox and go somewhere the wind can boss us around. A drawer at mine. A drawer at yours. A toothbrush that isn't the one still in its box." He swallowed. "The dot when I can't talk. You counting ships instead of ghosts. Me showing up when I can and explaining it like a bloke who learned how to use words."

"And," I said, finding my breath again, "you don't disappear. Not into work. Not into yourself. Step outside and count something. Ranges if that's what you've got. Nuts and washers if you're stuck in a shed."

"Nuts and washers," he said, a little croaky, letting the joke hold his hand. "I can count them all day."

He reached into the pocket over his heart and brought out a small, plain thing - a stainless-steel washer on a bit of black cord, the kind you see a hundred of every day if you live where we live and never see properly once. He put it in my palm like it was the only delicate thing he owned.

"I stamped it," he said, suddenly shy. "Just a dot. To remind me not to be clever when simple will do."

It was warm from his shirt. In the failing light the raised puncture winked like a private joke. I rubbed it with my thumb the way I rub the edge of Lionels driver's license when rooms take up too much air.

"You don't have to wear it," he said, still making me a doorway even while he was brave. "Tie it to your keys. Or we can chuck it in the gorge and let it rust somewhere beautiful."

"I'll wear it," I said. "And if it rusts against my collarbone, I'll call it patina."

He laughed, relief moving through his shoulders like weather. We stood while the day tucked itself in, the washer a small moon in my hand.

Behind us someone whooped and apologised to the gorges. Laughter unravelled and knit itself again. The smell of steak tried for a second chance. Someone asked if anyone had packed tomato sauce and three of us said yes because we're not animals. A bat traced its signature on the evening.

I looked up.

It's a strange kindness, the way a thing you met in a city can be truer far from where you first shook its hand. The star we've borrowed for Lionel is everywhere, that's how the night works. But here, above this country, it sat just-so. I found it the way I always do now, two over where my thumb wants to go, one down like a step. It is very slightly brighter to me because I've given myself permission to see it that way. The universe may not care for my rituals. My heart does.

Lionel, I said in my chest, not my mouth. There are words for inside because the air outside already has enough to carry. *Thank you for loving me into this.*

The tide came in the way it has learned, not to drown me, but to rearrange me. It brought back its flotsam, his laugh, gum in his eyelashes at nineteen, the ICU beeps that don't care about jokes, and set them gently on the beach of me, then stood back. I looked. I touched each one. "Safe travels," I told the bits that needed it. I put the cord around my neck, the dot found the little hollow where the throat asks its questions. It felt like a new place to breathe from.

I turned to Big Russ. He didn't ask for an answer with words. He asked with how he stood, unrun, unhidden, hands empty, yes ready to receive a no.

"Yes," I said. Plain on purpose. "Yes to a season. Yes to ranges and dots and toothbrushes with opinions. Yes to learning your weather and letting you in on mine. Yes."

He made the quietest sound and tried to cover it with a breath because he is still learning that his joy doesn't make a mess. He set his forehead to mine and kissed me like a person who had read the manual and thrown it away. Careful, funny, not performative. Mango and dust and something that might be the word after.

We walked back to our foolish family and were mocked precisely the right amount.

"Finally," Sharon said, rolling her eyes fondly. "We thought we were going to have to run a sweep."

"Who had 'Karijini rim at civil twilight'?" Peter asked the sky. "Pay up."

Gavin took a photo of our shoes next to each other because he is an artist whenever he forgets to be a clown. Robyn brought me a serviette with "Strong. Black. Two sugars" in biro and pretended it was a formal document. I pressed it into my notebook later because not all paperwork is clinical.

Night dropped proper. Ken wasn't there to do his Official Tour of Everything That Matters Above Our Heads, but I stole the bits he allows me to carry and handed them out like lollies. The Emu in the Sky was black and enormous and kind, and Big Russ traced it with a finger and did not say its name because he remembers the rules. The River spilled the way it always has. The Pointers did their signposting. Crux was itself. Achernar sat where it sits. Canopus did its old-friend trick. Someone claimed a satellite, someone else insisted space station. We let both be right because the night is generous.

We ate the second round of steak sandwiches and the first round of too many biscuits. We poured billy tea and called it a crime scene and then drank it anyway because sugar redeems much. The phone died at exactly the right time. People drifted in and out of conversation like tide pools, the long, low talk of men who don't need to perform, the fast, bright chatter of women who finally took their boots off. A baby, three rugs over, made that small asleep noise that resets your day's maths.

Big Russ and I took the long way to the edge once more, just to say goodbye properly. I held the washer and felt the dot's small steadiness. He took my hand and looked at the star and didn't look away when my eyes filled for exactly three seconds. He didn't fix a thing. He stood, like a good roof.

On the track back to the cars our head-torches choreographed legs and dust. We carried out what we carried in, the way you should. The fairy lights failed bravely at the last minute, Sharon bowed, we applauded as if they'd performed. Someone dropped a fork, and then immediately picked it up, because that's who we are now, people who leave things right.

At my car he did the Pilbara version of tucking me in, checked my water bottle with ridiculous seriousness, moved the esky so it wouldn't decapitate me on a pothole, put his palm against the bonnet and told a machine "good girl" like a man saved by steel more than once. He leaned into the door and kissed me quick, because goodbyes on edges are for quick, not forever.

"Roster cards," he said, tapping my forehead then his.

"Dots," I said, tapping the washer then his chest.

"Ships, when you can't do ranges."

"Ranges, when you can't do ships."

He smiled like a man who has built a deck board by board and knows it will hold.

The convoy hopped back down the dirt in a spray of red glitter. I drove slower than the signs suggest because wallabies have poor judgement and some nights deserve the longer way home. At the bitumen I pulled over for the other ritual. The port was far, but the count still matters anywhere.

No ships here, I thought, and smiled. Plenty of stars.

Back at the donga, Robyn had left a piece of damper in my fridge with a note: *KEEP THE NIGHT SWEET.* Peter's head-torch sat on my step because I always forget mine. I washed the dust from the back of my neck and the mango stickiness from my fingers, then stood in the dark a moment, watching the dot in the mirror throw a tiny shadow on my skin.

I opened the red-dirt notebook and wrote the lines that make tomorrow behave:

- Karijini said slow and we did.
- Pilbara promise: rosters, drawers, dots.
- Lionel's star brighter than grief, love grew bigger around it.

I tucked the biro under the elastic, slid the DonateLife brochure back behind the page like a talisman, and lay under the sheet while the air-con did its faithful dog impersonation. A moth adored the wrong bulb like art.

Outside, the land breathed the way it breathes when it approves. Somewhere past the highway a man set his morning alarm and, for once, didn't dread it. Somewhere in a kitchen a girl wrote "A Star to Remember" on a water bottle and liked her own handwriting. Somewhere on three steps a nan put my pamphlet under a magnet and said, "We'll yarn about that when we're ready."

I lay on my side, pressed my palm to the dot, and looked through the wall that isn't a wall to where the star sits like a kept promise.

"Thank you for loving me into this," I said again, because gratitude is a muscle you train.

Then, quiet, certain as Crux, "Yes."

We will check the ships again tomorrow. We will count the ranges when ships are too far. We will lay our roster cards like constellations on a fridge and learn the names of the bright bits as we go. And when the tide comes, as it will, it can find me here, with a washer at my throat, a promise in my mouth, and a star to keep.

Epilogue

The first hot wind of the build-up comes in sideways and bossy, rattling the louvres like a kid who's decided patience is for other people. The fridge hums, the roster cards on it look like a galaxy, my shifts in pink, his in pencil because he still doesn't trust highlighters, our overlaps in little sticky stars that make Peter groan when he sees them and then secretly ask where we bought them.

There's a toothbrush in my donga that isn't mine and a washer on a cord at my throat that has learned the shape of my collarbone. The dot sits where a voice would if I were a radio. I touch it when the smoke alarm has opinions about my toast, and when the port stacks five ships like promises, and when the clinic is fuller than the waiting room can handle, and when someone calls me Sister with gratitude, and when someone else calls me Sister with fury, and both of them are right.

Thursday nights, if the wind allows, the clinic waits open an hour longer. We call it Cuppa & Yarn because "community education session on organ and tissue donation" made the poster look like homework. We put the kettle on. People come because there's aircon and because Robyn's biscuits are famous and because grief sits easier when the room knows what to do with it.

Sometimes we talk about the paperwork. Sometimes we don't. Sometimes an Elder closes her eyes and sings three notes until the room remembers how to breathe. Sometimes no one comes and I make tea strong/black/two sugars and take it down to Aunty June and we sit on her step and talk about anything except death until we've talked about death without noticing.

Tonight, after the last cuppa, the lights in the clinic make their soft goodbye click and the corridor sighs. I wipe the table twice, not because it needs it, but because ritual turns rooms into friends. On my way out I leave a fresh stack of DonateLife pamphlets under the magnet with the turtle on it. A teenager with a lung scar still pink left a thank-you note there last month, "for people like Lionel." I keep it pinned behind the turtle so it doesn't have to be brave in public.

Outside, the wind lifts the hair at my neck, and a dust devil crosses the car park with more confidence than it deserves. Across the road, the port cranes hold their yoga poses and pretend they aren't nosy. I do the thing the old-timers taught me because superstition is just experience with its hat on. I check the ships. Four and a tug. Honest work.

My phone buzzes. A photo from Russ: a bolt so clean it could be a wedding ring, two greasy thumbs-up in the background, and the caption: "Counted washers. Didn't disappear."

I send back the other half of the sentence: "Counted ships. Didn't drown."

Three dots, then: "Rosters next quarter. Drawer upgrade. You free to argue about shelf heights on Sunday?"

I grin into the wind like a loon. We have learned the way to fight with our hands open. He brings coffee at 04:30 when my face still has the pillow stitched to it, I stand on his workshop floor and point at a safety poster until he admits it should be at eye level and not behind a rack of steel. He is teaching me patience with the kind of bolts that don't care how pretty your plan is. I am teaching him the names of stars one at a time so the sky stops being a ceiling and starts being a map.

We drive out on our one-phone-in-the-glovebox Sundays and argue about which gorge is bossiest and who makes the better damper (Robyn, obviously) and whether Emus in the Sky are laughing at us or with us. We check the ranges when the ships are too far and the ships when the ranges are a rumour. We go quiet when quiet is the only language that makes sense.

The promise we made on the rim, drawers, dots, dinners, one photo a day of something that isn't a person, has held. It creaks sometimes, like any good timber. We oil it with stupid jokes and serious apologies and cups of tea made the way the other likes. Once, in a week where the site ate him and the ward ate me, we stood in the smokers' door wind with our shoulders touching and said nothing for six minutes. It was the best conversation of the month.

A text lands from Sharon: "Point Samson on Friday? Gavin owes us chips." Robyn replies before I can: "And a public apology to the soup." Peter sends a photo of a roo that is definitely the same one from the jetty, more self-important than ever. The thread is a family bible in memes and weather.

I put my hand to the dot and look up to where I've taught my thumb to land, two over, one down. The Star that carries his name isn't brighter because it is, it is brighter because I am permitted to say so. When I spoke at 'A Star to Remember' I said the line that finally matched the shape of our days, grief doesn't shrink; love grows bigger around it. It keeps proving itself true in domestic ways, roster magnets, a steady hand on a small of a back, a drawer with too many screwdrivers and the good scissors we pretend not to hide from Peter.

The convoy is quieter these days. Some nights it's just us and a thermos and the kind of dark that isn't dangerous. Some nights the whole town turns up with fairy lights and accusations, and someone brings a guitar and plays two chords until we all learn a third. On one of those nights, under that familiar map, I tucked a hospital wristband under a plaque and said thank you for loving me into this. The tide came, rearranged me kindly, went on with its job.

A ute rolls past and someone leans out and says, "Night, Nurse," like it's a title you can inherit. I wave. I watch the tug nudge a ship like a small truth moving a large one.

When I get home, there's sawdust on my step. Inside, a flat-pack box leans against the wall with a note in his handwriting: "For shelf heights we will both pretend not to care about." On the table, a paper bag. Mango cheeks wrapped in cool cloth. I laugh, peel, fail to avoid wearing half of one, and suck the stone like it owes me money. I wash my hands and the dust and the day and sit on the edge of the bed with the red-dirt notebook open. Three lines, because three has always felt like enough:

- Four ships and a tug; didn't drown.
- Drawer upgrade pending; promise holds.
- Lionel's star, right where we left it.

I slip the notebook shut and the washer warms under my palm like a small moon. Through the louvres the night does its old breathing trick, and a moth decides to love the wrong bulb. Somewhere across town a kettle boils and two people who don't know yet that they're brave talk about donor cards without flinching. Somewhere a boy with a new scar runs until his lungs forget they ever learned fear. Somewhere a man in hi-vis sends a photo of a bolt because he has learned that showing up looks like small things often.

Tomorrow we'll check the ships. We'll count the ranges when ships are too far. We'll pin the next roster cards like constellations and argue good-naturedly about the best angle for the toaster. We'll get it wrong and fix it. We'll keep love big enough for grief to sit inside without making a scene.

I turn off the light, keep the star, and let the season go on.

Acknowledgements

Marinda, Aimee, Steven, and **Lily** - My Hearts and Souls. For your unconditional love and respect, and all the strength that I needed to carry on with this life. My Rocks. We held each other up when we didn't have the strength to stand on our own. You are the true LOVES of my life.

Muzzy, you always were, and always will be, my best friend, my soul mate.

Irene, with lots of love.

Strength is not the lack of grief, tears, or sorrow.
Strength is living each day with a broken heart that expresses honest emotions.
Strength is living each day knowing that love does not die.
- Tanya Lord

Mary and **Olive,** with love.

The loneliest people are the kindest.
The saddest people smile the brightest.

To anybody who has ever suffered through grief, shattered beyond repair, through loss, disbelief, and devastation, may you find peace.

About the Author

MAL STEVENS - THE AUTHOR was born in the small, country town of Geraldton, Western Australia, and at the very tender age of three, after discovering a love for reading whilst sitting at her Pops feet whilst he read in his library, decided that she would someday become an Author. Often her family and friends thought her weird because no matter where she was, she could always be found with her nose in a book…and if her nose wasn't in a book because of reading it, then it could be found in one of her many hundreds of journal notebooks filled with fanciful made-up stories, and vivid descriptions about her life in general, and poetry.

Today, I am a Registered Nurse by trade, a Mum 24/7, a Mining and Construction Industry Site Medic by day, and a writer by night. I rarely sleep. I find writing therapeutic, and I happily and passionately lose myself to it on a daily basis.

Shine, Shine, Shine. With Lots of Love xxx

An Excerpt from 'Atreia Rising - Book One' - 'Life-of-Life Series'

alea jacta est

Chapter One

Leaning out from over the Karijini National Park gorge's edge, Leena closed her eyes, stretched, and then unfolded her wings as far and as high as she could, and slowly turned in a full circle as she absorbed all the sights, and the smells and sounds that Karijini afforded her. The waterfall, the crystal-clear waterway leading to the green-coloured pool of water that lay at the bottom, and the stripes of red, brown, and bluish black of the gorge's rock wall in-between, that spread for as far and as wide as her eyes could see. The brilliant blue sky of a Pilbara dry season that encased her like a mother's overwhelming love and made her feel safe. She listened to the sounds of water trickling its very own journey, of gentle breezes, of trees gently creaking their appreciation of spiritual wonder, and of sounds that just had no names to her.

Hawks circled above her head, and their haunting cries began to intertwine with her own until she no longer knew where they ended, and hers began. As the sunlight gently touched her face, Leena inhaled deeply and leaned into the gentle breeze and let it slowly lift her off her feet and off out over the top of the gorge's edge. She beat down hard with her wings, and as she did, she felt the air lift her up higher and higher, her blonde hair flailing wildly around her. She moved in circles, slowly at first, higher and higher, then increasing in speed with her sheer desperation to fly through the clear blue sky towards the Sun. Away from the pain, and away from the cold injustices of life, and into the warmth of that Sun. 'No one can hurt me here, this is where I am free.' Leena flew for what seemed far too short a time, but had in fact been quite a few hours, wishing that she could stay here forever, and never again return to her waking life. For some reason, that life depressed her, it lay upon her shoulders like a heavy burden, even though those that surrounded her loved her very much.

***

I opened my eyes and turned my head and looked to the bedside clock, 04:57, another few minutes and the alarm would have gone off and woken me up anyway. Most times I am a morning person and I love to get up with the Sun, but these days it takes all my energy just to drag myself out of bed. I rolled over in bed and lay on my back and stared into the blackness of my bedroom up into the direction of the ceiling. My mind was full of thoughts about anything and everything and nothing.

I consciously willed myself to remember my dream. I remembered flying. For as long as I could remember I had been able to fly in my dreams. A lot of things I did I assumed everyone else could do. The more people I spoke to though, the more I realised this not to be the case.

I could still vividly remember my very first memory of flying in my dreams. The day had been a very profound day because it had also involved Andy. I knew that day that I was about to embark on a very significant journey. The voices on the wind had tried to speak to me, whispering to my mind their gentle secrets. Secrets that at the time I had been unable to grasp, and so they had slipped easily from my mind. Then that first night… my dreams had taken me far away from home - I had been to the stars. Sometimes I wished I could just go to sleep and wake up in five, or ten, or twenty years' time, and at other times I wished to just not wake up at all.

'I wish I never had to wake up,' I whispered quietly, knowing all the while that it was a very silly thing to wish for, and then I started to feel all my burdens return to me.

The bedside clock alarm sounded. I reached over and switched on the bedside lamp first before turning the alarm off. I caught a glimpse of my eldest boy Bandit as he walked past my bedroom door, heading in the direction of his younger brother Zander's room.

Zander was only ten years old and always sick, and we had been kept up half the night from his coughing. I felt like I had been hit by a bus! Sleep for me these days was never restful. Slowly I dragged myself out of bed and joined Bandit in Zander's room.

Bandit was fourteen years old and every bit his father's son. He was already a full head taller than me in height. His thick, silky hair, the colour of rich chocolate that fell in soft waves to his shoulders, and dark-lashed golden-brown eyes the colour of good Jamaican coffee, with the depth of a bottomless well. Both of my boys had inherited their fathers' brown eyes. I could see the dark-red rings around Zander's eyes, and I wondered to myself if he would ever get better. When Zander was well, he was dashing, his hair the same crisp blonde colour as mine. It fell in waves around his shoulders too, though at the moment it looked ratty and dirty, it had lost its sparkle and so had he.

Zander's bedroom was the smallest of the three. Our house was old but very much in line with the era for when it was built and for where we lived. It was built in the Pilbara in the 1970s. The window from Zander's room was the only bedroom window in the house that looked out over our back yard. It had a fairly large window that was draped in brightly coloured 'kiddie' curtains. He had asked me on more than one occasion to change them for him to something more 'suitable', seeing as now he was 'grown' up. In front of the window lay his most prized possession - his beloved DW custom-built drum kit that had once belonged to his dad. Above his bed hung model planes, planets, and a life-like replica of the solar system, and his ceiling was covered in stars that glowed when the lights were out. The floor was covered in a run-of-the-mill everyday carpet that was littered with floor rugs, and two of his bedroom walls were covered in shelves for all his bits and pieces. One day Zander hoped to be an astronaut and visit the stars.

My eyes were on Zander as I entered the room and walked to his bed. 'Hey, Buddy!' I lovingly brushed Bandit's shoulder as I walked past him to sit down on the side of Zander's bed. 'Didn't sleep well, huh? How are you feeling now?'

'Not good, Mum! I feel all light-headed and short of breath and I can't stop coughing. I'm sick of coughing!' Zander managed to say all this before another one of his coughing fits started.

'Morning, Mum,' Bandit interrupted.

'Morning, darl.' I turned and smiled to Bandit. 'Sleep well?'

'Mmm, not really! Zander coughed a lot last night.' Bandit headed towards the door, then glanced back to me to say, 'I will make him some breakfast, Mum,' before disappearing off into the direction of the kitchen.

'Thanks, darl,' I called after him as he exited the bedroom.

I focused my attention back to Zander as I spoke. 'I will make another doctor's appointment for you this morning as soon as the doctor's surgery opens, sweet. I love you.' I ran my fingers through Zander's hair as he lay in his bed looking back up at me.

We were both silent for what felt like the longest moment. I searched his eyes. What else could I do for him? How could I make things better? I sighed before leaning down and drawing him in close to me for a quick hug before standing. 'Is there anything else I can get for you, sweet?' I asked before leaving his room to join Bandit in the kitchen.

'Just something to eat and drink thanks, Mum. I'm starving!' Zander gave me his cheeky boy grin.

Zander's cheeky boy grin was the only thing I would ever need in this world to make my life complete. Bandit and Zander, and the bond and love we all shared as a family and nothing more. We were the three amigos! That was us!

'Right, my ole soldier. I shall check on how Bandit is doing in the kitchen then, shall I?' I smiled softly to myself as I left his bedroom.

***

Bandit had breakfast for both he and Zander well under way by the time I entered the kitchen, four Weet-Bix with milk, and a cold Milo!

I put the kettle on. 'I just wish I could do something more for him.'

Bandit stopped what he was doing to look at me as he spoke. 'Yeah, I know, Mum, don't worry, he'll be fine, you'll see.'

I smiled at his effort of breakfast. 'I'm going to ring the doctor's surgery as soon as they open at 08:30 this morning and make another appointment for him, hopefully for today,' Bandit scooped a hearty spoonful of the cereal into his mouth as I continued, 'and if they don't have any available appointments for today, then I will try for a cancellation instead and see how we go. Do you want me to drive you to school today, honey?'

'No, Mum, I'm all good thanks.' Bandit shovelled another mouthful of cereal into his mouth before he picked up Zander's breakfast. 'I'm meeting up with some of the other guys and we are all going to ride our bikes to school today.' And with that, Bandit turned and walked off to take Zander's breakfast to him.

I eyed off the fruit bowl sitting on top of the kitchen bench, overflowing with a whole pineapple and several oranges, apples, pears, and bananas. I picked up a single banana, and rather than cut up a bowl of fresh fruit for breakfast this morning as was my usual morning ritual, I decided instead to do a quick smoothie before going off to shower and get my day started. I measured out the almond milk and poured it into the blender, I then added some flaxseed, oat bran, my broken-up banana pieces, and a handful of frozen blueberries, blitzing it all for about ten seconds. I poured it into a cup and then downed it all in one swift gulp. I filled the kitchen sink with warm soapy water to soak the dishes and then headed off to take a shower.

***

The shower today was gloriously hot. I stood beneath the massaging warmth of its spray and as I washed myself, my thoughts returned to my scattered, fragmented memories of last night's dream. I could remember feeling a 'presence' beside me in my dream, that I had not been alone. I had turned to look but had seen nothing, and then suddenly the words *Leena, my Life'* had rung through my mind. I smiled to myself as I remembered the feeling from those few words, gentle and loving and nothing to fear. There was something very familiar to me about them. I wondered also about the name Leena. There was something very familiar to me about that too. Leena from Atreia and Michelle from Earth were one… but not the same. The first night that I had flown in my dreams I had been with others, but I remembered nothing of them, except the whispers of a promise. I flew as I had done many times before, but this time something was unusual and different, about the 'presence' that is, I could feel it stronger this time than at any time ever before. Yes, I had felt it before, but I had always passed it off as just my imagination, but this time it was almost a touch, *'see me'* it seemed to say to me. I turned around at the time but had seen nothing other than the blue sky that surrounded me.

'Oh well,' I hung up the shower sponge, 'something to ponder on until the next time I dreamed.' I turned off the shower and hopped out, pulling the towel around myself, and drying quickly as I went. I got dressed. Trying to pull my knickers up over wet legs was no easy feat. 'Should have just dried myself properly to begin with!' I mumbled quietly to myself, frustrated, as I continued to strategically hop and manoeuvre myself around the tiny little bathroom, trying to fix my damn knickers into place.

I mindlessly finished dressing myself, then hurried with some makeup, catching glimpses of someone I did not recognise in the bathroom mirror. I wound my hair up in a loose bun atop my head, and then I paused for a moment to stare deeply into the bathroom mirror, only to see the dull eyes of unhappiness staring right back at me.

All I could see was the battered soul. The effervescent woman whom I put on display for the entire world to see was not at all whom I appeared to be. This had become my daily routine, for as long as I could remember.

I hid them very well! My scars! Performing beautifully, day after day so as not to reveal any part of the depths of my soul that I had desperately tried to keep hidden for all these years.

***

Loud banging on the front door startled me back to the present now. I glanced quickly at the bedroom clock as I hurried past on my way towards the front door. *'It's 06:30 in the morning, no one ever knocks on my front door at this time of the morning!'* My initial reaction was to panic. But that panic immediately turned to giant elephants stomping around inside my stomach as soon as I opened the front door, to find Andy Russo standing there. HOOOOOLY CRAAAAAAAAP! My heart pounded so deeply that I was positive he could see it jumping around inside my chest like crazy just beneath my shirt, and if he couldn't see it, then I was positive he sure as damn well hell could hear it. 'I think I'm going to be sick!'

Andy Russo was knocking on my front door at this time of the morning and turning my world completely on its head for what felt like the umpteenth time in just as many years. Actually, it was ten whole years to be exact! But I certainly wasn't counting! Andy Russo was definitely not who I had expected to see standing on my front porch when I opened my front door this morning that's for sure. Tall, clean-shaven, gelled back dark-brown hair, those soul penetrating blue eyes, and smelling oh-so-good. I traced my tongue slowly over my bottom lip before biting it. He was leaning to one side against the front verandah of my house, in an unforgettable way to me that only Andy Russo could deliver. He really was master and king of not only his own universe, but according to him, everyone else's as well.

'Miiicheeeeeeeeelle,' his voice purred, 'what have I told you about biting that lip!' He looked me up and down, and then raised both shoulders as he lifted his hands slightly upward and away from his side as if to gesture an embrace.

'Andy.' I squinted at him. 'It's barely light.'

'I know,' he added, more serious now, 'but a 200-tonne crane went over just before dawn. Regulator's on site at nine. I need help.'

His voice intoxicated me, and momentarily I was drunk with him. Our paths had crossed on and off briefly over the last ten years on more than one occasion. Each time leaving me filled with feelings I couldn't explain. Feelings that felt so right, yet the timing never seemed to be. I could feel it instantly the moment I opened my front door. That undeniable pull between the two of us was still there! It permeated every cell of my entire being like sizzling thunder. Rising within me, and then paralysing me briefly for a moment until I was able to regain some composure. I prayed with everything I had in me that he didn't see the effect that he had on me.

'Andy! Well, aren't you just a …' I stopped myself-sight for sore eyes was what I was going to say, but that would have just meant that I was actually very pleased to see him, and at this point in time I was in no way ready to admit that yet. Actually, at this point in time I don't think that had even registered in my brain yet,

'…vision of loveliness!' I quickly followed this up with a forced smile across my lips and a raise of the eyebrows. I spoke as calmly and as controlled as I could. I steeled myself against him with everything I was made of all the while desperately pushing away feelings that were invading my body, and memories that were flooding my mind about Andy Russo, and of the last time that our paths had crossed. The Pilbara dry heat, the wilderness against our naked bodies, and the taste of salt from his golden tanned skin. 'And to what do I owe this pleasure, Andy?'

'Cuppa tea'd be nice.' A cheeky smile passed over his lips as he nodded his head up and down in a 'yes' fashion. He then raised his eyebrows up and down once as he gently tapped a finger on the belt buckle of his jeans. Then there was just silence. His expression turned more serious as he again began to speak, breaking the awkward silence that had begun building between us. 'Work, actually. Word on the grapevine is that you could be interested?'

'Work!' I repeated, the warmth of his body having an intoxicating effect on me. 'You're here to talk to me, about work-on my doorstep at dawn?'

'If it could wait, I'd have called,' he said, lowering his voice. 'We'll be shut down if I don't front with a credible plan by midday.'

Andy Russo was head of mining safety operations at Hampton Industries in the Pilbara, Western Australia. He was their main man. Any concern about safety standards within the mining operations was a responsibility that lay squarely on his broad shoulders. Andy was first and foremost, always passionately motivated about his work, he held the reputation as the 'go-to' man within the industry. He had a proven track record that had taken him twenty solid years to build up. I did feel extremely flattered that he was standing on my front verandah wanting to talk to me about 'work'. I had my own share of successes within the mining industry as a site safety advisor though. I prided myself on maintaining a company's 'Zero Harm' policy, and I worked tirelessly every day to maintain work environment's that supported the health and safety of its own people, whilst at the same time minimising any impact that the company may have on the environment.

A smile slowly formed across his lips as he watched me, and the tingles started to run furiously throughout every cell of my being. Andy Russo was well and truly aware of the things his smiles did to me, and right now he was all in with both guns blazing. I refused to let my guard down.

Taking a deep breath in, I stepped aside and gestured with my hand for him to come in. I was interested to hear what he had to say-but I held up a palm as he passed. 'Ground rule, Andy, work is work. If I say yes, that's the hat we both wear.'

'Fair,' he said, nodding once. 'As you are aware Michelle, Hampton Industries is in the process of the construction of the new $15 billion mine right here in the North, and the project is now almost 77 per cent complete.' He eyeballed first, then sat down on my lone, beaten-up, old couch that sat against the far wall in the small family room area of my home, just inside my front door. 'In the last couple of months, I have been inundated with safety issues at the mine. Bloody head office has received several notices from the Western Australian Department of Mines, with the last of the notices that I received being issued earlier this month and relating to elevated work platforms and working at heights.' He reached into his satchel and produced a manila folder that was overflowing with paperwork. 'I need to re-assess the site policies before we kick into the next stage. Your background in heights work-permit systems, EWP, crane lifts-fits the hole I've got to fill today.'

He passed me the folder. I pulled over a kitchen chair and sat as far away from him as I could without looking obvious, as opposed to right next to him on the couch. 'So, what's in all this for me, Andy?'

'Apart from another opportunity to work closely beside me?'

I rolled my eyes. He kept it business. 'There's no denying this contract will look impressive on your resume. And as far as I am aware, at the present moment, you are 'between' employment, are you not? And I think you will agree the salary on this contract is a hell of a lot better than any salary you might've previously earned. Also-regulator wants to see corrective actions by noon. Help me steady this, and I'll back your framework across the project.'

'You've had a lot of press about safety lately,' I said, refusing to be dazzled.

'We've earned some and copped some,' he admitted. 'But audits last month still called our overarching approach "excellent." We've had a couple of serious incidents-cranes, EWPs-and I need your head in the room to close the gaps before they close us.'

With Andy's business with me done, he stood in preparation to leave. 'Do we have a deal, Michelle?'

I took a breath, felt the pull, and kept my footing. 'If I say yes, I'm saying yes to the job, not…anything else.'

'Understood,' he said, softer.

He extended his hand to me, and I shook it without a second thought.

'We have a deal, Andy.'

As I shook Andy's hand, I couldn't help but feel like I was doing a deal with the actual devil himself. I saw Andy off, and then finished the morning routine before Bandit and his mates left for school. I checked the time. Still half an hour until the doctor's surgery opened for the day. Poor Zander, he will have to miss yet another day of school.

I smiled to myself as my thoughts then returned to my dream.

An Excerpt from 'The Dark Night of the Soul'

Condemnant quo non intellegunt

Chapter One

Before something breaks, it rehearses the sound of breaking.

They say when your life is about to change forever, you don't always notice the warning signs. Sometimes they arrive quietly, dressed in ordinary clothes, disguised as a day like any other.

In September of my forty-first year, the day looked perfect. Sunlight pooled on the kitchen tiles and the kettle stuttered to a boil. Birds outside repeated their old, rehearsed lines as if nothing new would ever happen to anyone. The sky wore its best blue. The jacaranda shook loose a handful of purple confetti. Even the breeze pretended it had nowhere urgent to be.

From the outside, it could have been any morning. But inside me, a different weather had gathered, low, electric, waiting. I stood at the sink with my coffee cooling in my hand and felt the kind of silence you don't make on purpose. Not the soft, restful kind. The watchful kind. The kind that presses a palm over your mouth and says, *listen.*

For years I'd been moving through life like glass, transparent, careful, easily shattered. My marriage of twenty-two years had sanded me down to a dull edge. Alcohol. Violence. Infidelity. Lies. A family with barbed wire in their mouths. We once tied white ribbons around our promises and called them forever. Over time each ribbon rotted into string, then thread, then nothing.

I slept beside betrayal and woke to it wearing my breakfast smile. Told myself this was love. Told myself I was lucky. Told myself a thousand small stories so I could keep living the big one.

I was stubborn though. Stubborn enough to keep putting one foot in front of the other. Stubborn enough to choose lipstick over truth on most mornings. Stubborn enough to mistake endurance for devotion. Even as the bruises faded into that sickly yellow and his words rang in my bones - *you're useless, you're nothing, you'll never be anyone* - I clung to scraps of meaning like a woman clutching fabric on a windy cliff.

Back then I still believed that commonsense would save me. That if I made the lists, paid the bills, smiled at the neighbours, folded the towels just so, the universe would notice my effort and reward it with peace. I didn't understand yet that commonsense has no jurisdiction over chaos.

That September morning I didn't know it, but I was about to lose even that small illusion.

The warning didn't come how you might imagine. No thunder, no omen. Just light. It was the way the sun hit the garden path, clean, hard, and honest. In that brightness something inside me cracked and spilled a picture across my mind, my body thrown at a wrong angle, skull split against brick, blood thin as watercolour.

It happened in a heartbeat, sudden, complete, and it didn't feel imagined. It felt like memory. Like I'd already done it. Like I was already gone.

And the strangest part? For that sliver of time, it was beautiful.

No performance. No fear. No waking up to the same argument inside a different day. Just silence. Like stepping out of a costume that had grown heavy as iron. Like slipping into water and not needing air. It wasn't dramatic in my mind, it was simple, cool, inevitable. The thought rested against me with the tenderness of a hand on a fevered forehead.

Then the world snapped back. The kettle shrieked. The dog scratched at the laundry door. Somewhere, a lawnmower argued with the morning. I breathed, shaky, guilty, and set the coffee down untouched.

Life, I reminded myself, doesn't let you leave just because you're tired.

I put on my shoes, the jacket with the loose button I kept promising to fix, picked up my handbag and keys like a woman who knew where she was going and why. It was the performance I'd mastered, the one where my body moved the right way while my mind lagged behind in the shadows.

The radio chattered as I drove. A voice selling insurance. A song I used to love before loving it became impossible. Every red light felt too long, every green too short. The world carried on as if my life wasn't cracking at the edges. Mothers pushed prams, a man washed his ute, school children crossed with backpacks bouncing against their spines, all of them breathing the same ordinary air that suddenly felt foreign in my lungs.

I had an interview. The kind you attend because people who love you insist you must be doing something about things. A fresh start, they said. A new chapter. Words for greeting cards from people who've never had to rebuild from splinters.

The building was small and square, smelling faintly of toner and stale carpet. "Take a seat, Lena," the receptionist said, smiling with her mouth but not her eyes.

The leather chair tried to be kind to my back. I tucked my hands together so they couldn't betray the tremor in them. The clock on the wall ticked with the smug patience of bureaucracy.

The man who arrived to interview me was small and balding in the precise way of men who love their pen collections. He asked about experience, strengths, goals. My mouth shaped passable sentences. My knee juddered under the desk, so I gently pressed it down with my palm.

"Is something the matter?" he asked, voice clipped with a Monday's impatience.

Yes, I wanted to say. *Everything. The whole of it. There's a fault line running through the floor and it's humming.*

But I shrugged instead, and it looked like indifference.

He studied me the way people study a recipe they don't trust. "If you don't want to be here, you're free to go."

So I did the least sensible thing and stood up. Left my empty smile on his desk between the stapler and the neat fan of post-its. Walked through reception with my head down, feeling the fluorescent lights turn my skin to paper. No one stopped me. Why would they? To them I was just another woman in a neat jacket and cheap heels, someone's wife or mother, sliding through a life as ordinary as office carpet.

Outside, the air hit my face like clarity. I got into the car and sat for a long time, engine off, hands slack on the wheel. I thought about calling someone, anyone, but who do you call when you don't yet know what's ending?

I don't remember turning the key, only the sudden sound of the indicator clicking like a heartbeat. The world moved around me, and I followed because stopping felt too loud.

I drove without direction with the suburbs peeling past me in slices, school zones, shopping strips, and driveways glossed with sprinkler water.

At one intersection, an old man with a walking stick waited for the green light, and for some reason the sight of him undid me. The tenderness of his slowness. The patience. I wondered if he had once loved someone the way I had, hard enough to lose himself in the effort of it.

By the time I reached the coast road, the sea was that bruised blue it gets when it's thinking about rain. I pulled over, let the wind slap my face, and watched waves muscle the shore. The horizon looked like something you could step across if you wanted it badly enough. I thought about the image from that morning, my body, the brick, the blood, and wondered how many women had stood in this exact place rehearsing their exit in silence. The world wouldn't even notice, I thought. The tide would carry me away as gently as a rumour.

Then the wind changed. A burst of sea spray, cold and stinging, smacked me full across the face, and something primitive inside me barked, *No. Not yet.*

So I turned inland.

The car seemed to know where to go when I didn't. It took me to the kind of pub that exists at the edge of every town, the one that smells of fryer oil and defeat. I walked in because it was easier than turning around.

The bartender gave me a nod that meant I won't ask. There were four other people scattered along the bar - men in work boots staring into their schooners like the answers might be floating at the bottom. The TV murmured a muted horse race. Somewhere in the corner, a jukebox blinked like it couldn't remember what decade it was.

The first sip bit. The second eased. The third made promises it would never keep.

The glass in my hand was blessedly honest, cold, heavy, and unpretending. It didn't love me, but it also didn't lie. I liked that about it.

I thought about how many times I'd sat across from Marko in pubs like this one, watching him charm a room, buy another round, and tell stories that made people forget he was dangerous when the night turned. I used to love that part of him, the way he could light up a crowd. It took me years to see that the light he gave off wasn't warmth, it was fire. And I was the thing left smouldering at the end when it went out.

The bartender slid another drink my way without being asked. "On the house," he said. I nodded, too tired to decline, too polite to refuse comfort when it came disguised as habit.

By the time I left, the day had dissolved into a bruise-coloured evening. The car park shimmered with heat that had nowhere to go. I sat behind the wheel and stared at my reflection in the rearview mirror, eyes swollen, mascara gone rogue, and a woman rehearsing calm.

"Commonsense," I said aloud, testing the word like it belonged to someone else. "You'd think I'd have more of it."

The voice that answered was my own, but quieter: *You had survival, love. That's not the same thing.*

The drive home was a blur stitched together by taillights and denial. I don't remember traffic lights or songs, only the way the steering wheel felt, hot, slick, and foreign under my hands.

My jacket slid off the passenger seat in a tired slump. Somewhere between the highway and the driveway, I lost the thread that held me upright. I turned into the street too fast, braked too late, and the car stopped a metre short of the garage door.

I sat there a long time, engine humming, breath coming shallow and quick. The house glowed with that false warmth of lights left on to pretend someone cares.

When I finally made myself move, my legs didn't want to hold me. I tripped on the first step, palms out, catching nothing, and went down hard on the coarse mat. My knuckles split. The sting was a mercy. It reminded me I was still here.

I knocked, gentle and foolish.

The porch light flicked on and the door yawned open like a lesson.

Marko stood there. His eyes were wide and red, the skin beneath them bagged from nights that hadn't known sleep. There were bags at his feet - two cheap duffels and the suitcase we'd taken to Bali the summer we pretended sunsets could fix us.

"I-" I started, but my voice cracked on the smallest word in the language.

He stepped around me.

The sound our wedding ring made against the doorframe as he brushed past was so soft I almost imagined it.

I grabbed his ankle, absurd, desperate, and childish. My cheek pressed to the cool tile, humiliation burning its way down my spine. No word I could think of would make this moment smaller. None could enlarge me enough to fill the space between us.

He shook me off like you shake off a dog you don't want to kick. Then he carried the bags to the car.

I watched him drive away through the blur of my breath on the glass. Stood there long after the taillights sank into the road's black mouth, and the empty street steadied its face for the neighbours.

There's a kind of quiet that follows a door closing like that. It isn't silence, it's the sound of a life that has just realised its shape.

The house held its breath. Every object seemed to lean away from me, the photo frames, the couch cushions, even the dog's empty bowl.

I walked through the rooms like a stranger touring the ruins of her own home. The kitchen smelled faintly of lemon cleaner and loss. A single plate sat on the counter beside an untouched sandwich, its edges curled.

I poured a glass of water and didn't drink it. I lit a candle without knowing why. I thought about calling my sister, but what would I say? *He's gone again, but this time it feels permanent?* She'd heard it all before.

So, I sat on the floor, knees drawn up, and stared at the small flame until my eyes blurred. The wax pooled like a wound, and I thought, absurdly, that even candles know how to bleed gracefully.

When sleep came, it was jagged and brief, the kind that forgets to be merciful. I dreamt of the sea again, of waves closing over me, cool and heavy and kind.

When morning came, it came without mercy. The light was too clean, too honest. It didn't care that my eyes were swollen or that my mouth still tasted of last night's salt. The house looked both smaller and emptier, as though grief had already started eating through the walls.

I moved through it like a trespasser. The kettle, obedient as ever, clicked on, and the sound seemed obscene. I poured coffee I didn't drink. The dog nosed my leg, confused by the rearrangement of loyalty in the air.

Outside, the jacaranda had dropped half its flowers overnight, small purple casualties scattered across the path. I thought of the sun the day before, the way it had cut across the tiles, that clean slice of light that showed me my own end. Maybe that had been the warning. Maybe every woman knows when the story's about to change but doesn't have the language for it yet.

The clock on the wall coughed its seconds. The fridge hummed. Somewhere, a truck reversed, beeping like a machine learning to apologise.

I should have cried, but I didn't. I was too tired for performance, even my own. Instead, I just stood there, breathing in, breathing out, and tried to remember the last time I'd felt uncomplicated joy. The memory wouldn't come.

By mid-morning, the phone began to ring. It was my sister first, then a friend, then silence again. I didn't answer. What would I say? *He's gone, but I can't tell if that's a tragedy or a reprieve?*

The dog barked once at nothing, a small defiance. I almost thanked him for it.

I thought about cleaning. Cleaning is what women do when language fails. We polish, wipe, fold, stack, as if order can replace meaning. I started with the kitchen bench, moving things that didn't need moving, aligning the canisters, refolding the tea towels, trying to trick the universe into symmetry.

But the air stayed wrong. Every sound had an echo. Every shadow a memory.

I sat at the table and stared at the phone. The part of me that still believed in reconciliation whispered, *He'll call. He always calls.* But the part of me that had been paying attention knew better.

It wasn't rage I felt because rage would have meant energy. It was something quieter, the hollow thud of finality.

Hours passed in their strange elastic way. I must have stood. I must have moved from one room to another. The sky outside shifted from white to pewter. A storm was coming. The kind that makes you believe the earth is capable of weeping.

I lit another candle because I couldn't stand the overhead light, it was too clinical, too witness-like. The flame wavered, small and sincere.

That was when I heard it.

Three small knocks against the wood. Polite. Too polite.

For a second I thought maybe it was him, maybe he'd forgotten something, maybe regret had turned the car around.

But even before I opened the door, I knew.

The silence behind it had a weight. A heaviness that waited with folded hands and didn't care if I was ready.